cheryl

I'M COMING BACK

AUNT GEORGIA LEE

Sapphic Silhouettes
an imprint of Onyx Lee Publishing
Company address:
Onyx Lee Publishing
P.O. Box 953
Alpharetta, GA 30009

Cover Art - MidJourney AI
Design: Humble Nations
Printed in the United States of America

❀ Created with Vellum

contents

introduction

Hello, sweet dahlings! It's me again, your Aunt Georgia Lee, ready to tell you the first story in the *My Day One* series.

In this musical masquerade, contemporary gospel diva Cheryl Rose Campbell learns *tis so sweet to love the Lord and the woman you can't let go of*—even though there will be a price to pay for the lesson!

Cheryl is on a course of redemption and hopeful reconciliation with a woman who stole her heart over praise and worship. Cheryl knew the moment she created her first song with Tabitha Scott the music director and minister had the power to break down her walls.

Cheryl had been wearing a mask for years, in fear that her authentic self would not only destroy her successful career but would threaten her family's safety. American-born but of Nigerian descent, Cheryl's mother, Ola, migrated to the U.S., carrying Cheryl in her womb, and with her teenage son, Ayodele. Their mother's love was strong and unwavering as she gave up everything she owned, including her career as a principal, to seek asylum in America. Because of Ayodele's mother, Cheryl's brother was saved from persecution in a Nigerian prison or death by stoning for identifying and living as a *yan daudu*, a "man who acts like a woman."

Young Cheryl grew up fearing the repercussions of such a fate, even in America. The Black church might not beat the lesbian out of her, but Cheryl knew her career would suffer if she were open about her sexuality like Christian artists such as Whitney James.

But the price of her secret included the loss of Tabitha Scott. Until one day, Cheryl decided it was time to walk in faith. When she convinces Tabitha to help her with her latest album, Cheryl hopes that this reunion will include rekindling a love she's never forgotten.

Will Tabitha walk down memory lane with Cheryl and trust the woman who broke her heart? Find out as their story unfolds in Book One of the My Day One series.

Happy Reading!

Trigger Warning: For the sake of the story, this book contains content that includes transphobic hate speech, depictions of a hate crime, and instances of forced outing. Reader discretion is advised.

I write these acknowledgments on a day when my heart is filled with mixed emotions. There is both joy and sadness in my spirit right now. Despite the conflicting emotions, I will always first give thanks to the Lord, who is the head of my life!

This book has been a long time coming. Over 20 years ago, I had an idea for a book entitled *The Minister's Wife* that was similar to the preface of this story but not exactly. Indeed, God comes not when we want him to but right on time, and so this story at this time in my life. So, thank you, Lord, God, for the vision and the resources to put Cheryl Rose Campbell and Reverend Tabitha Scott's story on these pages for these readers who are blessing it with their patronage.

My life and my love of the Lord and gospel music wouldn't have been possible without the inspiration from my chosen grandmother and my biological mother, who raised me in the church on gospel music and the faith that God would make all things possible! As a child, I sat in the pew of Mt. Gilead Baptist Church in Atlanta, Georgia, and fell in love with gospel music. I also fell in love with a gospel singer, and I was introduced to the beautiful voice of another visiting singer/organist that I would later learn was my first introduction to a transwoman.

In my youth, I understood God's love through this

music, and later in life. I learned through my life experiences and the word of God provided by ministers like Bishop Dr. Barbara Lewis King, founder of Hillside Chapel and Truth Center, Bishop Carlton D'Metrius Pearson, Christian minister and gospel music artist and pastor of Higher Dimensions Evangelistic Center Incorporated, and many others. Their ministry promoted inclusion, love, not hate, and to speak life into each other. I thank these spiritual leaders for instilling in me the importance of this powerful message from God.

I also am so thankful for my chosen family of the author, W.L. Tracy, my furbabies present and past, my QWOC Books community, and the artists who have provided inspiration and realness to the characters of this story. Please enjoy the music during or after you read the story. There is an entire soundtrack available on download streaming services near you. These artists include American singers/songwriters and Nigerian and Zimbabwean singers. Experience this story through their praise and worship.

I am also truly thankful to everyone who reads this story, whether you like it, love it, or don't feel it's for you. My life's mission is to give a voice to the voiceless. So many people within our LGBTIQA+ community are being targeted, suffering, and struggling to remain positive in their ability to be their true selves. If this story helps to shed light on our community's desire to be loved just as we are— to be respected and treated fairly without others using religion and laws as a nemesis against those they choose not to see as simply a different version of themselves, then I pray God will say to me well done one day.

I end these acknowledgments with a call to action for everyone who lays hands on this book to speak life wher-

ever you go. No matter how hard life is, we are all struggling. So, let's speak life into ourselves and into each other.
   Amen

This book is dedicated to those who aren't afraid to openly be their true selves and those who love you just as you are. Love is love, and that's all there is to say!

quotation

"Politics or should I call it parlor tricks? Y'all taking advantage of mankind's racism and hatred to win favors. Don't you know God said you should love your neighbor? Seem like the Ten Commandments are just a way for you to make paper." - ***Isaiah, God As A Nemesis***

1998 atlanta, georgia

ROSE AGWUEGBO TIPTOED into Mount Paul the Baptist Church, like a thief in the night, trying to hide her misdeeds, with her choir boy crew of Mitchell Suttler, Dameon Foster, and Rodney Williams as her backup. Even as she slid into the back pew, young, mischievous Rose didn't miss the melodic sound of the stranger willing the ivory keys to her will and her way.

She also didn't miss her mother's disapproving stare from the front row or her brother's sheepish grin from the choir stand. The Agwuegbo family weren't church royalty, but they were darn near close to it. Ola Agwuegbo was the head of the Deaconess board and confidant to the First Lady, Marianne Palmer. Ayodele was the choir director and a virtuoso with the organ and piano. Ayodele was also a taskmaster when it came to his leadership of all three choirs: junior, young adult, and senior.

The pleasant surprise of hearing the magnificent masterful playing of the guest pianist made Rose's weary body perk up and her spirit excited about the anticipation of getting to know the pretty woman. *Well, was she merely pretty—more of a sexy femme with an edge, skin like dark brown sugar, and curves that made Rose sit up and take notice!*

The stranger was definitely soft in all the right places, but she also exuded command and control. Rose loved herself a femme aggressor—a strong woman who would take charge, put her in her place with confidence, and then lay hands on her in the most authoritatively sinful way!

Rose caught the giggles and whispers that wreaked of E&J from her sidekicks' breath. She glanced at them to see what all the chatter was about. These clowns were going to spill tea laced with pungent cheap liquor all over the church if they didn't quiet it down. She hadn't devised a clever plan to slip out of her mother's home to meet her boys at the corner to hitch a ride with them to Lola's and dance the night away with the children at the most popular Black gay bar in Atlanta, just to be reprimanded for disrupting church instead of breaking the law by entering a nightclub and drinking alcohol at the age of 20 with Mitchell 18, and Dameon and Rodney 16!

"Sshhh! You know my mother will beat our behinds if you keep it up. What's so funny anyway?"

Mitchell sat the closest to her. He was her favorite choir boy and the bravest to speak up whenever the boys disagreed with Rose's demands of them—which Rose often had many demands of most folks, whether they obeyed her or not. It was also the reason they were boycotting the young adult choir because Rose was petitioning to be the main lead singer. But Sister Janine Hathaway was the choir's primary piano player, and her daughter had been the lead singer for the past two years. And come hell or high water, that's what Leah Hathaway was going to be!

"Nothing, Rose, gurl. We just see something, or *someone* has caught our sistah's eye, and we just taking bets to see if you gonna do something about it," Mitchell teased.

Rose rolled those irritated brown eyes and then returned her attention to the object of their conversation.

"*Proverbs 16:28, a whisperer separates close friends*, Mitchell. I have no idea what you're referring to, but I'm just minding my own business."

Mitchell snickered, "*Rude Boys' It's Written All Over Your Face*. Gurl, you can't fool yo boyz, it's clear as rain. That ain't all you minding, Rose. But okay, gurl, I'll leave you be."

Rose couldn't keep the smirk off her face or the snickers from her lips. She'd deal with those messy church queens another time. Her attention was best focused on being less obvious about her fascination with the honey-rich contralto voice that was smooth as cashmere yet penetrating enough to awaken feelings in Rose's being she shouldn't be experiencing in the house of the Lord!

Her posture was rigid as she bopped her head along to the words of the song the pianist belted out with emotion that reverberated in every Christian heart. Rose was just as captivated by the silky, dark shoulder-length hair that draped beautifully across powerful shoulders, the flawless chocolate skin just begging to be touched, the inviting neck that flexed strong muscles with each note she released, and those deep brown eyes that seeped into her soul every time their eyes would meet.

As those heavenly hands caressed the keys on the shiny black Yamaha grand piano, Rose wondered what they would feel like making beautiful music along her instrument. The piano was Ayodele and Sister Janine's pride and joy, and they often fought over who would let it use them to minister to the congregation. Rose was glad that neither had won their usual battle today. Instead, the stranger had been allowed to let one of the church's most exquisite instruments use her skills.

* * *

"Reverend Tabitha Scott, I want you to meet my wayward daughter, Rose, who I'm sure wants to apologize for disturbing your beautiful performance this morning. Don't you, Rose?"

Rose did her best to appear contrite, but her lowered, teasing brown eyes hid the sparkle of mischief as Ola Agwuegbo chastised her daughter with tart words that didn't reflect the mother's love for her precocious child— who was much more grown than Ola wanted Rose to be. In those sweet brown eyes, she still saw the beautiful little chubby baby she sang lullabies to and swaddled close to her heart.

Her spoiled little beloved flower had always been beautiful, bright, and bold in her walk in life, and at age 20, Rose was still stirring up trouble no matter the circumstances. But her mother's heart swelled with love and pride as Rose turned on the usual charm. She briefly laid her head on Ola's strong shoulder, then shot her those pleading innocent eyes that feigned regret.

"Oh, Mommy, really? *Wayward?* Certainly, I haven't been that awful. Mitchell couldn't help his car had a flat on our way to church. You were right yesterday when you said I should come to church with you and Ayodele. But my friends have been so sad since we've had to take a strong stance against the Philistines working against us."

Ola's eyes brightened with embarrassment. And so it began, even in front of company such as the awe-inspiring, talented minister, her daughter couldn't hold her peace.

"Rose, we'll discuss this later. Let's not be rude. I'm so sorry, Reverend Tabitha."

"Please, Deaconess Agwuegbo, call me Tab. And you weren't rude at all. I am curious about these *Philistines*, which Rose is battling with. It sounds pretty interesting. Hello, Rose. Nice to meet you."

Tabitha didn't miss the heat from those hooded brown eyes doing a quick once-over of the minister. Although it was mere seconds, Tabitha felt like she'd had the most pleasurable, thorough examination that filled her with something less than holy! And the soft hand that caressed her palm, vibrated her secret places so powerfully that she felt like dropping to her knees to pay homage to the sweetest temptation before her.

Holy Father!

"Welcome, Rev. You played real nice today, and you're not too bad with your vocals either."

Tabitha stifled her laughter, but that raised eyebrow, which had been perfectly contoured by her favorite aesthetician at Brazilian Waxarama, couldn't hide the truth. The minister was intrigued and aroused by the sassy Sister Rose.

"So, not too bad, huh? Well, your mother tells me you have a beautiful voice yourself. I look forward to hearing it, maybe next Sunday?"

It was Rose's turn to be surprised by the pleasantly unexpected news. Her body was filled with abundant joy to know she'd have another shot—an opportunity to get further acquainted with the minister.

"Well, I'm sorry to disappoint you, Rev, but I'm officially boycotting the choir stand until my demands are met."

"Rose, please. Let's not trouble Reverend Tabitha—I mean Reverend Tab with private church business."

Tabitha empathized with Ola's distress over her daughter's boldness. Still, the intrigued minister enjoyed Rose's fire even more than she had enjoyed stealing glances at that beautiful, brown-skinned body from a distance. It had taken all her willpower and a few silent prayers to remember the keys and lyrics of each song as her eyes and thoughts wandered to the temptation that was beyond her ability to ignore without her Lord, Jesus, Savior!

"It's okay, Deaconess Agwuegbo. I'd like to know more about this *boycott* if it's alright with you."

Ola's expressive brown eyes begged the curious minister not to push the subject, but her head nodded in agreement. Luckily for Rose and Tabitha, the Deaconess was called away to care for more important church matters. Most of the congregation had dispersed into the basement kitchen and commissary, where the Mother Board was having a bake sale. Tabitha looked forward to satisfying her sweet tooth with a few slices of pie and cake that Mother Wallace and Mother Jones had promised to save for her.

Other than the three young men lingering around in the back, doing their best to cover their spying eyes, whispers, and laughter at Rose and Tabitha's expense, the rebellious singer and the dutiful minister were alone.

"So, Rose, do tell, why are you boycotting this beautiful choir that sings like angels?"

Rose snorted, then flashed Tabitha a warm smile to cover her displeasure over the traitors who had chosen to remain loyal to Sister Janine and her spoiled daughter, Leah.

"Nepotism runs rampant in this church, and it's time somebody stood up for what's right. I'm a much better singer than the current lead singer, yet I get fewer leads than the piano player's daughter. Sister Janine also overrides my brother's direction when it suits her. So, until a fair process is implemented, me and a few choir members are protesting."

Tabitha glanced at the three young boys, who were no longer interested in their conversation and were slumped over in the back pew, taking a nap. She could tell by their glazed eyes during service that Rose's posse probably had something more than communion wine before attending church. Rose seemed surprisingly sober but still charged with indignation.

"So, you're a quitter?"

Rose's eyes couldn't hide her surprise and irritation with the bold minister's accusation. Was she a brave soul or a foolish one? Rose wasn't sure, but clearly, the presumptuous minister needed to be set straight.

"Quitter? Do I look like a quitter?"

Tabitha was silently enjoying the fire even more in Rose. She could only imagine how much heat they could ignite together in different circumstances.

"Aren't you? Why not prove your point by remaining dedicated to the cause? With the songs you are allowed to sing, make them so magnificent there won't be a dry eye in this sanctuary, and lost souls will be saved by your musical ministry. Make them take notice not by your rebellion but by leaning into your calling and showing them in those few moments that quality is way more important than quantity. And certainly, don't cause more confusion by destroying the unity of your choir family, Rose. Those young boys need a leader who guides them with wisdom and humility."

Rose wanted to shout and stomp her feet with a less than holy dance at the audacity of the fearless, determined, eloquent, undeniably sexy, charming, phyne ass, Tabitha Scott! Instead, her breath quickened with desire, and her body hummed with delight as the fiery minister gave her the business!

"Well, I guess you got everything all figured out, including me, huh, Rev?"

Tabitha expected more fight in the feisty femme, but the fire in those brown eyes warned her Rose was not one to be played with—no matter how enjoyable the amused minister knew it would be to do just that.

"Nope, Rose. You already know what you should do. But duty calls, and I must greet some of my new congregation. See you around, Rose."

* * *

When Rose stepped into Mount Paul the Baptist Church's choir room, she never expected to see the now familiar face of Reverend Tabitha Scott sitting at the piano. The room was already buzzing with the noisy sopranos, gawking at her and cackling like hens. Mitchell was sitting dutifully on the front row near the other sopranos but with complete allegiance to his gurl. Dameon and Rodney sat on the last row with the other bass and tenors.

Rose also noticed Sister Janine wasn't present for this pleasant surprise from the good minister. But her joy was soon destroyed by Leah's sudden appearance from the side entrance, sprinting her way to the only remaining front-row seat next to Mitchell, who caved underneath the tired heifer's tyranny.

"Good afternoon, Sister Rose. Your timing is perfect; we were just about to start practice. Please take a seat."

Rose shot a deadly stare at Leah and then turned on her southern charm with Tabitha. Her smile was warm and laced with a sweetness that promised to reward the good minister with a private session of their own if Tabitha corrected the egregious attack being made against her.

"Afternoon, Rev. Today is just full of surprises, ain't it? Imagine seeing you here. Maybe you want to fill me in on where my brother is, and Sister Janine? And why my seat seems to be mistakenly occupied?"

Rose could clearly hear the snickers from the bitchy sopranos, but one deadly shot from her fiery brown eyes quieted the mutinous bunch, except for her trifling nemesis.

"Rose, if you had been here last Saturday, Sister Janine would have informed you that I will be taking over the choirs as the new Minister of Music. Brother Ayodele is coming in later and has chosen to take over the permanent position of pianist and organist for the church. Now, please take a sit in the back. There's room for you there."

The good news spilling from the sexy minister's lips was bittersweet when Tabitha ordered her to the back of the choir!

"*Excuse me?* I'm a soprano. Why would I sit in the back? I've always sat on the front row. I know you're new here, Rev, but surely Ayodele must have told you our seating arrangement."

Tabitha and Rose heard the loud stage whispers and giggles, but the battle that had begun between the two drowned out the spectators who were eager to see who'd win the first of many feuds. Tabitha quietly stilled the heat rising in her body as that sharp tongue of Rose Agwuegbo got her hot and bothered, even in the midst of contesting her new leader's authority.

Rose was pushing her buttons, and usually, Tabitha detested disobedience, especially in the younger generation, even though the spoiled soprano was only ten years her junior. This pushback would be Tabitha's first impression on the rest of the choir, and first impressions were always lasting. It was imperative she made a lasting impression on Sister Rose to ensure their future dealings were more in favor of the good minister's methods.

"Rose, yes, I'm fully aware of the previous seating arrangements and that you're a Mezzo-soprano. But today, you will sit with the bass and tenors. As your new Minister of Music, I will determine future seating arrangements. And I know we all agree *that there be no divisions among you, but that you be united in the same mind and the same judgment.* Amen, Sister Rose?"

Rose was more than familiar with Corinthians 1:10. Her mother had recited it to her and Ayodele often when they were growing up and were trying Ola's patience with their petty little squabbles. Her mother's love and constant course correction ensured her children worked together for the good of the Lord. Rose silently acquiesced this time, but she wouldn't be so pliable to the sexy minister's will unless her submission brought her more pleasure than pain at this moment.

"Sure, Rev, *teamwork makes the dream work.*"

* * *

"Well, Rev, do you plan on telling me what I've done now? Why am I being held in detention?"

Rose gave her best performance to appear displeased by Tabitha's request she remain after the one-hour choir practice instead of allowing her to go for a kiki with her choir boy crew. Being alone in what now felt awfully small for the spacious choir room with the stern but sexy-as-hell minister was much better than spilling tea with Mitchell,

Dameon, and Rodney in the parking lot of Denny's on Cheshire Bridge Road. The home of the famous Grand Slam breakfast was their favorite after-hour hangout once Lola's was closed for the night. Rose knew she'd prefer a side of Tabitha Scott than her favorite creamy grits.

She unconsciously licked her lips as she took in that phyne body of the new Minister of Music, and then those curious brown eyes caught her in mid-moan.

"Rose, your mother has asked me to give you piano lessons."

Rose's enjoyment of openly drooling over the sexy minister ceased at the sound of the preposterous idea that she'd need any such training.

"*What?* Why would she ask you to do that? And why am I the last to know about major changes impacting *my life* these days? First, Ayodele is being reassigned from choir director, and then you are banishing me to the back row like I'm some useless tool!"

Tabitha tried to stay strong when Rose locked eyes with her. Those dark brown eyes twinkled mischievously and refused to hide their intent to break down their senior's resistance to Rose's charm. She felt the temperature rise in her body when a hint of Rose's tongue played peek-a-boo with her, and the sound of a moan escaped from Rose's lips. Rose's relentless teasing was enough to make Tabitha take a pause and silently pray for strength before continuing their private session.

Lord, God, help her!

"Rose, I apologize if this is news to you. I thought Deaconess Agwuegbo had informed you and that this was something you wanted."

Rose snorted and crossed her arms in protest of her mother's usual meddling in her career plans.

"Yes, well, I guess it's not your fault. Mommy thinks she's helping, I know. But I have my own plans on how to expand my singing career."

Tabitha's raised eyebrow warned Rose that the uninformed minister wasn't only new to their congregation but also new to being in the presence of a celebrated rising star like Rose. Most of her fame thus far had come from local and a few national church singing competitions. But Rose knew in her heart that it wouldn't be long before she recorded her own music.

"What? You doubt my talent even though you've only just recently met me, Rev? Don't sweat it. I've shut down many naysayers in the past and will continue to do so even now."

"Then show me what you got, Rose Agwuegbo. Make me a believer, and let's run through some scales."

"Really, Rev? That's your challenge? Rudimentary child's play? Why not a more interesting challenge? And if I exceed your expectations—which I have no doubt that I will, you buy me lunch at Denny's."

Tabitha had to give it to Rose. She was clever and clearly enjoyed a challenge. But would the young, sexy body that serenaded her with a melody of babymaking music ever since their paths had crossed be too dangerous to take Rose's bait? Yet, that's precisely what Tabitha Scott did, despite her own discernment. Thank God she wasn't fertile and Rose wasn't a man, or she might end up carrying a bunch of little Rose's around in her belly!

"Fine, Rose. I'll play a song, and then you repeat it. I'll take it easy on you. It'll be a familiar song that most real musicians should know. I have no doubt you're familiar with the music."

"Um, Rev, you really need to stop underestimating me.

Play whatever song you want to, and I'm sure I can handle you—I mean, I can handle it."

* * *

Reverend Tabitha Scott soon learned never to wage a bet with Rose Agwuegbo after the young woman delivered what she had promised in their music competition. Although Rose wasn't a virtuoso like her brother, the cocky songstress had skillz, and Tabitha rewarded her with a date at Denny's. Well, not an actual date, a meal between friends —new friends, former strangers; she had no idea what they were to each other except clear temptation.

From that first challenge and winner's lunch, Tabitha had found herself spending more time with Rose at the piano for further lessons. The music lessons went beyond scales and notes; they also provided the curious minister with the opportunity to explore her innermost desires to be with Rose and to be her true self. She prided herself on not crossing the line, though she was tempted to indulge. Rose had made it clear their first Denny's date—*lunch meeting* that she was interested in the new minister. Tabitha had used all her willpower to reinforce the two's friendship. But the more they did *friendly* things, the more Tabitha's defenses crumbled and gave way to her body's need, which wanted more of Rose and more for Tabitha.

"So, when do you plan on preaching, Tab? You've been our Minister of Music for almost six months and still haven't had a trial sermon. What's the tea? Are you scurred, Rev, to shoot your shot?"

Tabitha almost squirted the mustard across her white blouse instead of the sesame seed bun of her burger. Rose never failed to throw her off her game with her constant sexual innuendos, or was it just the never ceasing horniness Tabitha felt when she was in Rose's company? It wasn't only her six-month anniversary at Mount Paul the Baptist church but their six-month anniversary of hanging out at Denny's after choir rehearsal. It seemed to be the only excuse Tabitha could make to spend time with Rose without it looking like a date.

"You, alright there, Rev?"

Tabitha felt the playful energy radiating from Rose's teasing brown eyes. But her libido was still distracted by her constant thoughts of capturing those spread lips and having them pressed against her own and running her fingertips along the swell of those more than handful breasts that were teasing Tabitha from beneath the plunging neckline of Rose's top. Amid the dense aromas of greasy burgers, bacon, and sugary confections, Tabitha could still detect Rose's signature scent. That aroma made her salivate for something much more satisfying than anything on the menu.

"Yes, um, sorry. This bottle is a little slippery," Tabitha responded dryly as she made a whole theatrical production of adding the French's mustard to her buttered bun.

"Okkayy, so what gives on the trial sermon?"

"Yes, right. Well, Reverend Palmer just thinks I need a bit more time getting to know the congregation and doing more ministry with the choirs before I take to the pulpit. It's fine. I'm patient. Remember, Rose, Corinthians reminds us not to *be anxious about anything, but in everything by prayer and supplication with thanksgiving, let your requests be made known to God.* God knows what I need and desire, and He always answers prayers."

Rose paused before responding in kind. Her mind briefly wondered why Tabitha, like her mother, was so fascinated with Corinthians. Her minister often quoted from that particular area of scripture whenever she wanted to reprimand Rose for something that displeased her. She wondered what area of the Bible Tabitha would quote from if Rose could ever have the opportunity to please the good and patient minister.

"Fugees' *Ready or Not.* Lauryn Hill's point is that sometimes you have to take what you want. Honestly, Tab, you never struck me as passive in any way. You radiated with power and heat the first Sunday we met at church. You know what I think? I think it's time you show some of those tomboy skillz you use on the basketball court in the pulpit. You deserve an opportunity to show them what I already know. You are a woman with a purpose and are destined to serve God from the pulpit just as much as from the choir room and choir stand."

Tabitha was primed to argue with Rose's assessment of the patient minister's need to take the bull by the horns of Reverend Palmer and the Deacons and insist she have her day in the pulpit with a trial sermon. Rose's seductive motivational techniques only made Tabitha feel even more aroused and ready to show just how much of a presence the commanding minister possessed.

At the moment, all she could do was try to stop blushing and smiling at her young defender's passionate proposal.

"Thank you, Rose. Lauryn Hill is a wise prophet in her own right," Tabitha half-teased.

Tabitha slowly glided her hand over to meet Rose's. Their fingers entwined in a gentle embrace, then quickly returned her wandering appendage to the safe space of her half-empty plate. Tabitha didn't miss the squeeze of Rose's slender fingers against hers during that brief moment or the fire in those eyes as they sparkled with interest.

"I'm serious, Tab. Don't brush me off."

Tabitha looked long and hard into those tempting brown eyes and held Rose's gaze.

"I'm incapable of brushing you off, Rose, even if I wanted to, and I have no interest at all in doing so."

* * *

Tabitha smiled at the petite, mocha-skinned cutie. She bopped her head to the beat as they danced on the packed dance floor. The air was humid and sticky, but no one cared when CeCe Peniston, Technotronic, Crystal Waters, and C&C Music Factory were blasting through the speakers. The tiny gay bar on Spring Street in Midtown was bursting with bodies and sweat, but Tabitha could see security ushering more people into the cramped space even in that chaos.

The converted warehouse was a favorite of the Black gay community in Atlanta, and a select Black straight women—*fag hags* who enjoyed hanging out with their best boyfriends in the trendy spot, as long as no obvious butch women made a pass at them. Although aggressive in manner, Tabitha had always been eye candy for her straight sistahs, whether at work in her corporate job or in the congregation at her church.

They enjoyed the cover she presented of a strong, straight Black woman who didn't take no shit off neither man nor woman. They all knew her secret and had no intentions of revealing it, in fear she might reveal their penchant for the sweet lips of another woman whenever they had a dick drought. But if they hung with Tabitha, her straight sistahs quickly learned all they would be doing was *hanging, not fucking!*

A few had convinced her to party with them and their gay male friends Saturday night. Ever since taking a supervisor's position for the Healthy-R-U member services call center at corporate headquarters, Tabitha had met a lot of gay family and their straight women fan club in the trenches. She had kept her distance for the most part, but a few of the boys had worn her down. Tabitha knew it was more of her desire to distract her mind and body from thoughts of Rose, who was always on her mind.

Although she had sworn a month ago that she wouldn't brush off Rose, the confused minister had been using any excuse not to have their lunch dates at Denny's and ghosting her after choir practice. Rose wasn't the kind of woman to take a hint or take defeat lying down. She had become stubborn in her demeanor toward Tabitha, purposely disobedient during choir rehearsals, and a few times close to imploding upon her choir director. Tabitha had done her best to ignore Rose's behavior and to avoid having a reason for a private discussion with her.

As she danced with Michelle from the Claims Department, Tabitha's thoughts wandered to the whereabouts of Rose Agwuegbo. She didn't know if it was divine intervention or the devil's handiwork. When Rose and her choir boy crew squeezed through the door of Lola's, the perplexed minister didn't know if she should stand her ground and face the music or run and hide in plain sight. She didn't doubt it wouldn't be difficult to pull Michelle into the sea of bodies and take cover from the storm that seemed to be heading her way. But something about the way Rose looked made her incapable of fleeing the ebony goddess cutting a path straight toward her and Michelle.

As a sultry, deep bass beat pulsated through the crowded club, Rose was weaving through the throngs of swaying bodies like she was the honored guest and the party was really about to get started since she'd finally arrived. Mitchell, Dameon, and Rodney trailed behind her like her faithful knights in shining armor. They scanned the crowd and parted the sea of bodies as if daring anyone to get in their way. Suddenly, the brazen bunch was only a breath away from her and Michelle.

Tabitha tried to ignore the heat stirring within her as Rose's hips rolled seductively, and her temptress shook that plump booty so hard that the poor minister thought she might catch a case of whiplash from craning her neck to get the best view of that powerful rump shaking!

Sweet Jesus!

Rose dipped her eyes seductively, and those devilish browns sparkled with delight at Tabitha's distress. She popped her hips, shifted her full attention onto Tabitha and her anonymous companion, and teased her misbehaving minister. Rose had no idea who the unfortunate heifer was to dare try to take her place, but she was determined to inform both misguided souls Rose had no plans to let Tabitha slip away from her.

Michelle must've felt the heat between them or the obvious brushoff from Tabitha and gave her dance partner a meek smile before retreating into the sea of writhing bodies. Tabitha could see the gleeful faces of Rose's entourage as they were overjoyed by Rose's defeat of the intruder on their sistah's territory. Tabitha had to give it to the three faithful friends; they never failed to look out for Rose. By the looks of Rose's naughty smirk, it was time for Tabitha to tap in.

Tabitha reached out without saying a word and tightly

pulled Rose into her arms. Rose put on a brief display of rebellion. When those powerful hands grasped her waist and drew her closer to Tabitha's soaking-wet cotton t-shirt and tight-fitted jeans, Rose melted into her minister's strong embrace.

Tabitha leaned down and ran her lips across Rose's ear before whispering, "I'm sorry I'm so wet."

Rose's body hummed with delight. If only Tabitha had gotten soaking wet because of her. Her lady parts clenched at the thought and the feel of Tabitha's hand squeezing her needy backside. Tabitha's mouth circled her earlobe, and then Tabitha's tongue slid down her face, leaving a trail of desire, which heightened when Tabitha's teeth marked her with tiny bites along her neck.

Rose grabbed Tabitha's plump, apple bottom and pressed herself into the depth of her minister's tall frame—creating twin moans from their thirsty lips. They danced, fondled, and kissed for what felt like an eternity, but in reality, it was only a few songs before Tabitha decided she couldn't take any more feverish flirting with Rose. She leaned down and gave Rose a slow, sultry kiss that made Rose tremble with a desire so powerful she thought she might literally pass the fuck out!

Tabitha's grip kept her upright and poised for that skilled tongue to dip inside her mouth and tongue fuck her like Rose knew it could thoroughly service her lower lips. Rose rubbed her aching breasts against Tabitha's sweat-drenched t-shirt, which revealed the white lacey bra, dark brown skin, and large erect nipples underneath.

Tabitha's hands were everywhere, caressing and pinching, until Rose was breathless and revealing the beggy bitch that she was! The friction of their nipple-on-nipple contact made Rose gasp with pleasure, and when Tabitha's mighty tongue was all said and done, Rose was surprisingly silenced by the fucking good foreplay! Tabitha smiled softly, leaned down to place one final quick kiss on Rose's forehead, and whispered, "I have to go now."

Tabitha released her hold on Rose but quickly discovered determined hands pulling her back.

"Where are you going?"

The music was loud, and Tabitha could barely hear Rose, but it was clear from the lip movement that her new dance partner wasn't pleased with the dip-and-dash. She grabbed Rose's hand and guided them through the thick crowd until they were near the club's front door. As the chill in the air caressed their bodies and created goosebumps along their feverish skin, Tabitha and Rose were abruptly made aware that the fantasy world they had created inside of Lola's had come to an end. They found themselves longing for more—more time, more touching, more flirting, much more.

"Rose, I have to go. Tomorrow's a big day for me at church. And I don't need to be distracted."

Tabitha could tell by the frown that quickly covered Rose's beautiful face leaving wouldn't be as easy as she had planned.

"*Distracted?* You haven't been distracted for a while now, ever since you decided I wasn't good enough for you! What is your fucking problem, Tab? If you don't want me, just say so. You don't have to play childish games with me, hiding from me, breaking our dates..."

Tabitha embraced Rose and quieted her angry Rose with another deep kiss before releasing the breathless and perplexed Rose.

"I'm sorry. I want nothing but you, and that fucking scares me. I shouldn't have behaved the way I have been.

I'm very sorry for that. But I haven't stopped thinking about you—wanting you."

"Then take me with you," Rose responded breathlessly.

Tabitha smiled warmly. She knew it was wiser to go home alone and prepare for tomorrow, but she couldn't deny Rose or her desire to be with the woman tonight.

"Rose, I'm doing my trial sermon tomorrow. I should've been home this evening preparing, but I couldn't get you off my mind. My co-workers gave me a reason to try to forget you for a moment. Even that didn't work."

Tabitha released frustrated laughter but didn't regret running into Rose at Lola's. Rose smiled brightly and then took Tabitha's hand in hers.

"Well, congratulations on the trial sermon. You were right; patience is a virtue. I'm happy and proud of you, and I know you will do well. But I can't stop thinking about you either. Please, Tab, take me with you. I promise I won't bother you."

Tabitha looked at Rose with a raised eyebrow, and they both laughed.

"Okay, alright, well, I do plan on bothering you just a little bit. But please, Tab. Don't push me away anymore. I'll do whatever you want—whatever you need."

* * *

Tabitha stood at her front door with a trembling hand as she willed her brain to cooperate with her libido. The key that led Rose to her private sanctuary was stuck in the lock, making her more nervous by the minute. Then, a soft hand pulled Tabitha's away from the door, took the key, and unlocked the door.

"Thanks. It can be a little sticky."

"I bet it can. Thanks again for letting me come with you."

"Yes, of course. I want you here, Rose. I know I haven't been clear about my feelings. Please, come inside."

Tabitha led her into the modest home, which was cute and cozy and held masculine energy with its Earthy tones but warm vegetation of various plants. The two-story duplex in Inman Park was in the middle of a trendy historic neighborhood and far away from their church and church-goers. Tabitha could easily have the necessary privacy for extracurricular activities such as the one they'd be partaking in this evening.

"Rose, can I get you something to drink, eat, or..."

"No, Tab. I'm fine."

Tabitha smiled nervously and then stood in silence before she decided she needed to freshen up and remove the sticky, sweaty t-shirt before getting any closer to Rose, who seemed flawless. The tight denim dress with a low-cut top showcased her ample breasts, and the tight-fitted bottom highlighted her hourglass bodiyati!

"Rose, will you excuse me for a moment. I just need to make a quick change—this t-shirt is a hot mess. I'll be back in a moment. Make yourself comfortable in the living room, please."

Rose nodded in agreement and watched Tabitha rush up the stairs to what she assumed was her bedroom. She didn't hesitate to familiarize herself with the downstairs, assuming she'd visit Tabitha's home more frequently after tonight, or so she hoped.

By the time she'd checked out the small kitchen, private study, hall bathroom, and spare bedroom, Rose was making herself at home in the living room. Her eyes spotted Tabitha's album and CD collection, and stereo. She couldn't stop herself from seeing if they had similar tastes in music. She was excited to see a little Will Downing, Rachelle Ferrell, George Duke, and her favorite tenor, Luther Vandross, in the mix. Rose decided the *Velvet Voice* was the perfect mood music for the evening.

She spotted her favorite album, Luther's 1985 *The Night I Fell in Love*, put the album on the turntable, and put the needle on the third song, *If Only for One Night*. Rose slowly hummed the song and danced to the soft beat as she silently hoped to spend more than one night with Tabitha.

Soft hands and a warm body caressed her backside and alerted her that she was no longer alone in the quiet, dimly lit living room. Tabitha's determined hands and strong frame embraced her like a protective shield that was soothing but didn't change her desire for fornicating with the enticing minister instead of merely falling asleep in Tabitha's arms. As skilled fingers continued to move over her aching breasts, she was absofuckinglutely certain that she'd rather be fucking than sleeping!

"Ooooh, Tab!"

Tabitha's lips painted Rose's neck with plum lipstick, leaving a trail of desire for her Rose. She felt Rose moving seductively against her, and the pressure made her less gentle and more demanding of having the woman beneath her.

"Come with me."

Tabitha pulled Rose quickly up the stairs to her bedroom, where she promptly moved Rose to the queen-sized bed and pushed her down onto the firm mattress. Tabitha's body followed. That now familiar tongue claimed her mouth and emphasized Tabitha's desire to show Rose just how much she missed her, needed her, wanted her!

Rose met Tabitha's desire with a matched intensity that

forewarned the eager minister she might need an extra cup of Green tea along with her Women's Formula vitamin in the morning to recover from the marathon young Rose was about to put her through. As she felt Rose's hands palm her eager breasts, then slender fingers stroke and twist her rising nipples, Tabitha moaned into those plump lips and tongue fucked her lover with an intensity that matched Rose's stroking.

Two sets of hands worked in complete harmony to rip clothes from horny bodies, limbs entangled in a heated battle to get skin-on-skin action, and aching honeypots whimpered to be nourished by thirsty tongues. Tabitha wanted to worship every inch of Rose with slow praise but quickly found it impossible to engage her discipline and practice.

Her mouth lingered just a little bit longer on those sweet, soft breasts that stood proudly against her face every time Rose arched her body at the slightest and most intense stroke from Tabitha's tongue. She gave each breast and hardened nipple one more stroke before setting her focus on other unknown terrain. Her fingers had only merely touched the surface of Rose's moist, honeypot and enjoyed the silkiness that coated the tips of her short-manicured nails, but her mouth hadn't been properly introduced to Rose's sweetness.

Tabitha didn't wait for permission, but if those thick thighs opening wide were any indication of Rose's desire for her to pay some attention to the moist treasure patiently waiting to be discovered, Tabitha was all over that assignment with a quickness! Tabitha paid homage to every inch of Rose's body she traveled along before reaching the center of her desire. Rose's moans and words of encouragement were like music to her ears as Tabitha gave that special sweetness her full attention.

As Rose's body moved against her face, lips, and tongue, Tabitha stayed on her knees, bowed, and never ceased to finish her mission to bring Rose abundant joy. If the screams that bounced against the silent walls, nails that dug deep into her bare shoulders, thick thighs that locked themselves firmly around her neck, and pelvic thrusting that shook her lover's body to her core were any indication, Tabitha had completed her mission with flying colors!

Tabitha was satisfied with their first night of love-making after hearing the contented purrs from Rose's lips as they hugged up later that night. But her little Rose had a mission of her own. When Rose took hold of Tabitha's body, the righteous minister was caught up in a rapture that not only quenched her horny body but opened her heart wider than ever before. Rose was her gospel and the song Tabitha would sing always, never forget or live with-out, ever.

* * *

Sleepy brown eyes and pouty lips made Reverend Tabitha Scott contemplate snoozing through her sermon, but Rose Agwuegbo was having none of that. Surprisingly to Tabitha, her Rose had been up bright and early at 5 in the morning, preparing to vacate the premises. It was Tabitha who had pleaded for Rose to stay a little while longer in her arms, nestled in her bed. After 15 more minutes of cuddle time, Rose pulled them both out of bed, made coffee, and then headed for the door in her rumpled nightclub attire.

Tabitha grabbed her hand. "You're in a hurry to get out

of here. I guess I didn't satisfy you as well as you sounded last night."

Rose blushed and then gave her minister a kiss that was long enough to express her pleasure in last night's events but short enough to prevent any reoccurrence of said event before Tabitha's big day.

"Rev, you need to focus on your sermon and getting to church on time. I need to do the same."

Tabitha tried to give a long face and realized she was behaving like the former spoiled soprano. *Had their roles reversed so quickly after one night of fantastic fucking!*

A memory of that night flashed in her mind, and a smile claimed her face. If she was being childish, Tabitha didn't care at the moment. She'd never felt this way or this good before, and she didn't want it to end.

"Do you think I'll be any good today?"

Rose smiled brightly and didn't stutter, "If you give the type of performance that you did for me last night, the congregation will be kneeling at your feet in praise! See you soon, Rev."

sinner in me

HAPPY FORTY-FIFTH BIRTHDAY! Cheryl Rose Campbell stared into the bathroom mirror. She counted the laugh lines from both sides of her nose to the corners of her mouth, noted the heavy bags underneath her tired brown eyes, and pulled at the soft flesh at her neckline to detect any wrinkles and sagging that might require a nip/tuck.

As a darker-hued Black woman—well, sort of middle of the road, not bright enough to be called high yellow and not too dark to be called blue black, Cheryl still held to the adage that *black doesn't crack*, even if she might require a bit of surgical help to ensure she retained her melanin inheritance of graceful aging.

As she eavesdropped on the sound of controversial but prophetic comedian Kat Williams on his NetFlix special, she had to admit Kat was right about those cursed 40s! As soon as she celebrated the big 4-0, her former youthful body took a nosedive and became an unruly caretaker of one of her prized possessions.

The aches and pains, accidental minor injuries, weight gain, and tone and tightness that were no longer in sight constantly reminded the gospel diva she was simply getting older and not aging like fine wine!

Thank God her voice was still in supreme condition!

Because of her adoring fans, money hungry managers, and faithful church family, Cheryl would have just as successful and long career as the gospel greats like Aretha Franklin, Shirley Caesar, The Clark Sisters, Dorothy Norwood, CeCe Winans, Tasha Cobbs, and Mary Mary—although she patterned her appearance, fashion, and overall style after Karen Clark Sheard.

Although the First Lady of the Church of God in Christ and successful businesswoman was much more her senior in years, Cheryl adored Karen's musicality, personality, and ability to retain her stardom regardless of age. Now, Cheryl would never share this secret adoration with anyone, including the First Lady. This diva had learned at the young age of 10 that it was more important to flex your own Black girl magic than to worship at someone else's feet—unless those feet were of the Lord, Jesus Christ, her Savior, or the person that held a special place in her heart, but she'd never confess that truth, so help her God!

The soft laughter from her guest reminded Cheryl she wasn't being the most hospitable hostess. She blamed her birthday blues for even putting herself in this awkward situation. Cheryl checked her watch and pondered how long she'd have to play nice before sending the acolyte home. The sound of Ayodele's ringtone gave her the needed distraction from disappointing her date.

"Sister, what are you doing answering your phone? I thought I would surprise you with a voicemail song to cele-brate you being older than me yet again!"

The raspy voice of Ayodele, with her usual quip about

Cheryl being the eldest, was refreshing—even though her dear sister was the *old lady* by 14 years, to be exact!

"No, sister. It would seem that your menopause has made you forgetful. I'm still the hot auntie, as they say these days, but you, sister, are G-Ma status!"

The deep, hearty laughter that filled Cheryl's ears with Ayodele's amusement at their familiar game of teasing made her miss home. Cheryl had no doubt that if she were back in Atlanta, the two of them would be out getting into some good trouble, having premium cocktails, eating their guilty pleasures, and dancing the night away at some 90's House Music pop-up club.

Then finish the night, they'd celebrate over Cheryl's favorite four-layer Red Velvet cheesecake, which Ayodele would make especially for her, as their mother had done since she was a child.

"Sister, is everything alright? You've gotten quiet on me. What are you doing to celebrate the day the Lord brought me, my little angel?"

Cheryl felt her face warm, and the impending tears threatened to ruin her stage makeup, which was still perfection even after finishing a three-hour set at the Shrine World Music in Harlem. Although the popular venue is dedicated to indie musicians only, they had allowed Cheryl to use the venue for a special benefit fundraiser to help her close indie artist friend, Liz Wittmore, who was now battling pancreatic cancer.

The event had been emotional and exhausting, but well worth the energy and time to openly support the frail dying woman, who stoically sat through the entire event. Most days, Cheryl did her best to keep her heart close to her chest, but Liz was one of the few people who knew her deepest feelings—Ayodele was another.

"I'm fine, really. It's just been a long day. We had the benefit for Liz tonight, and it was..."

"What? Why didn't you tell me it was happening so soon? One minute, you were talking about planning it, and now you've had it. You know I would have been there for you if you'd just clued me in."

"I know, Ayodele. I'm sorry. Honestly, things have been all over the place with the new album dropping yesterday in the midst of wanting to do this for Liz and spending time with her. It won't be much longer, you know. At least, her family will have the money to..."

"I understand. You are loyal, my sister. But someone needs to be there for you. You know? I should be there for you."

Cheryl wiped the tears away and did her best to pull herself together. Perhaps it was she who was experiencing perimenopause, or God forbid, menopause! The knock at the bathroom door motivated her to gather her wits and put on the performance she was known for as the charismatic diva her world adored!

Before she could stall a little bit longer, the bathroom door swung open, and the youthful body, barely concealed with only wisps of sheer undies, paraded the birthday present her acolyte had promised. Had it been too many lime margaritas, too much marijuana, or just too much realness about how short life could be that had made her take this young woman to her hotel room? Cheryl couldn't say, but the deal was done, and now she had to decide if she really wanted to do the deed with this stranger?

"Cheryl, I'm getting lonely. When are you coming to bed?"

Cheryl could hear Ayodele in the background asking her for clarity on what was happening in hotel room 501, but for once, she'd have to keep this little secret. Cheryl couldn't bear to reveal she had sunk so low at the height of her career. She raised her index finger in the air like she used to as a child in church, signaling that her bladder couldn't wait for the two-hour-long sermon to end. She gave her guest a sweet smile and waved her away before shutting and locking the door behind the tasty-looking backside, making a smiley face with the string down the crack.

"Sister, it's time for me to complete some unfinished business. I will call you tomorrow, and we'll talk then. Thank you for remembering my birthday. I love you, Ayodele. I'm coming home soon."

* * *

Never did Cheryl imagine her promise to return home to Atlanta would be sooner than later. The morning greeting of knocks at her hotel door, the buzzing of her cell phone, and the glaring sound of the loud volume of the hotel television made her throbbing headache threaten a full migraine.

She rolled over into the comforting softness of the down pillow and considered ignoring the bugaboos threatening her peace, but the frizzy hair piece that fell into her face caused her to sneeze and scratch her oily skin. Cheryl snatched the honey-blonde hairpiece and threw it across the room. Even the pricey coverup that gave her hair that extra volume from its normal thinning state had abandoned its duty to maintain the delusion she had retained her youthful beauty.

"Lord! I swear before God if these people don't stop!" Cheryl screamed, reluctantly threw her aching limbs out of bed, grabbed her robe, and dragged her listless body toward the door to deal with the noisy knocker. As she passed the boisterous television, her ears and eyes got wind of the main topic of discussion on TMI, and Cheryl Rose Campbell couldn't believe she was the hot topic of their conversation!

"Sweet baby Jesus!"

Images of barely clothed figures shrouded by darkness but clearly distinguishable to her weary eyes flashed across the screen. Then, that familiar face of the unruly menace to this madness appeared on the TV. Cartier, the young, ambitious, but annoyingly persistent artist, was slinging so much dirt on Cheryl even she couldn't imagine being able to climb up out of that well like the farmer's donkey.

The pictures were accompanied by the clip from an Instagram reel Cartier had dedicated to Cheryl with a song that was cutting and meant to damage her in the most humiliating and brutal way.

CHORUS
Hey, Rose, you hurt like hell,
dark as coal,
you broke my heart,
I call you a rose with thorns,

crown with pain,
that's just who you are.

VERSE
You keep acting like you are really a saint,
you pick younger girls and break their hearts,
word of mouth,
you put a track on them,
you found them back to back,
then you kick her out when you are done,
you have a heart of stone,
damn, you wear a crown of thorns,
your words like arrows that pierce,
your tongue like bullets that shoot,
and you got a target in your heart.

How in the world would she shake off the dirt that was being dumped on her not only by Cartier but now TMI and soon others who would help to bury her old, useless body? Cheryl heard the persistent sounds of her manager and what she assumed would be his entourage of assistants, social media managers, and strategists—all of them feeding at her table with every percentage they received on top of her profits. Well, today would be the day they would earn their fees, or they'd find themselves going hungry!

She dusted off her shoulders, straightened her robe, and prepared herself to find a way to not be buried alive by this bitch!

"Cheryl, what the fuck, diva! What the hell have you done this time? Can you imagine what I thought when I saw that video on my phone at 4 am in the fucking morning! C'mon, this is too much even for this queen!"

As Ben paced back and forth with his favorite Cold Brew with a dash of cinnamon and a whole heap of oatmilk foam in one hand and his iPhone in the other, Cheryl did her best to remain silent as he berated her for the mess Cartier had created. But her temper was rising, and the migraine was seeping into every part of her body. She wanted Ben to shut the fuck up and fix this shit in the most Christian manner possible.

Ben Castrelli was far from a saint and more of a sinner than Cheryl was. She didn't hire him for his virtue but for his victories, which he accomplished by any means necessary. Today was one of those days that she needed him to pull out every weapon he had in his arsenal to put this scandal to bed!

Shit! Why was her mind even thinking about that fucking bed!

Cheryl gave him her most angelic smile, the one she'd used ever since childhood while covering the most devilish acts behind that sweet innocence. But her eyes were sharp, and her demeanor was less than meek and mild.

"Ben, I don't need a lecture. I need you to do your job. As much as I've been lenient with your frequent need to put me *in my place*, I am not your servant but the master of not only my fate but of yours as well. So, calm the fuck down and tell me what you plan on doing to fix this shit!"

Ben sipped his $6.00 Venti coffee from Starbucks, and then, with all the sugar his queenie body could ooze out of those deep acne pores, Cheryl Rose Campbell's manager fired her from his client list of overnight sensations and megastars.

"Cheryl, sweetie, you've gotten this all wrong. I'm

merely paying you a courtesy visit. I've done all I can for you, but enough is enough. From the diva digs on the red carpets and bratty behavior with the paparazzi to your refusal to record the songs the record company wants instead of the ones you chose, we've *ALL* had enough of Cheryl's Way! Monument Records has asked me to inform you that in light of your recent *behavior*, you've broken your morality clause, and therefore, they've terminated your contract. And, if this new album falls short on the sales to accommodate your advance, you will be paying it back in full. Now, my lecture is done, and my bill will be served sooner than later. Good luck, Cheryl Rose Campbell. You're going to need all you can get."

Ben and his entourage didn't wait for a response from Cheryl, who surprisingly was speechless. They paraded their band of six out the door and left her with the dirt that would continue to pile over her head without any hope that she'd survive.

The phone calls continued, and more visitors came to her door, but Cheryl remained in hiding the rest of the day. She wouldn't even answer Ayodele's calls. As the harsh brightness of the daylight faded to dusk and then the darkness of the night surrounded her yet again, Cheryl thought of her friend Liz and her family and allowed herself to mourn the loss of someone's life other than her own.

Cheryl searched around the hotel until she found her cell phone and steadied her nerves before she placed the call to Angie Wittmore. Liz's daughter had been estranged from her mother, but over the past few months, she was the only real family that Cheryl's friend had been supported by other than the family she had created in the artist community. Now, as she heard the tearful voice of Angie Wittmore over the phone, Cheryl thought about her own mother's passing years ago and the regret she had felt not choosing to spend more time with Ola Agwuegbo.

Ola had given Ayodele and Cheryl their freedom by risking her own life to carry them far away from persecution—and Cheryl had repaid her mother's love and loyalty with distance and empty promises. She hung her head low in shame as she did her best to force warmth and hopefulness within her voice.

"Angie, I'm so sorry I'm calling so late. I just listened to your message. What can I do for you? May I help you with the arrangements for Liz? Just tell me, and I'll do whatever you need."

Angie's response was far from what Cheryl expected. She had anticipated the tears, even wailing and words of shame and pleas for understanding. Cheryl was more than familiar with the prodigal daughter's guilt. Instead, the cold, dismissive words that would ring in her ears throughout the night would have never come to her mind from the grieving daughter of her good friend.

"There is nothing that you can do, Ms. Campbell. I'm not trying to judge you at all. But you have enough problems of your own. I think it's best you take care of your situation, and I'll take care of mine. My mother needs to be remembered for the life she led, not the one you're leading. Like Mom used to say, don't hate the sinner, hate the sin. I will pray for you, Ms. Campbell. Only God can help you now."

god as a nemesis

"CHERYL ROSE CAMPBELL, my name is Ayda Kohn, and Reverend Tabitha Scott asked me to contact you. She said you needed some specialized assistance, and that's my area of expertise."

Cheryl hadn't expected to hear that name again unless the righteous minister was preaching hell and damnation for her sins. But it would appear that Tabitha didn't think Cheryl was too lost to be redeemed—and she was definitely not forgotten by her *old acquaintance*. A smile crept over Cheryl's face for the first time in the past few days, and a small sense of hope was restored.

She hadn't intended to answer the unknown caller, but that slippery iPhone screen had swiped to answer instead of sending the caller to voicemail. She could only assume it was divine intervention.

"Thank you for calling, Ms. Kohn. I'm familiar with the help you provided Whitney James and a few other artists in the community. But I have to be honest and say I'm surprised that my dear old friend, Tabitha, sent you to me. We haven't spoken in some time."

"Yes, well, good friends are hard to come by these days. But Tabitha Scott is one of the good ones. I'm sure you agree."

Cheryl could hear the determination in the highly sought-after talent manager's voice. Although Ayda was knocking at her door, Cheryl was connected enough in the community to know the *Queenmaker*, as they referred to this petite, seasoned powerhouse, wouldn't waste time on someone she didn't believe in or knew she couldn't help.

"Yes, you're right. Good friends are hard to find and keep. So, should I consider you a new friend, Ayda?"

The amusement could be heard in Ayda's voice, and even a little bit of joy could be felt in Cheryl's body.

"Yes, Cheryl, you should. It's time you come out of hiding and kill the rumors. If you had good management and the right type of support, this would have already been handled. So, let me do this for you. It's time for you to return to Atlanta and start in a new direction. I have a lot of ideas on how we can make that happen."

"What if I don't want to come back to Atlanta? Surely, your reach goes as far as New York. Why can't we do damage control from here?"

This was the second time she had been asked to come back home, and she was still not convinced that it was the best thing to do. Atlanta held too many bad memories, broken promises, and a woman she'd hurt but still wanted. How would returning to her past mistakes make her wrongs right?

"Yes, I could help you from New York, but you need to be on familiar ground, where you can reinvent your brand in familiar surroundings with people who want to support you."

Cheryl snorted. "I doubt that's true. I've already

received the harsh sentiments from the church communities in Atlanta, and my former Atlanta fanbase is quite vocal of their disgust with their former diva."

"I agree; it's not going to be easy, Cheryl. But no place will be a walk in the park for you. Atlanta is where you were born, and it's where you'll be reborn. So, hear me out, please. I have two other artists who are also on their own individual roads of redemption. I'm sure you're familiar with R&B artist Roxanna and perhaps hip-hop artist Dymon Stud."

Although Cheryl had her doubts about Ayda's proposal, her ears perked up at the sound of the two controversial artists. She was more than familiar with their character being questioned in the public eye, and the three of them definitely had drama and fair-weathered followers in common.

"Yes, I don't know them personally, but I do know of their similar issues as mine. So, you want the heathens to join a group together? Is that your idea of redemption?"

"Cheryl, I am more than aware of your resistance to this idea, but it is true that birds of a feather flock together. This is a good thing, believe me. You aren't heathens; you are human beings, and there's not one person on this planet who hasn't made mistakes and isn't in need of redemption. *For all have sinned and fall short of the glory of God.*"

So, Ayda Kohn knew her scripture. Cheryl was at least pleased to hear that her potential future talent manager had her own walk with God. Ben Castrelli may have been good at burying the bodies, but those evil deeds always had a way of resurfacing when she least expected it. Maybe it was time she practiced what she preached.

"Alright, Ayda. You've piqued my curiosity. What is your proposal?"

Cheryl could hear the smile in Ayda Kohn's voice. She imagined the Queenmaker's success wasn't built on failures but her resilience and determination to get what she wanted. Cheryl would need a fighter like Ayda on her side for perhaps both professional and personal reasons.

"Good, Cheryl. I'm glad you're open to the possibilities. How do most artists appeal to their disillusioned followers or increase their following? Good question, right? Simple, they write more music and create a new album, and not just any album, but one that speaks to their challenges. We need to do this for you. Even more, we need to unite you, Roxanna, and Dymon as collaborators on a few of the songs. But that's not all; we need to do a whole redemption tour with three strong women on the road to a better life and taking their fans with them on this journey."

Cheryl had to admit the new album and tour were great ideas—especially if her latest album tanked. She would definitely need an additional income source to pay back the money she owed to Monument Records. But how would she finance the production of a new album? Ayda was two steps ahead of her on that concern as well.

"Dymon has her own recording studio, so the album can be done under her label at no cost to you. I'm sure I can arrange that, of course, as part of the deal. How does that sound?"

It sounded too good to be true and something Cheryl didn't feel she really deserved—but she was in no position to deny God's mercy. There was just one more thing that she needed from Ayda Kohn in order to seal the deal.

"It all sounds perfect, maybe a little too perfect. But I'm interested and would be completely on board if you can guarantee something else."

"Yes, Cheryl, of course. What else do you need?"

* * *

"Ayda, absolutely not! When I asked you to help Rose, I didn't mean that I was a part of that arrangement. I don't have time to co-write music with her, and I honestly don't want to work with her."

Ayda paused for a moment and looked up toward the heavens from the skylight in her living room as she did her best to mix business with pleasure. It was her only real day off from saving the careers of talented artists, but she needed to have one other conversation before closing the deal with her new artist—and Cheryl Rose Campbell wasn't going to take no for an answer.

"Tabitha, how can I do what you ask if you don't help me to do it? If you didn't want to truly help Cheryl, you wouldn't have come to me. I don't understand the history between the two of you, and I will only pry if it is important to helping Cheryl get back on track. She needs you, Tabith. I need you to help make this right for her."

Tabitha grimaced as she sat in her office at the Unity House of Worship Love Community Church where, at the moment, she felt less unified and loved by the idea that Rose was requesting an ill-fated collaboration between them yet again. It had taken her years to have some semblance of peace without thoughts of the woman's smile, eyes, voice, curves, touch, and how Rose made her addicted to her taste!

She silently chastised herself for even thinking about Rose in that most intimate way in God's house. But no matter where she was these days, Tabitha saw more of Rose than she had seen in some time and not in a good way. This proposal was insane, and only a mad woman would consider getting tangled up in Cheryl Rose Campbell again!

"Nope, Ayda. We've got to find another way—that is, you've got to find another way."

Ayda released a deep sigh and then forged on. "There is no other way, Tabitha. The woman I spoke with this morning doesn't seem all that eager for course correction. She seems broken, and honestly, that's expected. She loss her fight, and although I hear a shred of hope in her voice, Cheryl needs something, someone to keep her inspired. Isn't that what you do, Reverend—provide inspiration for healing? Cheryl needs to be healed. Won't you help her?"

Tabitha cursed under her breath and then, within seconds, prayed to God for her own deliverance. What Cheryl and Tabitha needed and wanted was more than a God-inspired healing. The healing they would ignite together would have nothing to do with God if Tabitha didn't reinforce her determination to put as much distance between her and her addiction.

"Fine, Ayda. But I have my counter, and it's a deal breaker if she disagrees."

Ayda smiled with victory and then sipped her mint tea. This arrangement was going to be even more fiery than her most recent success between Dymon Stud and Layla Joy. Ayda had no doubt she would be just as successful in turning sinners into saints in the public eye.

"Yes, Tabitha, of course, it's to be expected. What do you need?"

* * *

Cheryl threw her last toiletries into her overnight bag and rushed to the door. She hadn't expected the driver to be so prompt in New York afternoon traffic. The pounding at her door was a sign her time was up. She was homeward-bound whether she was ready or not.

The tall, dark archangel standing before her would not be whisking her away to the John F. Kennedy International Airport at the moment. The serious look on Ayodele's face warned her sister's mission was more of a captive nature at this time. The hotel manager must have feared the same, but Ayodele had him in tow behind her, vehemently persisting she did not disturb the former celebrity per Cheryl's orders. His weak grip on Ayodele's solid arm was no match for the mighty crusader.

"Sister, tell your little friend he needs to take his grubby little hands off me before he loses a finger or two!"

Cheryl was shocked and amused by Ayodele's surprise visit, but her humor faded at the sight of Michael Voortman's less-than-amused face. She couldn't tell if he were in the midst of an asthma attack or ready to blow a fuse over Ayodele's ability to effortlessly emasculate the petite gentleman.

"Ms. Campbell, I'm so sorry for the interruption. I told *this person* that you were not to be disturbed. But he insisted he knew you. I can call the authorities if needed."

Yes, the amusement was definitely gone from this peculiar situation as soon as Michael Voortman had reminded Cheryl of the frequent attacks against her sister. The name-calling, the stares, the bruises, and the hatred in those eyes and words from strangers who had no idea of what a beautiful spirit her sister really was. Nor did they know of the actual fighter that Ayodele could be until they dared challenge her patience with their transphobic cruelty.

Despite what she really wanted to say or do to the manager in Ayodele's defense, Cheryl remained calm and reminded herself there had been enough trouble at this hotel for one week. Her savior had come to rescue her as always, but she would first have to rescue Ayodele.

"Michael, thank you for being so loyal and supportive of my needs. Please, release my sister's arm. Forgive me for not telling you she was arriving today to take me home. But she's here now, and no need to worry. As you can see, she can take care of me from now on."

Cheryl finished reassuring the small man with her usual warm, angelic smile and an added touch of her hand softly caressing his grip, then plying those fingers from Ayodele's sturdy arm. Ayodele didn't seem worried about what could have happened if Michael Voortman didn't stand down. She was still ready to show him just what *this person* would do to his scrawny ass if he took things further.

But she needn't worry because her little angel took care of this bullshit with the charm and elegance that retained Cheryl's diva status, no matter what the Philistines said! Now, she would give her angel the support Cheryl needed to walk with dignity and return home to heal from this mess.

"As you wish, Ms. Campbell—as long as you're sure..."

"Boy! If you don't get your little ass back to your desk..."

Cheryl released her hand from Michael and placed it on Ayodele to steady her sister.

"Ayodele, it's okay. We know that Michael was just doing his job. Go ahead, Michael. I don't want to keep you from more important things. We're fine."

Michael Voortman looked at Ayodele with venom in his eyes, but he knew there was no bite to back up his stare. Instead, he gave Cheryl a saccharine smile.

"As you wish, Ms. Campbell. Have a safe flight."

Cheryl pulled Ayodele into the hotel room and shut the

door quickly, and only then did she fall into the welcoming arms of her giant crusader. Ayodele secured that hold and reassured her little angel that nothing would harm her again—and for once, Cheryl released the tears of humiliation and fear into the security of one of the few people she could trust.

"It's okay, sister. I knew you needed me. Did you think I would just let you sit here and suffer alone? Ayodele will always be here for you. Don't you know that, sister? You are my little angel, and I will always take care of you, whether you want me to or not. So, let's get your things and go home."

* * *

Ayodele was sitting by Cheryl's side in the green room at the *Atlanta Alive* studio, just as she had done on their trip home and the nights at Cheryl's condo, which her protector quickly informed her she wouldn't spend alone. As her nerves got the best of her, Cheryl held the strong hand that gripped hers tightly for the strength to face Taylor Horton's Saturday morning audience as they judged the wickedness of this woman.

"Ms. Campbell, they're ready for you on the stage. Please come this way."

Cheryl motioned to rise, but Ayodele held her hand tightly and whispered, "Don't worry, sister. No one has the right to judge you but God. Remember, Jesus said, Your sins are forgiven. *Your faith has saved you; go in peace.* We all make mistakes, sister, but it is your faith that saves you. So, head up, proud chest, and give 'em hell! I mean, you know what I mean."

Cheryl gave Ayodele a reassuring smile and then tried

remembering her sister's encouraging words as she walked onto the stage to greet Taylor Horton and her TV audience.

"Good morning, ATL! It's your gurl, your favorite auntie, Taylor Horton, coming to you from *Atlanta Alive* at the crack of dawn, where we do nothing but thrive! Now, for you early birds and those who will be streaming this later in the day, I have a special guest who needs no introduction but does need our prayers and love. Let us all give a warm welcome from our team here in the studio and our family watching us on your TVs, computers, cellphones, wherever you are, to the celebrated gospel diva, Cheryl Rose Campbell."

Taylor gave Cheryl a warm, tight hug and then ushered her to the couch to sit beside her. The popular weekend Atlanta personality had been gracious in extending Cheryl the opportunity to tell her side of the story, complements of Ayda Kohn securing the interview on her behalf.

Ayda sat calmly in a front-row seat in the otherwise empty space generally reserved for a live audience. She granted Cheryl a reassuring smile and nod before turning her attention to the prosecution—or so it felt, even though Taylor was known for being fair in her interviews.

"Thank you for having me today, Taylor."

"Oh no, Cheryl. It's me who is grateful for your presence. I know this is a difficult time for you right now, and we want to give you a safe space to lift some of the weight off of what I'm sure are heavy shoulders. Would you like to say a few words before we begin?"

Cheryl smiled warmly and then shook her head. The confidence that Ayodele had tried to encourage and the thirty-minute pep talk from Ayda Kohn on their ride to the studio had not sunken in just yet. The empty studio was just as intimidating as if a large audience were ready to persecute her.

"No, not at this time. I'm ready to answer your questions," Cheryl finally uttered.

Taylor gently squeezed her hand and then began the inquisition.

"Thank you, Cheryl. So, after a week of the news leaked by hip-hop artist Cartier of the images we just shared, there are a lot of questions that I'm sure many people have asked of you or are discussing with or without your permission. We want to help reduce the noise and stories and suppositions created without true knowledge of the facts. So, take your time, Cheryl, but please tell us if those images are real?"

"No, they're not."

Cheryl's quick response surprised her benevolent host, Ayda Kohn, and Ayodele. Ayda had advised a more thoughtful yet deliberate approach to her response, and Ayodele had expected a more detailed explanation. Taylor Horton wasn't satisfied either with Cheryl's brevity and began her journalistic discourse to get to the bottom of that unfortunate event.

"Cheryl, do you mean that you're not in those images and video or that what the images imply is not real?"

"Yes, I'm in the images and the video, but Cartier's implication and accusation that we slept together are not true—well, they are partially not true."

Ayda did her best not to show the panic expression unequivocally covering her face better than her trusty foundation!

"Then, Cheryl, what is the complete truth?"

"Did we sleep together in the same bed? Yes. I fell asleep in that bed next to Cartier. Did I have sex with this young woman that night, or ever? No, I didn't, and her claim that we did is a lie."

Given Taylor Horton's history with the controversial Cartier, her reporter senses told her Cheryl was speaking the truth. As she silently pondered for a brief moment which route she wanted to take with her next line of questioning, Taylor's need to have the whole truth about Cheryl Rose Campbell outweighed her desire to show her some grace and leave her private life, private.

Taylor knew if she didn't uncover the real story, some other hungry and less scrupulous reporter would, and they wouldn't hesitate to destroy this woman's life. And that was neither on Taylor's agenda nor did she want to assist someone else in doing so because she was complicit in hiding the truth.

"I see. So, you fell asleep in bed with Cartier but didn't have sex with her. Then, Cheryl, you should already know what my next question will be and what others have pondered."

Taylor paused and allowed Cheryl to spell it out for her and the audience without forcing one of her favorite Christian singers to come out of the closet. Cartier had already shoved the six-time Grammy winner, chart-topping, glam diva of gospel music out that proverbial closet door, and there was no way for Cheryl to find another place to hide. So, she silently prayed her guest would confess the truth on her own accord.

"Yes, I know what you and others want to know. For many years, I have worried about when this day would come. When I would have no choice but to face my truth and share it with people who have grown to love my music, my ministry, and I like to think, love me. But within this same community and family, I have listened most of my life to words from the Bible, words that people give credit to God used against people like me. I have feared the retribution, not so much from God, but from those who say they represent his words and his beliefs."

Cheryl paused, cleared her throat, and then continued to confirm the truth her jury already knew.

"And I have supported others, in my own way, who were brave enough to stand in their truth regardless of the repercussions; one of those brave souls is my sister, Ayodele. But I failed to do the same. Now that Cartier has chosen to indirectly free me from my self-imprisonment, I don't blame her for her actions. We all make mistakes, and I'm not absent from making horrible mistakes in my life that I regret. I won't make another one and try to deny who I am any longer. You all want to know if I am a lesbian. Yes, I am a lesbian. I know that God is by my side. I will no longer allow people to use the Bible or God as a nemesis against me and others to serve their own ulterior motives. God doesn't teach hate but love of ALL people. And if *God is for us, who can be against us?*"

speak life

"AYDA, IS THIS REALLY NECESSARY?" Cheryl slowly stepped out of Ayda's car and braced herself for her second day on trial. This time, she wouldn't have a closed set and privacy from the condemning stares and whispers. Reverend Tabitha Scott had demanded her attendance at Sunday morning service. She had no option to decline if she wanted the talented minister's help writing her next album.

Dressed in her finest Sunday attire, which honored the tradition of Black women over the ages, Cheryl was at least covered with a protective armor against whatever would happen on this holy day. Although the navy blue suit accentuated her mature body, Cheryl still had beautiful curves that respectfully put on display her sweet femininity and desire to seek attention from one particular church member. The beautiful wide-brimmed matching blue and white hat sat perfectly on her honey-blonde hair, which was pinned up to showcase the preserved fineness of her smooth neck despite the lines of aging. Her face was beat to perfection, and those kissable lips granted a soft smile to a few church folks passing by them.

Cheryl emulated confidence and devotion to bringing the good minister to her knees, so help her God! But her insides were nothing but nerves. She did her best to wipe away the sweat from the palms of her hands before formally greeting some of the fine church folks of the Unity House of Worship Love Community.

"Don't worry, Cheryl. Things will be fine. I have invited a few good friends who will make you feel right at home. Trust me, neither I nor Reverend Scott want you to feel uncomfortable. But getting back into the congregation— one that would welcome you as their own is a brilliant idea from Tabitha. So, let's do our best and try to enjoy the service. You never know; it might feel just like old times, right?"

The thought of her *old times* with Tabitha Scott brought back memories that weren't decent enough to think about as she entered the house of the Lord. Cheryl silently promised to do her best to think only the purest of thoughts during service as she worshipped below the enticing minister's pulpit without any mindful meditation on how she'd like to praise Tabitha.

"Yes, you're right. Just like old times."

Cheryl slowly walked up the steep steps leading to the church entrance with Ayda by her side. If Cheryl's memory served her correctly about Tabitha's need for punctuality, they had made it just in time for praise and worship. She could hear the beautiful sounds of Ayodele on the grand organ, filling the modest spiritual dwelling with jubilant harmony.

Ayodele's natural ability to exude just the right emotions from the congregation through her reverence to the Lord was only enhanced by her dedication to her musical artistry. Cheryl wasn't blinded by the music; she saw the expressions and heard the voices of the congregation as they were some of the few chosen to see the scorned songstress in person for the first time since *the incident*. That was what Ayda Kohn had chosen to refer to it as in their marketing and communications campaigns.

Cheryl allowed Ayodele's music to guide her on her path to being absolved by Reverend Tabitha Scott, whose absolution she assumed was a part of their deal. She spotted a few empty spaces near the back of the mostly crowded service, but Ayda propelled her along to the front of the church. Cheryl's heart sank, and her nerves reawakened as she realized too late that she was expected to be a spectacle on program, in the spotlight of these watchful, prying eyes!

"You're doing great, Cheryl. Don't panic. Look who has joined us. These women have come to give you the strength you need."

Ayda ushered her to the front row seating, where familiar faces she only recognized in passing at various entertainment events or from their public notoriety greeted her as if she were a member of their family. Contemporary Christian jazz artist Whitney James was the first to greet her with a warm hug.

"Morning, Sister Cheryl. You looking mighty fine today. I'm glad we could finally meet, and what a perfect place to do so."

Then Congresswoman Mikail Rollins shook her hand briefly before Ayda encouraged her to take her seat. Cheryl obeyed the quiet command and briefly glanced at the pulpit. She spotted the attentive minister's silent request that she remember proper church decorum. Those deep brown eyes that watched her closely conveyed more than Tabitha's desire for Cheryl to be a good little church girl. Cheryl quickly looked away before she willingly offered the desired sacrifice.

"Roxanna and Dymon will be here shortly. They tend to be a bit tardy, but they wouldn't miss the opportunity to support you today. Layla Joy will also be here," Ayda whispered before turning her attention to the service.

Cheryl was beginning to understand why Ayda Kohn was so successful with her clients. She truly made them feel special when they felt so small and defeated—the way Cheryl felt even amid the serenity in the church Tabitha had built from the ground up. She admired the stained glass that was handcrafted for the building by an artist friend of the beloved minister. Another collaborative artist had etched the pews with some of Tabitha's favorite Bible verses.

The pulpit and choir stand were just as majestic as the rest. Their regalness and stature granted the church members who sat below them the feeling as if the prophetic minister was preaching from the mountaintop and the choir were angels singing from the heavens! It was breathtaking. As Cheryl listened to Ayodele sing one of her favorite songs, the emotions she had been doing her best to contain overwhelmed her.

The perfectly applied makeup on her beautiful face was in the line of fire from the tears that flowed freely from her eyes. Throughout this tumultuous week, Cheryl had done her best to present a confident appearance. The damage that had been done to her spirit, career, and credibility was heightening her sensitivity to a song that encouraged people to believe God would never forsake them and to speak life, not death, into their spirits.

Yet, Cheryl couldn't stop thinking of the cruel words from Cartier's song and how the rejected young woman was helping to bring death to the life that she knew. Ayda handed her a beautifully embroidered handkerchief, and Cheryl hesitated, soiling the delicate material with her sinner's tears.

"Go on, Cheryl. Take it," Ayda encouraged, then took Cheryl's free hand into her own.

Cheryl held on to the older woman's firm grip and was rewarded with Whitney James's supportive arm around her shoulder.

"Take your time, sis. It's tough right now. But it will get better. The Lord's got your back, and so do we."

VERSE
When the going gets tough,
When it seems hope is lost,
Remember,
He will never forsake you.

When the sun won't shine,
Cloudy days won't pass,
Remember,

God's word is true.

There is power when you speak,
So much power,
Just confess his words.

HOOK
Speak life 3x,
Just speak life.

* * *

Reverend Tabitha Scott watched in silence as she did her best to resist the urge to offer Rose the comfort Tabitha knew only she could give the woman who had broken her heart. Even with the memories of the former celebrated contemporary gospel artist's refusal to be open about their relationship and her own sexuality, Tabitha's heart still wanted nothing more than to belong to Rose.

She watched Rose find comfort in the words and affection of the women surrounding her—and Tabitha took comfort in knowing that she had helped to offer substitutes for her own affection. She had insisted Rose face her and the congregation without much regard for Rose's need for privacy or healing before confronting the judgment of a religious community.

Had she meant to hurt her or punish Rose in some way?

If she were honest with herself, Tabitha knew it was because of her desire to be in the woman's presence, but at a safe distance with the watchful eyes of her community, keeping them both proper in their behavior. At the moment, her safety net seemed unreliable as she clenched her hands on the arms of her chair to resist leaving the pulpit and rushing to Rose's aid.

Perhaps it was God divine that her desires were interrupted by the arrival of her guest performer and the popular social media influencers, who had the church's young members awestruck. Tabitha had no doubt that her daughter and sons sitting behind her in the choir stand were just as enamored by their appearance—especially Isaiah, who was now an artist on the record label of his new friend Dymon Stud.

Tabitha gave a quick nod and smile to Roxanna, Dymon Stud, and Layla Joy as they took their seats next to Cheryl's entourage. She gave silent thanks to the Father for the needed distraction and opportunity for Rose to compose herself without all eyes on her distress. Tabitha looked into those teary brown eyes only for a moment—hoping to will them to brighten until she could offer her shoulder to lean on, ears to listen, and body to surround and protect her, in, of course, a Christian sort of a way.

Who was she fooling? Certainly not Rose, who returned a look of longing to Tabitha's empathetic gaze.

Tabitha averted her attention to Nichelle, her junior program coordinator, signaling it was her turn to introduce Roxanna's special performance. The vibrant little 13-year-old was waving her hands up and down, trying to get the distracted minister's attention. The young girl was lighting up the space with her huge grin and need to take the microphone and do the task she had rehearsed for the past two weeks.

Nichelle's pure joy brought a smile to Tabitha's face, and she silently thanked God again for letting the young return the sunshine to the emotional moment. Tabitha gave Nichelle a nod to proceed with her introduction, and after a few nervous stumbles and giggles, the junior program coordinator got her big spotlight on the program.

Tabitha was the first to applaud her performance and encourage the rest of the congregation to celebrate the young girl's debut. Then Nichelle ushered Roxanna to the front of the room and handed over the microphone. Although it had only been a few weeks since the infamous R&B artist had been released from rehab after her own public fall from grace, Roxanna stood before the congregation with confidence and a peaceful grace.

Tabitha was glad to witness Roxanna's serenity and strength. She had been offering the very troubled yet talented artist, private spiritual counseling since leaving rehab. Tabitha was proud of the woman that stood before them—still healing, yet stronger just the same.

"Morning, church. Thank you, Nichelle, for that beautiful greeting. You make me feel so welcome, and your joyful energy is contagious. I can't help but smile when you smile. Don't we all need that type of sunshine in our lives? Amen, church?"

Despite her troubles, Roxanna was still much loved by her fans in secular and Christian environments. The congregation was just as excited to hear her perform and responded to her in kind.

"Thank you, Reverend Tab, for inviting me to share my new music with the church. Y'all know where I've been and who I was, but it's time I show you where I'm going and who I'm becoming. In this world, people will try to define you and tell you what to think and who to be, but only you and God know what lies within you. So, this song is for those who judge us, yet don't see their own sins, but are good at pointing out ours."

VERSE 1
Love your neighbor as yourself,
Don't go round judging nobody else,
That's in the Bible, you don't gotta take it
*   from me,*
You say you love God, but that's not how you
*   treat me.*

CHORUS
It's like all you can see is the sinner in me,
But if God can love you, He can surely love me,
All you wanna see is the sinner in me,
I hope God judges you just like you judge me.

VERSE 2
Always judging me,
Saying how could God use me,
Say, come as you are, then suddenly,
You condemn me for everything,
Let he with no sin cast the first stone,
Before you judge me, better judge your own,
If you look deep inside,
I'm sure you'll find,

Your sin is no different from mine.

* * *

As Reverend Tabitha Scott stood at the podium, she was pleased to see that it was well within Rose's soul. The once solemn demeanor seemed lighter, surrounded by the support of women who joined her this day to stand in support of her deliverance. Now, it was her turn to give Rose hope for brighter days—and maybe even a little wishful thinking of her own that those days would include a better connection between the two of them.

"Let the church say, Amen. Thank you, Sister Roxanna, for reminding us that no sin is greater than the other and that we all have to go before God for true judgment. It's not our place to ridicule and ostracize those in need of grace, but rather, like Sister Ayodele sang so beautifully, we need to speak life into each other, not death, with our words. And that's what I'm asking all of you to do with me: speak life into our Sister Rose. I know she doesn't mind me calling her by that name, as I've been addressing her that way since we were young women in the church ministering together through song. I know this spiritual being by no other name because she is the true meaning of love."

Cheryl did her best not to break her composure again, but the good minister made her insides weep with joy. She hadn't expected such kind words granted to her from Tabitha. She hoped they were authentic and not just out of a need to shower her with sisterly love. Cheryl didn't dare look around the congregation to see if any naysayers were against Tabitha's endearing support to *her Rose*. She didn't doubt that there was more than likely a strong consensus that all didn't agree with Tabitha's adoration.

Instead, Cheryl focused on Tabitha and only her minister as the woman and minister who wanted to heal her heart.

"Now, none of us are unaware of Rose's recent struggles or a particular individual that would counter my words in accusation that Sister Rose is more treacherous than trusting. But I ask this congregation to search within your heart for the real truth—not what you've heard or seen on TV or social media, but what you already know about this woman and yourselves. We've all had crosses to bear, mistakes we've had to recover from, and a need for the love Christians profess they have to support those in time of need. Let us show Sister Rose and those who come against her that Christ is within us, and display what Jesus Christ would do. Church, stand with me as I welcome Sister Rose down front for a special prayer."

The congregation was quick to respond to Tabitha's calling, but Cheryl was a little delayed in obeying the request. Although remorseful, she hadn't expected even more attention drawn to her pitiful state. When Tabitha walked from the pulpit down to the congregation and beckoned Cheryl to join her, there was no way she could deny the determined minister.

"And Sister Roxanna and Sister Whitney, please join Sister Rose. You know some of the challenges she's going through, and you've been kind enough to be here today to offer her your support. Stand with her, as the Unity House of Worship Love Community stands with our family member."

Roxanna and Whitney didn't hesitate to join Cheryl. Though her legs felt weak and her heart beat fast, Cheryl gazed into those concerned brown eyes and found the courage to stand tall.

"Let us bow our heads," Tabitha continued.

She gently placed her right hand on Cheryl's bowed head and tried her best not to get distracted by the sweet softness. Her fingers were tempted to stroke and pull on the thick hair and soothe Cheryl's worries with less talk but more action. Tabitha cleared her throat and then refocused her demeanor. She was supposed to be praying for Cheryl's soul, not laying with her!

"Father, God, surround Cheryl Rose Campbell with your love, mercy, and grace. Let her feel your love and know you are neither judge nor juror. You are her protector, her Father who loves her no matter when she is wrong or right. Let her feel the love in this congregation, the protection of this community, who understands the importance of having a unified spirit. We come to you in prayer that Sister Rose's spirit be redeemed and her honor be redeemed; in your name, Father, God, in Christ's name, we pray. Amen."

Tabitha's words broke the small shred of confidence Cheryl had restored during Roxanna's performance. But it was the minister who wiped away her tears with a firm hand that provided a soft caress against her skin and then strong arms that pulled her into an embrace of Christian love. The smell and feel of Tabitha's skin against her own made her dizzy.

What was only a brief moment felt like forever as Cheryl was transported back to the time when she first laid eyes on Tabitha Scott. Back then, the minister was the Minister of Music at their former church, and where she first heard that voice serenade the congregation at Mount Paul the Baptist Church with her powerful praise. Tabitha might have been singing to those faithful church members that Sunday morning, but Cheryl felt as if those songs had been dedicated for her enjoyment only. Even then, ten years younger than the 30-year-old Tabitha Scott, Cheryl knew Tab would belong to her one day.

Tabitha's supportive arms were slowly removed from her body, and the distance put between them jolted Cheryl back into their present state with all eyes on them. Although Tabitha was better at hiding her true feelings than Cheryl was, those eyes weren't deceiving this time. Cheryl hadn't been the only one touched by the brief connection, which made her even more determined to make more than a comeback within her career, but to also come back to Tabitha Scott—and she would pray without ceasing.

my everything

CHERYL'S RELIEF to finally be out of the congregation's watchful gaze was momentary bliss. She had spent the rest of the service and almost another hour trying to remain on her best behavior. Although she appreciated the support from her new woman warrior circle, trying to remain hopeful, kind, and attentive to the young artists, congresswoman, and her talent manager was exhausting—especially since she really wanted a more private conversation with the good minister.

To her dismay, Ayda informed her that Tabitha was in the middle of a church meeting, but the busy and very popular minister would make time for her that afternoon. Cheryl hadn't overlooked Reverend Tabitha Scott's admirers. The women, both young and old, of various races in the nondenominational church were deeply caught up in her sanctified swag! Cheryl couldn't blame them.

Even now, at age 55, Tab was, as Cheryl's mother used to say, *a tall drink of water!* Cheryl couldn't help thinking about climbing that tall fountain of water to quench her thirst. Tabitha had put on a few pounds, but the extra weight for the 5'7" woman was perfectly distributed over her body, which was more firm than soft. Cheryl assumed Tabitha was still playing regular pickup games with her loyal crew of female jocks. No matter how old those studs got, they never seemed to tire of one-upping each other on a basketball court, even if it might dislocate a hip or two or sprain an ankle!

Cheryl was reminded of the many times she'd taken Tabitha to urgent care due to one injury or another the former high school athlete had experienced from the neighborhood basketball court. Except that one time, her injury came from playing a private game with Cheryl, which literally blew the poor minister's back out! Her private amusement and inability to contain her laughter over the memory, alerted the two women of her presence, even though they seemed deep in some sort of intimate contemplation.

Standing at the door of Tabitha's office, eavesdropping on her conversation with the young girl who sang so beautifully in the choir, wasn't her idea of the welcome home Cheryl anticipated Tabitha would give her. Her former smile quickly changed to a more curious or agitated look as she considered whether the tantalizing minister might be interested in even younger women than herself these days.

"Rose, come in. I didn't see you there."

"Yes, I can see that, Reverend Scott. I apologize for the intrusion. It looks like you're busy. Perhaps I should pay you a visit another time?"

It was Tabitha's turn to find amusement in the woman standing before her. She knew Rose well enough to know the woman was spinning her own tales about who knows what. But that tone of disappointment, laced with the need for Tabitha to place the diva center stage in this moment, was clear as rain.

"No, Rose, this is the perfect time. I'm sorry I couldn't see you earlier, but I had church business to take care of."

Cheryl granted her a raised eyebrow as she did another cursory glance over Tabitha and the young woman. "Right, is that what you're calling it now?"

"*What?* Um, Tiffany, can you excuse Ms. Campbell and me? We'll finish our conversation later."

Tiffany wasn't doing a good job either of hiding her amusement with the familiarity and tension between her elders. She might have been deep in her own distress, but Cheryl Rose Campbell and the patient minister confirmed the rumors she had heard in choir practice ever since it was announced the clickbait celebrity would be dropping by Unity.

"Sure, Tab."

Tiffany stood up without hesitation and headed toward Cheryl with a huge smile on her face. She was a fan and had been since she discovered the old CDs that Tabitha and Cheryl had made together. Tiffany wanted to be just as famous as the beautiful diva had become—except with much less drama.

"Sorry, Ms. Campbell. I didn't mean to take up too much of your time. It's so good to meet you and have you here. I love your music, and I believe in you. I hope to see you later."

Cheryl wasn't doing a good job at hiding her true emotions today. She blamed it on the fatigue from the entire week or Tabitha's young friend's reference to the adored minister in such a personal manner. The young woman's genuine kindness forced her to rethink whether she would plot to push the little girl off Stone Mountain if she even thought about getting in her way of reclaiming *Tab*.

Tiffany gave her an unexpected hug, and Cheryl's evil plot to destroy her melted in the warmth of the young woman's embrace.

"Thank you, Tiffany. I'm happy to be here, too. Your song was beautiful and needed."

Tabitha was relieved Tiffany's spirit had seeped into the lioness about to pounce on her and calmed Rose down. As her daughter floated out of her office on Cloud 9 from the small compliment Rose gave her, she silently reflected upon the power of Tiffany's voice and her empathy for others. Tabitha was thankful God had brought Tiffany into her life.

"Rose."

"*Tab*."

"Okay, Rose. What is it that you want to say? I can sense you have something on your mind. Is it time for a confession? I'm not a priest, but you can certainly lay your troubles at my feet."

"Are you sure, Tab? It seems like someone else is already lying at your feet. I knew you liked them young, but damn, that young?"

And there it was again. Rose quickly reminded her of why they never could agree on most things. Cheryl Rose Campbell's boldness and hypocrisy were challenging to deal with without prayer and preparation.

"Okay. How about: *Hello Tabitha. Thank you for helping me salvage my career after being accused of the very thing I'm accusing you of.* Doesn't that sound a little bit more like the gospel, Rose, than what you're preaching?"

"Then who is your young friend, Tab?"

Tabitha smirked, then extended her hand to Cheryl.

"Come have a seat, Rose. You've been gone way too long—and haven't paid much attention to your people back home. You probably don't remember her because it's been a while since she arrived at the church. You were just making a pitstop into my life, as usual. Tiffany is not my young lover. She's my daughter. I took her in and two other refugees from Nigeria."

Cheryl couldn't hide her surprise or her embarrassment. Tabitha was right; she'd spent most of the past twenty-five years building her own little empire beyond her albums by diversifying her money into franchises, hair products, and a few unmemorable reality shows while making more albums and touring worldwide.

Even though she filled her life with distractions that gave her a financial return on her investments, Cheryl hadn't been able to completely bury her feelings for Tabitha or what she wanted to one day have again with her minister. She kept telling herself she'd take that step and come out someday. Maybe when she was as famous as other celebrities who weren't openly gay but were accepted by the Black community without questioning.

As each year went by, Cheryl grew older, as did her ways of remaining stuck in silence and loneliness. Had it truly been that long ago when she'd been introduced to the shy, sweet child whose body had been battered by a brutal stepfather but whose spirit rejoiced every time she opened her mouth to sing?

"Okay, you're right. I can admit when I'm wrong."

Tabitha chuckled. "Really, can you, Rose?"

"Yes, of course I can. Clearly, I needed clarification in this case. I will say she's continued to grow into a beautiful young woman. I don't doubt that she has a ton of admirers —so do you, it would seem. The lovely Christian ladies of your congregation seem like they're ready to have a catfight over who gets to claim you."

Tabitha secretly enjoyed the fight resurfacing in the cat standing before her. She didn't want their reunion to be one of strife, but Ayda was right. Rose needed to regain her fight. If making her jealous would bring back that fire, Tabitha didn't mind being the catalyst to do it.

After all, the observant minister had been paying close attention to Rose's career. Tabitha had caught the photo ops with various men by her side or the occasional mystery lady who was introduced as just a *friend*. These women looked more like the type of *special friend* Robyn Crawford was to Whitney Houston!

"Well, that shouldn't trouble you, Rose, since I'm none of your business."

Tabitha didn't miss Rose's shocked expression or the devilish grin. What was her Rose thinking? Maybe she'd gone too far with the teasing?

Cheryl walked closer to Tabitha, only a breath away from those beautiful, sweet lips that had brought her so much joy in the past. She couldn't help but wonder if they'd want to do it again.

"What if I made you my business?"

The sinful thoughts that crossed the intrigued minister's mind made it hard for her to resist pulling Cheryl into her arms and making it her business to give the woman the proper homecoming she so deserved. She wasn't as brave as she was pretending to be. Her body was nervous, turned on, confused, and overstimulated by Rose's familiar fragrance and the heat that emanated from her voluptuous body, teasing Tabitha to reach out and touch it.

"You don't have time to do that, Rose. They want to see you now. I told them I'd bring you after church."

Dayum! Why did the woman's command to take her to yet another inquisition sound so sexy and appealing coming from those lips?

"And I guess I have no say in the matter? This is just a part of our deal?"

"You guessed, right. Come on, you know they don't like it when we're late."

* * *

Cheryl and Tabitha could hear the *Gospel Girls* before they actually stepped foot into their private party at their renowned elder, gospel singer Dorothy Banks' home in the prominent Cascade Avenue-Road community. Dorothy had lived there during the community's humble beginnings as one of the best places for affluent African American people who wanted to remain within the city limits of Atlanta.

As Atlanta had grown immensely with transplants from around the country, the Cascade community had become even more affluent, with Black business owners, politicians, entertainers, and some questionable entrepreneurs with homes valued in the range of 600k to a few million. Dorothy had purchased her home for a mere $150k in the early 70s with the royalties from her tenth gospel recording. Both the value of her home and her music had prospered well beyond her expectations.

As her special group of women friends referred to her, Dot was the leader of their saints and sinners circle. Although the small group of six were prominent figures in the Black church—some gospel singers like Dorothy, others ministers, and one the recent head of an independent record label, they didn't deny their individual walks with

God weren't always paved with good deeds but salacious secrets they promised to keep amongst themselves.

As Cheryl entered the beautifully preserved history of the gospel greats inside Dorothy Banks' home, their leader questioned how long those secrets would be kept when their wayward daughter had pulled the type of stunt Cheryl had recently done. Today, the statuesque gospel diva with beautiful silver feather-soft hair cascading around her shoulders, dressed in her *Come-to-Jesus garb* of a form-fitted satin knee-length dress, black nylon stockings, and black patten-leather kitten heels, didn't hesitate to instigate the inquisition.

"Come on in here, Rose. Don't slow drag. We've been waiting on y'all for a minute. Tab, what the hell took you so long? You know most of us old heads are on borrowed time!"

The women cackled at their feisty leader's joke. Although they were all of various ages, the average age for the group was 60, with Dot being the eldest at age 70; none of them lacked energy or the inability to give a young girl a run for her money.

Tabitha coughed on the strong Gunga permeating through the air from a blunt Patricia Whitfield, owner of Gospel Slam Records, was passing around. Cheryl wasn't surprised by the table overflowing with *refreshments* the women sat around. She would need a few puffs and a cocktail or two before this evening was over.

"Sorry, Dot, but traffic was bad in Midtown, even to get here. There's a concert at Piedmont Park."

"Well, y'all here now. No time to waste. Cheryl Rose Campbell, sit your ass down and tell us what the hell you were thinking, messing with that young pussy! I know it's sweet and tempting, but this new pussy is dangerous; they are all about spilling the tea on social media, as you can see now."

Cheryl walked around the table to the head and gave Dot a kiss on the cheek and a tight hug before taking the next pass at the blunt. She inhaled the sweet scent and released the smoke into the air before sitting in the empty seat next to Dot.

Tabitha stood in silence before joining the group. She was more interested in hearing Rose's response before settling in. When she saw the news report, and even after hearing Rose's confession on *Atlanta Alive*, Tabitha still believed in her innocence. Rose was a lot of things, but the accusation of Cartier seemed unbelievable to Tabitha, even with the damaging images and the mockery the young woman made of her in song.

Maybe she was just being a fool for love, yet again?

Tabitha needed to hear the words from Rose to truly confirm that she wasn't making a mockery of herself for giving Rose more credit and faith that she wouldn't do such a thing.

"Dot, it was a mistake. You have every right to fuss at me. I'm getting used to the ridicule. But believe me when I say I didn't touch that girl. It wasn't how it looked."

Tabitha watched the skeptical faces of the women around the table. It was clear none of them believed Rose's denial of fucking that young girl. But she still held on to hope that Rose was telling the truth.

"Then how did she get those pictures?"

Tabitha's soft request for Rose to share more details caught everyone's attention. The looks in their eyes confirmed they needed more information, too. Though she wished she didn't need to continue to prove her innocence by telling the humiliating story to the group, Cheryl needed Tabitha to believe her more than anyone else.

"Are you going to sit down, or are you waiting to hear what I have to say before you dump me?"

"Oooh, nah, child, don't tell me you two done started it up again, Rose? Tab, I knew you was still sprung on, Rose. I don't blame you, though. Y'all too cute together," Cleopatra Clarkston of the famous Clarkston Singers chimed in.

Cleopatra whet her lips with a few sips of her whiskey but couldn't wait to get more tea on Cheryl's busy love life and the revamp of the two lovebirds' rocky relationship. Cheryl wasn't bothered by their older sister's teasing. Cleo was addicted to gossip even though she did her best to keep her business hidden in the closet. Tabitha didn't seem amused at all. The prying minister was clearly more focused on getting the truth out of her Rose.

"Please, Tab. Sit down next to me. I will answer your question, but I need you to show me you're open to the truth."

"Oh she open alright—to you, Rose, wide open!" Cleopatra continued to tease.

"Hush, Cleo! You always starting some shit. Tab, gone sit yo ass on down here with Rose. She gonna tell us, girl," Dot commanded.

Tabitha obeyed their elder and sat between Rose and the usually quiet, introverted Reverend Carlotta Williams of Better Days Ministry.

"Good, now go on, Rose."

"Well, if you must know the whole truth and nothing but the truth."

"Yes, child, so help you, God!" Cleopatra exclaimed.

Cheryl giggled. It was evident Cleo was enjoying her whiskey. The 60-year-old could drink most folks under the table, and she could belt out a gospel song that would leave even the devil weeping with sorrow. It was still amazing to Cheryl how Dot and Cleo had become private friends when they spent so much time on the gospel circuit, being infamous nemeses vying for the spotlight of the greatest gospel diva despite many other notable singers' claims to that fame.

"I was tired. Tired of everything. I know I haven't had as long of a career as many of you around this table, but it feels like a lifetime. It was my birthday, and I wasn't feeling like celebrating getting older, no offense to any of you."

"Shit, no offense taken! You young, Rose, so you have no idea that at your age, it's a blessing. But we've all been there when you think your 40s is a death sentence, then you feel the same about the 50s; by the time you get to your 60s and 70s, child, you are just glad you breathing, and you can remember your lyrics and keep on singing!"

The other women in their 60s nodded in agreement with Dot. Even Tabitha had to agree that at age 55, she spent less time worrying about the signs of aging and more time living her best life. She vaguely remembered still holding on to the resentment of aging—and it didn't help that she started menopause early. Menopause was a bitch, but she didn't die afterward. So, she saw no reason to lament the time she couldn't get back and instead just appreciate what she did have.

"I know, Dot. But you asked me why this happened. I'm just being honest. I felt unattractive, old, defeated, and exhausted with my life. I was also in the middle of a fundraiser for a good friend who was dying. I wasn't doing a benefit to help preserve her life but to help bury her with dignity. All of it was a bit too real for me. Then Cartier approached me at the benefit, and she showered me with praise and adoration for my public persona. I tried to escape into the vision that she painted of me."

Cheryl saw the head nods and heard the mumbles of agreement. A few members of their group had dabbled in the drama and forbidden fruit of young girls. Carlotta had even married her young wife and, like Tabitha, was open about her sexuality—and that decision had come with its own price. Cheryl knew Tabitha understood how difficult it was to chase a determined young woman away. Tabitha had tried hard to resist Cheryl's youthful, lovesick aspirations to be her woman, but ultimately the Minister of Music had given into her charm back then.

"So you took her to your hotel room, and then what?" Tabitha persisted with the line of questioning. She wasn't going to be satisfied with Rose's story until she knew if Rose had been as weak as she'd been to fall for a younger woman.

"Then I spent most of the time in the bathroom stalling, trying to figure out what I wanted to do with her. I ordered food and drinks, and she occupied herself watching TV while I hid. Ayodele called me, and in the middle of our call, Cartier had grown tired of waiting and insisted I join her."

"Did you?"

Cheryl could hear the impatience in Tabitha's voice and also anger or jealousy, or maybe both. The rest of the group were less emotional about her story but more intrigued by the potential juicy tidbits.

"Eventually. I sat with her for a while but then told her I wasn't feeling well and went to bed. She came into the room and asked if she could lay with me, maybe help me fall asleep or comfort me. I didn't decline her offer. But when I tell you that I never touched that girl, I mean it. I did fall asleep, and when I woke up, she was naked in the bed with me, and she was clear about her intentions."

"Then Rose, what did you fucking do!"

"Okay, Tab. Calm down, child. Let Rose speak. I know you getting hot and bothered by this story, but let your woman speak her truth," Dot interjected.

Tabitha snorted. "Clearly, Rose isn't my woman."

Tabitha hated letting her anger get the best of her. As much as she prayed and tried to work on her temper and patience, God wasn't through with her yet. Clearly, Rose re-entered her life to show her that she had much more work to do in those areas.

"Dot, it's okay. I would have been pissed to know if there was any potential that somebody else was lying with Tab too. But that's another discussion for another time, just between us two," Rose said, hoping to share some truth and humor to lighten Tabitha's mood.

"But I won't belabor this story. I didn't fuck her, nor did she fuck me, Tab. I told her that I needed her to leave and apologized for miscommunicating. I offered to call her an Uber, and she, of course, was angry, and we argued. But in the end, she left. One of my many mistakes was assuming that the argument was the last I'd see or hear of her. I never imagined it would escalate to this. But in truth, as I've had a hard time dealing with the fallout, I'm strangely relieved. I know that sounds crazy to y'all, right?"

Cheryl looked around the table and surprisingly found mutual understanding in their eyes. It was the smallest of the loud voices in the group who uttered words that resonated with her feelings.

"We all understand where you've been and how you're feeling right now, no matter what choices we've made. Although God offers everything we need, sometimes God isn't everything we want. It wasn't easy to come out in the Methodist church either; even though we may display an air of more literate sophistication, Black churches are based on the same ideology no matter how we sing a song or how we praise. Leviticus 20:13 is the most common passage in the Bible used against us to damn our souls to hell for loving someone of the same sex. Yet Exodus 20:14 and Matthew 5:28 specifically refer to adultery in a marriage, which is often skated over. We all struggle with our desires —our need to want more than God. Because we do need love other than God, and in my mind and heart, there's nothing wrong with that, Rose."

Everyone was laser-focused on the mild-mannered minister Carlotta as she spoke some of the most sage advice.

"Well hell, Carlotta! I guess it's true, it ain't quantity but the quality that matters. You said a mouthful right there! And y'all know I've had my struggles with my walk with God too. But I know he loves me no matter how much I also enjoy the love of the sweetness of another woman. I just ain't trying to lose these coins out here by spreading that sort of gospel. Rose, Tab, and Carlotta, I admire your courage. And I stand by you in any way that I can," Dot interjected.

"Me too, y'all! I stand by you, too. But can we lighten up this mood, sisters? We didn't come here for a prayer meeting. Our Rose is back in town, and we should enjoy this nice spread Dot set out for us. After listening to Reverend Talbot all afternoon preach from the same verse John 3:16, I know I'm hungry as he conveniently compared God's sacrifice to Jesus as the minister's need for us to fork over our earnings to him. But I'm tired of that man pimping out Jesus every time he needs to upgrade his ride!"

The Gospel Girls burst into laughter as they all appreciated the comic relief Cleo always provided. Over the next hour, they gave their personal summation of the events in their lives that Rose had missed over the years. Although seasoned sisters, her friends had been just as busy in their personal and professional lives as she had been. Her keen attention was focused on Tabitha, who she was silently pleased to learn hadn't referenced any admirers she might be interested in. There was no ring on her finger, so she was still single and hopefully ready to mingle with Cheryl!

"Do you want to take a taste with me?" Cheryl teased Tabitha as she held the well-used blunt to her minister's face.

Tabitha's mouth watered at the thought of what she really wanted to taste from Cheryl, but the woman was clearly amused by her struggle to remain composed amid temptation.

"Go on, Tab, get you some! Loosen up that collar, Reverend Scott! Ever since you and Rose took a hiatus, you been pure as the driven snow! Bring that old Tab back!" Cleopatra teased.

The other women nodded in agreement and then waited to see if Tabitha would crumble under the peer pressure.

"I promise I'll be gentle. Just a little, Tab," Cheryl continued to seduce her.

Tabitha slowly nodded in agreement and held her breath while waiting for Rose's sweet lips to touch hers. She licked her lips in anticipation, and that small gesture brought a sparkle to Rose's teasing brown eyes. Rose took a big toke of the blunt and then leaned in to Tabitha's lips and beckoned her minister to open wide enough so she could come inside.

The sweet scent of the Gunga flowed through their nostrils, and soft lips upon softer lips passed the powerful smoke in a gentle kiss that sent the most electrifying, wonderful feeling to their nervous systems. The touch of skin on skin, the euphoria of the weed, and the wetness of their salivatory glands ignited the fire inside of them that neither wanted to extinguish.

Cheryl pulled back from the tasty minister's lips long enough to exhale deeply then dove back in for another deeper kiss. She could hear Tabitha's moan of satisfaction and feel her minister's determined hand stroking her face and cupping her chin to deepen the kiss.

The rest of the Gospel Girls were enjoying their special performance with catcalls and giggles. Tabitha and Cheryl didn't give a good fuck about the spectators when all they wanted to do was take things further.

"Go ahead, Tab, you betta get you some of that sweet Rose! Yasss, praise God, that drought is finally over!" Cleopatra shouted.

"Yes, to God be the glory, 'cause Rose is back in your story! I knew my girls would find their way back to each other!" Dot chimed in, not to be outdone by Cleopatra's boisterous bragging about what God can do!

Patricia and Carlotta just shook their heads as their two older sisters carried on their antics. Although they were genuinely amused and happy to see the two back in each other's arms, the Methodist bunch prided themselves on a more refined display of emotions than the Baptist bunch. They had accepted that Dorothy and Cleopatra would often show up and show out even though they'd prefer a less obvious display of their joy. No matter how they reacted to this good news, the Gospel Girls all prayed that the two would stay together this time.

"I've been waiting all day to do that, Tab," Cheryl confessed breathlessly once she released Tabitha's irresistibly soft lips.

Tabitha blushed and couldn't contain a silly grin of joy forming on her face. She was in complete agreement with Rose's need for that kiss and more. Amid the joy, the good minister knew they weren't ready to explore anything further. But God help her if Rose didn't tempt her with more!

"Take me home, Tab. It's time to go."

shining my light

WHEN TABITHA SCOTT rose the next morning, she soon discovered she would have her homegrown paparazzi to contend with. The three pair of watchful eyes clicked their lenses with each movement she made into the unusually noisy kitchen. Tabitha knew she had to thank her youngest son, Isaiah, for the loud morning reception of laughter, clatter of dishes, and serenade of his latest lyrics for an upcoming album.

As much as she'd accepted his decision years ago to further his career in a more secular environment and move away from their family home to New York, the boy's big personality and ability to get her out of her comfort zone had been truly missed. She smiled brightly at the joy that filled her heart to see her three little ones—well, not so little ones anymore, fill the space with the love and happiness she had wanted to share with them when she first decided to adopt them years ago.

Tabitha absentmindedly smoothed the soft curls that were precision cut into a beautiful pixie style for her salt and pepper crown. She nervously tugged at the olive silk blouse. Then adjusted the belt, which secured her athletic figure into a pair of tailored black cashmere slacks. Tabitha walked as normally as possible into the kitchen to greet her family—even though her feet were doing their best to adjust to the newness of the five-inch shiny black heels that increased her 5'7" frame just a tad bit taller for the statuesque, handsome minister.

Her efforts to polish the rough diamond that was the Reverend Tabitha Scott didn't go unnoticed by her spectators. Isaiah was the first to call attention to Tabitha's new look. Her face full of makeup, not too gaudy but just enough to highlight the attractive minister's natural assets on soft chocolate skin that blushed at the sound of her youngest son's teasing.

"Morning, Rev! A little late to rise on this day the Lord has made, eh? But now I see why. Looks like you got a pretty date early this morning, Tab and somebody's gonna be happy with you, diva! You fire, Ma!"

Tiffany giggled at her brother's teasing. Jerome, the eldest of the three, handed Tabitha her usual cup of black coffee and a soft smile, ignoring his little brother's antics as usual. Still, he couldn't ignore the new look and attitude of his Mother, Minister, and Savior. She was looking exceptionally beautiful today.

"Morning, Rev, you do look beautiful. Coffee?"

Tabitha couldn't hide her pleasure over her children's approval of her appearance. Although the extra special effort was devoted to pleasing another, their feedback gave her even more confidence that she'd please her intended audience.

"Thanks, Jerome." She took the cup of her favorite Pete's coffee and sipped a little before responding to the speculative eyes waiting for the explanation behind her Monday morning majestic.

"Isaiah looks like we're both in for a surprise today, son. I didn't expect to see you here this morning. Actually, I hadn't expected to see you here so often. With your big fine house and all, what are you doing hanging out with the likes of your little old family?"

Isaiah chuckled, then walked over to Tabitha and grabbed her around the waist for a big hug before returning to his plate full of fluffy pancakes, cheese eggs, and grits. His skinny little body could devour massive amounts of food without adding an extra pound or two to his lean frame. Tabitha silently envied his successful battle with the bulge—too bad she wasn't as lucky without putting forth a concerted effort. She grabbed a banana from the fruit bowl on the kitchen island and settled for a more meager start to her day.

"Ah, Ma, you know Isaiah ain't forgot his real fam! I was over here doing the Christian thing, helping my lil sis with her class project. You know Tiffany done waited to the last minute to finish the music video for her final project. And what kind of big bro would I be if I didn't use my skillz and help bring home that 100? We were up all night creating that fire reel, right, Tif?"

Tiffany frowned. She couldn't hide her normal irritation with her big bro's loose mouth. He was supposed to be helping her in private to finish the project she had sworn to Tabitha would be done well in advance this time instead of her usual last-minute ditch efforts. But Isaiah had just blasted her screw-up again. After her confession to Tabitha about her conflicted relationship with Tyanna, she knew Tabitha would assume her mad dash to finish the project was due to the troubles in her love life.

"Tiffany, is that true? Isaiah was helping you finish your video for Mr. Summer's film class?"

"Yes, Tab. But it was almost done. Isaiah was just helping me fix a few technical issues, that's all. I did most of the work on my own."

"Eh, she right about that, Tab. Lil sis put together a banger! But you know I put that extra fire in it for her! You gotta see it. Maybe after you come back from wherever you going today?"

Tabitha didn't miss Isaiah's slick redirection to her new look. Jerome seemed oblivious to his brother's antics. However, her eldest was taking in all the tea being spilled as he surfed through the latest stock alerts, Apple News, in between church emails as her official church Treasurer and acting Head of the Deacon Board. Jerome was doing a fine job of presiding over the deacons, who were much older than his 30 years. Tabitha knew her son was determined to make his mark and replace Deacon Reynolds even after the 70-year-old got back on his feet after a recent fall off his roof, which caused him to break his leg in four places.

"You are going somewhere today, ain't you, Ma? Or is somebody pulling up to see the Rev? Somebody like *Cheryl Rose Campbell*?"

Isaiah mumbled Rose's name as he continued to tease Tabitha. He hid his sheepish grin by stuffing his face with his favorite banana-nut pancakes, complements of Tiffany, as a repayment for his help.

"Son, you know, Thessalonians 3:11 says, *those who are idle or not busy are easily led to sin*. I'm gonna need you to get back to work on your own album and let me take care of my business. And if you plan on hanging around here so frequently, I'm going to start charging you rent again."

Tabitha tempered her words with a huge smile. Sometimes it was difficult to detect when the good minister was genuinely pissed with them or if she was simply showing her brand of teasing. Either way, they all knew whether she was disappointed in them or proud of them; Tabitha Scott loved them always.

"Rev, it's time we get a move on. We have a meeting with the bank this morning at 9."

Although Jerome was more than busy and never spent too many days idle as one of the minister's trusted advisers and protectors, he would also revisit this reunion with the infamous songstress Cheryl Rose Campbell, who was putting a different shine on his mother.

"Right, Jerome. Thanks for the reminder. Alright, you two, go get into some good trouble. And yes, I want to see this video, so come by the church later today and show me what you put together."

"Thanks, Tab. Will Ms. Campbell be there?" Tiffany asked tentatively, hoping she'd get to see the gospel diva too.

All eyes turned to Tabitha to confirm that Cheryl was, in fact, the reason for her shiny new look and personality.

"Yes, Tiffany. Ms. Campbell will be there. I'm sure she would enjoy seeing your project, too. Come around lunch, and we'll take a look."

Tiffany's smile grew even brighter, and Isaiah gave her a high-five over their mutual excitement for the chance to get the full optics on Tabitha and Cheryl.

"Now, your brother has told me that I need to get a move on. I'll see y'all later."

Tabitha grabbed her laptop bag and headed behind Jerome to the car—but not before doing a double-take with Isaiah.

"You sure I look alright?"

Isaiah gave her a sly wink. "Ma, you fire! Chery Rose Campbell gone be all in your snack!"

"Isaiah! Language," Tabitha playfully reprimanded.

"But thank you, son. And be on time."

* * *

Cheryl Rose Campbell was more than pleased by the snack that stood before her in Unity's choir room. Although Tabitha had chosen to tease her instead of please her the other evening, the vision of one of God's most magnificent creatures was apologies enough. Cheryl Rose Campbell was no quitter; patience was a virtue she often lacked, but Tabitha was clearly worth the wait.

Tabitha checked her watch as she nervously awaited a reaction to her new look other than those cloudy brown eyes, which were checking out her every nook and cranny. She had no doubt Cheryl appreciated her new outfit, but a verbal compliment wouldn't hurt either. At least it would drown out the palpitations of her frantic heartbeat, which was overstimulated by the sexy diva's appearance. The determined minister wasn't the only woman who came to sway another to her will and her way!

"Morning, Rose. Right on time."

Cheryl enjoyed the appreciative minister's watchful gaze as those deep brown eyes caressed her skin as if they were really penetrating her body with their thorough inspection of the dip in her smoky gray v-cut blouse. They trailed over her healthy curves, journeyed to her slender waist, rolled down to her plump hips and backside, lingered between the modest slit in her black pencil skirt, then slid down her smooth legs to the 6-inch red bottoms before returning to Cheryl's mutual hungry expression.

They had a few more hours before lunchtime, but Tabitha's stomach was already growling with a hunger that Mother Florence's catered lunch from Mama Flo's Soul Food Kitchen around the corner wouldn't satisfy.

"I'm glad I didn't disappoint you, Tab, as you did me last night. As you see, I'm not holding your disappearing act against you. I can turn the other cheek."

Cheryl punctuated her playful banter with a view of her backside as she turned away from Tabitha and dropped her purse and coat into one of the choir chairs. Tabitha didn't miss a chance to get a repeat glance at that plump apple bottom before Rose caught her looking.

"You, on the other hand, must have gotten your beauty rest with not a care in the world, looking all Denzella Washington. What are you trying to do, Tab? Catch you a *Minister's Wife?*"

Tabitha cleared her throat and tried to moisten her dry orifice, which was parched and in need of a libation from Rose's private well.

"I think somewhere in there was a compliment? So, thank you, Rose. You look lovely as well today, but then you always do, even when you're mad at me. From your tone, I think it's the latter today. I'm sorry about last night. I didn't mean to misrepresent my intentions. I just think we need..."

"I know, I know, Tab. You want to take things slow. No need to repeat that virtuous verse to me today. I heard you loud and clear, and fine, slow it is. But I know your time is precious, with all the church ladies laying in wait for your attention. I'm ready to get started if you are, and I promise I'll behave."

Tabitha shook her head but refused to counter Rose's sarcasm. As much as she wanted to keep them focused on the business arrangement for now, she silently admitted she was disappointed Rose wouldn't continue teasing her into a willing submission to the woman's charm. Being a good girl was the last thing Tabitha really wanted Rose to be.

"Right, you're right, Rose. Let's talk about what you want to achieve with this album. I agree with Ayda that it's a good way for people to refocus on why they love you and need your music. But given the circumstances, have you considered the message you want to share with this new music?"

Tabitha held her hand out to Cheryl and led her to the piano in the center of the room. They sat at the keys, and Tabitha did her best to keep their focus on the music, not the feel of her thigh against Rose's, Rose's aroma, and those eyes that watched her intently as she did her best to remain appropriate.

"I have thought about it. Actually, I thought about it a lot last night after being with Dot and the rest of the girls. Roxanna's performance also had me thinking about this new album's music and message. One thing I know for sure that I want to convey is a positive message. I'm so tired of hate speech, anger, and brutality in this world. Not just with actions but more with our words. Whatever we create, it needs to be about speaking life, like Ayodele's song. No more bringing death to each other through our words."

Cheryl wasn't expecting Tabitha to be completely moved by her initial thoughts, but she didn't expect the huge grin.

Did the good minister find her ideas childish, too simplistic?

It wasn't surprising that Tabitha disagreed with her; they had often fought over the concepts, lyrics, and even melodies of music they had created together. But in the end, they always came to a happy resolution. The music they made at the piano, in the lyrics and chorus, evoked spiritual awakenings and were often celebrated by the sexual awakening in the music they created between the sheets!

"What? I'm sure you have a better idea, Tab. At least you always think you do."

Tabitha grabbed Rose's hand to quiet the active brain and mouth, ready to punish her collaborator over an assumed offense.

"Rose, I love the idea. I'm not amused by your ideas. I'm consumed with abundant joy by them. You're absolutely right. We need more music that speaks of shining a light for the glory of the Lord. What you've described is the Book of Isaiah. It's poetic and prophetic and imagines the glorious future of Jerusalem and the people of Israel. Even now, we still pray for the same in today's society. Even when we profess to share good news with our neighbors, family, friends, co-workers, social media, movies, and music, it all sounds the complete opposite. It's sad and melancholy and laced with bitterness. You're brilliant, Rose! It is time for some good news!"

Tabitha's excitement got the best of her, and without any thoughts about her promise to pace herself with Rose, she leaned in to those former pouty lips that were now smiling bright and rewarded them with a deep kiss. When she finally released Rose's lips, the twin sparkle in their eyes confirmed their mutual desire for the direction of the new music and the revival of their relationship.

"Rose."

Cheryl caressed Tabitha's face and returned a soft, quick kiss, long enough to convey her mutual appreciation for the inspiration and short enough to ensure she kept her wits about herself. As much as she wanted a more private collaboration, Cheryl was just as intrigued about the music concept as Tabitha was. They'd have time to play later.

"Yes, Tab. Let's talk. I'm glad we see eye to eye. I love your idea."

Tabitha smiled brightly and silently thanked Rose for keeping them focused on the current need.

"Good, glad we could get on the same page quickly. I even think the main song needs to be titled *Shining My Light*. Rose, I know it's hard right now, but you are a light to so many, and we don't want to let Satan or anybody darken that. It's also important to remind the people you touch that the person who gives light also needs to receive it. We need to speak life into you, too. As Isaiah says, *you feel me*?"

Cheryl granted Tabitha a raised eyebrow, then giggled.

"What? What's so funny?"

"Are you teasing me? Where does the Bible say, *you feel me*?"

Tabitha joined Rose in the laughter. "Sorry, I meant my son, Isaiah. By the way, it's been a long time since you've seen him and Jerome. Isaiah and Tiffany are coming by in a few hours to have lunch with us. Jerome will be dropping by in a little while. They're excited to hang out with you if that's okay."

Cheryl found Tabitha's smile contagious. She was pleased to know her minister wanted to include her more in her personal life as much as in this professional arrangement. She promised that this time, she'd focus on what and who was important in Tabitha's life instead of what she needed or wanted.

"Yes, Tab. It's fine. You never know; maybe they can help us brainstorm on the album, too. They all have beautiful voices and songwriting skills. I guess they got that from their mother."

Tabitha beamed with pride. "A little. But they're naturally gifted. And they will love the opportunity to show off their skillz. In the meantime, let's work on a melody and some lyrics before they get here."

"Yes, Rev. Whatever you say."

* * *

Jerome Wright watched silently at the door as he admired the picture of perfect harmony between his faithful mother, Tabitha Scott, and the unpredictable temptress, Cheryl Rose Campbell. The music that flowed between the two was spiritually fortifying, and if this was just the start of the scorned singer's new album, redemption was just a streaming download away! Jerome couldn't help worrying about the day the album would be finished, and Cheryl would no longer need Tabitha's help. Whether Cheryl had good intentions or not toward his mother, Jerome knew he'd be there to help her pick up the pieces just like all the other times before.

"I don't know, Rose. Something's missing. I love this first verse and chorus, just as they are, but we need something more. This is where we need to bring home the point that you need others to give you the love you give to them."

Cheryl agreed but didn't want to sound too needy or desperate for attention. She couldn't deny that she often felt lonely or wanted someone to be by her side, too, but she wasn't about to present herself as weak.

"I hear what you're saying, but maybe we just repeat the first verse and then be done. It's a strong verse, and the overall song is strong enough to set the tone of the album."

"Or, you could do another verse like Tab recommended. May I?"

Tabitha and Cheryl were surprised by Jerome's unexpectedly strong assertion about what they thought was a private conversation. They nodded in agreement as he walked toward them and requested Tabitha to swap places with him.

When Jerome began to repeat the melody that Tabitha had created only an hour earlier, Cheryl was pleasantly surprised by his natural ability to pick up music without sheet music. Her amazement expanded when he took a few minutes to create the perfect verse.

"How about something like this..."

VERSE
I strive to be a light to those in need,
And share the love of Christ in every deed,
But sometimes it feels like no one's there,
To give me love and show they care.

"Then we return to the chorus."

CHORUS
I'll keep shining my light every day,
And pray that others will find their way,

To let Christ in and be a light, too,
And together, we can make our way through.

"Dang, bro! You always trying to glow up. Mad respect though, Romey, them lyrics fire, bro!"

What was once a private session of two quickly became a family affair as Isaiah and Tiffany joined them in the choir room carrying the bags of soul food from Mother Florence. Tabitha and Rose couldn't agree more with Isaiah on Jerome's amazing work in such a short time to finalize their initial version of *Shining My Light.*

They also couldn't deny their tummies were ready for some of Mother Florence's mouth-watering savory dishes. Tabitha could smell the peppery gravy, cheesy macaroni, and smoked turkey that she was sure Mother Florence had packed for her favorite minister.

"Isaiah's right, Jerome. That was a beautiful verse. Thank you. We might need your help on some of the other songs if you're interested," Cheryl chimed in while still keeping her eye on the enormous bags of delicious-smelling food.

Jerome did his best to retain a modest disposition, but Cheryl Rose Campbell's flattery didn't fall flat on his ears. He loved making music just as much as he enjoyed working with numbers and securing the good minister's calling.

"I wouldn't mind being of service to this project if Tab thinks it's a good idea."

He also didn't hesitate to make Cheryl aware that he took his guidance from his minister, not her tempting offer. On the other hand, his brother and sister were salivating at the potential of being a part of the album, too, more than they were waiting patiently to get their mouths on some of Mother Florence's banana pudding.

"Ma, we can help, too! We have that fire, too, Ms. Campbell. We even have an audition sample. Don't we, lil sis? Let's set up that music video we just created."

Tiffany frowned as her brother did his best to ride her wave. "Um, you mean my music video, the one where I composed the music, wrote the lyrics, directed the video, cast the actors, and did the final cut?"

"Ah, Tif, why you being extra. You know, I put that fire on it. Forreal, sis. Give Isaiah his props now!"

"Okay, okay, enough, you two. Rose, forgive my children. Let's blame their ill manners on the fact we are all hungry, and Mother Florence's food is making us all not think straight. So, let's take this to the table in the back and discuss these ideas over a good meal after I bless the food and these misguided souls."

The hungry bunch burst into laughter, but they all agreed that nourishment and further mediation over who would get a chance to participate in the new album was needed. By the time they were finished devouring the food and their bellies were filled, the euphoria of the spicy, savory dishes made them all more content and agreeable.

Instead of debating who was worthy of a spot on the album, Tiffany and Isaiah showed off their work on the music video, and Tabitha and Cheryl praised them for their excellent work. Then, the three siblings decided it was time to investigate their elders' relationship further. It was even more evident that they were cuffing. Cheryl was fixing Tabitha's plate, Tabitha was wiping sauce from Cheryl's mouth, and they were giggling at their own private jokes like two little lovebirds.

And inquiring minds needed to know the real tea!

"So, Cheryl Rose Campbell, wassup with you and Ma! Y'all know we ain't blind, right? We can see something firey going on between you two. How long has this been going on?"

"Isaiah, watch your mouth, son."

Cheryl grabbed Tabitha's hand to temper her minister's words. She wasn't ashamed to share her feelings about Tabitha with her children. Cheryl could feel Jerome's trepidation toward her even though he did his best to hide behind the civility in his words and expression—but it was clear he didn't trust her, and she couldn't blame him. The eldest of the three, Cheryl imagined had a good memory about the *pitstops* she'd made in Tabitha's life and the impact of her flighty behavior on his mother.

"It's okay, Tab. I don't mind sharing with your family if you don't mind."

Cheryl searched Tabitha's embarrassed eyes for confirmation that she had her permission to answer Isaiah's questions—and hopefully any questions that her minister might also have.

"Only if you want to, Rose."

"Yes, I want to, very much."

Tabitha blushed. She wanted Cheryl to express her feelings, which was just as apparent to the watchful eyes amused by the sexual tension between their two elders.

"I think I fell in love with Tab the first day she sat at the piano at Mount Paul the Baptist Church one Sunday morning. I was much younger then, probably about your age, Tiffany. And your mother was so goddamn—I mean, beautiful. She *is* very beautiful."

Isaiah gave Cheryl a sly wink, and she giggled under his scrutiny. Tabitha was less amused by Cheryl's overly candid words in their holy sanctuary. But her mind enjoyed the walk down memory lane just the same. Honestly, she had found it just as difficult to concentrate on the lyrics on the page and the keys on the piano as she attempted to spread the good news amongst the small congregation over 25 years ago.

The then-20-year-old Cheryl Rose Campbell was way too young for the 30-year-old Minister of Music. Still, that hadn't stopped the precocious young singer from wrapping Tabitha around her fingers within less than a year of being introduced during that faithful revival evening. Tabitha had done her best to resist Cheryl's flirtations and full-blown assault on her senses. That body, smile, voice, and hands filled her with more than the Holy Spirit every time they were in close proximity!

"Tabitha didn't make it easy for me to get to know her other than the choir rehearsals and private piano lessons my mother hired her to give me as I started my recording career. But practice turned into writing songs together and spending more time together, and I tried to obey Tabitha's wishes to keep things professional. Then, one night, I was out with some of my choir boys. We snuck out to this hot gay nightclub one Saturday night, and I saw Tabitha there for the first time. For a while, I wasn't sure if she was gay, although I had heard a few rumors from other church friends who were in the closet like us."

"So, what happened? What did you do, Ma, when you saw Cheryl there?" Isaiah was impatient. He wanted to get the real tea sooner rather than later, and Cheryl was taking way too much license with teasing out the information.

"Son, don't interrupt grown folks when they're talking. This is Rose's story."

Cheryl threw a little side-eye toward Tabitha. "Oh, is that right, Tab, *my story*? Am I telling it wrong? Why don't you share what happened next?"

Tabitha could hear the teasing sound in Rose's voice,

but she knew all eyes were on her, and she didn't doubt they questioned her side of the story.

"No, Rose, you've been telling the truth. I saw Rose, and at first, I was worried about what she'd think and if she'd tell anyone about seeing me there. I wasn't open about my sexuality at the time, and it was one of the reasons I did my best to stay away from Rose intimately. I knew the moment I saw her that I wanted her, but not just in a sexual manner. Rose was the kind of woman that would make me want to give my all to her. Remaining in the closet and sneaking around wouldn't be enough for me—and as you can see, it wasn't enough, that is, for me."

he will never let me go

"SAINTS, thank you for signing up for this glorious opportunity to walk our way into spiritual excellence. Now, most of you know the *Woman Thou Art Walking* challenge has been an annual event that our loving minister, Tabby, has given me the honor of presiding over. For those of you who are new to this spectacular event at Unity, don't worry, the Rev and I got yo back. Isn't that right, Tabby?"

Cheryl cringed every time Eloise Montgomery butchered Tab's name with her pet name, which was laced with a lecherous lust the pretentious prayer princess didn't have the authority to display toward her minister!

"If she keeps on touching Tab, Sister Eloise is going to fall down and not get back up! Mama, say knock the devil out, and that's what I'm going to do if yo gurl don't get her spirit right."

Mitchell Suttler and his husband of two years, Paul, cackled over Cheryl's stage whisper as the diva continued to express her displeasure for the blatant flirtation their substitute diva was displaying regarding Tabitha Scott. When they saw Cheryl head into Unity earlier that morning, Mitchell and Paul couldn't wait to crash the women's only volunteer meeting just to connect with their gurl. Well, Cheryl was more Mitchell's girl from back in the day. Now that Paul was his new hubby, *mi casa su casa*, or something like that!

"Cheryl, gurl, you know you a mess! You ain't been back but a minute, and already you trying to stir up trouble."

Cheryl snorted as she kept her eyes stead on Eloise and her wandering hand. The good minister didn't seem to mind Eloise's hand running over those broad shoulders with a familiarity Cheryl didn't want to consider how Eloise had acquired. She just kept a watchful eye on the two as they sat at the front of the church conducting *their business*. Cheryl was about to make it *her business* if this foolishness persisted!

"Well, like the Bible says, *Don't start none, won't be none!*"

Mitchell and Paul almost spit out their energy drinks as they pre-gamed for a brutal workout with their trainer later that day.

"Cheryl, honey, where in the Bible do you see such a verse?"

Cheryl threw Paul some side-eye. He was a cute little blonde-haired Ken doll, perfect for her smooth, dark chocolate brother, Mitchell, who loved him some white boys. But Paul clearly needed to be indoctrinated into their dialect so he could better understand their secret language when they spilled tea and kiki about the good Christian folks right under their nose.

Mitchell chimed in, "Proverbs 3:30. *Don't pick a fight without reason when no one has done you harm.*"

He was more than familiar with Cheryl's Bible reference because they had often used it instead of her blatant translation. He could tell his sister wasn't taking the news well of Tabitha's many admirers during her long absence from the minister's bed.

"And she aiming for a fight. Like Isaiah said, *you feel me*?"

Mitchell and Paul looked at her dumbfounded. Was this yet another secret code reference?

"Cheryl, what verse in Isaiah are you talking about?"

From the first time since she'd sat down in this charade of a meeting, Cheryl cracked a smile. She had truly enjoyed her lunch with Tabitha and her family, and being with her minister for these few days was leaving a big impression on her.

"Tab's son, Isaiah, not the Bible."

The boys snickered, and the constant noisemakers' rude behavior had worn out Eloise Montgomery's patience. Cheryl could see Tabitha's displeasure as well, but she wasn't so inclined to care about the misbehaving minister's feelings right now when that green-eyed monster was directing her path.

"Excuse me, Cheryl Rose Campbell. Is there something you want to say? I'm sure we'd all love to hear what has amused you about the women's ministry's plight toward empowerment, health, and self-love. Want to share? Or is this just you passing the time before you head back to your real life?"

Mitchell and Paul grabbed Cheryl's hands to steady their indignant icon, ready to reign down hell on Sister Eloise. But Cheryl wasn't in the mood to remain silent as her territory was being threatened. She pulled away from their gentle grip, stood proudly without hesitation, and looked Sister Eloise Montgomery in her deceitful dark eyes.

"Why thank you, Sister Montlick."

"Montgomery, it's Montgomery, Cheryl."

"Yes, whatever. I was just overcome by your ministry and motivation. I feel like that old shouting farmer who couldn't hold his mule or his peace! But please, you just keep on saving us, saints and sinners. And I'll keep it all on the inside, as best I can. Amen?"

Mitchell and Paul completely lost their composure, and Cheryl could hear them cackling from their seats and then all the way to the hallway as they stood and held their index fingers up as a sign they needed to relieve themselves of the drama between two divas. Eloise and Cheryl's standoff wasn't complete until Tabitha stepped in and called a recess for the moment.

"Um, church, we're unfortunately running out of time for this initial meeting. Elle will schedule another one. As she mentioned, Elle graciously took on this huge program, and we are so grateful for all her work. So, y'all get ready for an even bigger and brighter event. Amen, church? Go with God, and please go in peace."

* * *

"Do you want to tell me what that was all about? Or are you just going to sit there in silence for the next 30 minutes?"

Cheryl hated the sound of disappointment in Tabitha's voice as they sat in the perturbed minister's office. But she wasn't the one who should be on trial here, considering Tabitha hadn't discouraged Eloise Montgomery's behavior—instead, she'd praised the woman for her volunteerism.

What else was she giving away each year she served underneath the minister?

"I don't know, *Tabby*, you tell me. What was that all

about in there? Did you expect me to just sit in silence while you let that woman nearly fuck you across the table!"

"Cheryl, language!"

"I'm not your child! Don't scold me."

"Then you need to stop behaving like a child if you don't want to be treated like one. You have no right to try to censor me or others when you wouldn't even be here if you hadn't needed my help, yet again."

Tabitha silently cursed herself for losing control. She was supposed to be setting a better example. Tabitha needed to defuse the threat of Rose's temper tantrum, instead she found herself experiencing one of her own.

"I didn't ask for your help, Tabitha Scott. You offered it! If you were going to offer support just to throw it in my face, I wish you hadn't done so. In fact, why don't I get out of your and *Elle's way* and let y'all keep walking into a better life of *empowerment, health, and self-love.*"

Cheryl was furious and hurt by Tabitha's constant reminder that she was simply a charity case when it suited the good minister to punish her for all the hurt Cheryl had caused her. Despite every attempt Cheryl made to show Tabitha she was trying to change and make up for the wrongs, it was never enough, it would never be enough!

She stood and marched toward the door and out of Tabitha's life permanently, but her minister wasn't done with her yet. The strong hand that pulled her back and pushed her against the closed door refused to let her go. Cheryl tried to look away from those firey eyes, which were still just as charged as hers, but Tabitha pulled her face toward her.

"Rose, I'm sorry. I don't want to fight with you. And I don't want to hurt you."

"Then what do you want of me? One minute, you're

helping me, acting like you still care about me, and then the next, you're pushing me away with harsh words and distance. What do you want?"

Tabitha licked her lips and tried not to want to kiss those pouty lips, but Cheryl's nearness was destroying her willpower to remain cautious. She wanted Cheryl, all of her, now and forever. But risking her heart and sanity again for a woman who could easily change her mind the way Cheryl often did was scary. How could she explain that to her Rose without showing her own weakness?

"Rose, you know what I want. You also know that I need time. Time to see that you're really committed to changing and not because of this incident. A part of that change must be you reigning in that temper."

Cheryl's raised eyebrow and smirk couldn't hide her amusement at the pot calling the kettle black. It was obvious that they were both firecrackers when the spirit moved them to be.

"What about you, Tab? You didn't seem so spiritually grounded a few seconds ago. I'm not the only one who has a short fuse. I don't like that woman touching you. I don't want any woman touching you like that except me. If that's non-negotiable to you, then what are we doing here? I'm not a child anymore, and I'm not playing a child's game with you, Tab. Whatever is going on with you and *Sister Elle*, put that shit to bed!"

Tabitha's amusement at Cheryl's choice of words didn't lighten the diva's intensity.

"Tab, you know what I mean. Correct that woman, or I'll do it for you."

"How will I know you want just up and leave like before? It seemed pretty easy for you to let me go to protect your career. What's to stop you from doing the same now?"

"Is that what you really think? That my remaining in the closet was just about my career?"

"Yes. The only reason you're out now is because someone did it for you, Rose."

Cheryl pushed Tabitha gently away from her to put some space between them. She knew if she remained so close to Tabitha's body, she'd not be able to concentrate on their discussion in a meaningful way. Even now, only a small distance apart, she could feel her body vibrating with the desire for her minister to touch her again, in any way and anywhere she wanted.

"I won't deny that my career was important to me. I was young and just starting out, and I dreamed of success and sharing my voice with the world. But it wasn't the only reason I remained in the closet. I was afraid of what might happen if my father ever found us. All of my childhood, my mother warned me of the horrors of Nigeria for people like Ayodele—for people like me. She hadn't sacrificed her marriage, career, or life just for me to throw it all away on love. I know that seems harsh to you, and it wasn't easy for me, but I loved my mother and sister just as deeply."

"I don't understand. You were safe here in America. You were born an American citizen."

"Yes, but they were refugees. And you should know because of Jerome, Isaiah, and Tiffany that homosexuality could be a death sentence in Nigeria, or at minimum imprisonment, beatings, rapes, and constant harassment. My father had sworn to kill Ayodele for being a *yan daudu*. He had promised to come home that evening and kill his son and the demon inside him. If my mother hadn't run that night, with me in her belly and Ayodele in tow, I might never have known the love of my sister. You might have never known her beautiful voice, music, and spirit."

Although they had survived violence provoked by the Shari'a criminal laws, Ola Agwuegbo refused to continue to risk her children's lives in this barbaric society. Ola had told her little daughter many times the story of how she had fled in the night with nothing but her children and a few items to a rescue ministry that secured their passage to the United States. It was ironic to Cheryl, as she grew into a mature woman and learned the African American history of slavery and imprisonment in the *home of the brave and free* that this land was now a refuge for freedom to Africans centuries later who longed for these shores.

"I grew up in fear of the day Abayomrunkoje would hunt us down like runaway slaves and kill his shameful family for their sinful ways. It is one of the reasons I've never traveled to the African country for one of my concerts and will never visit Nigeria to this day. I had to choose them, Tabitha. I won't lie and say I regretted protecting my family, and I'm not lying when I say that I never stopped loving you."

Tabitha had never seen such fear in the obstinate woman's eyes before, and she didn't doubt Cheryl's words were true. It was a similar fear she'd seen in the eyes of her children when she was first introduced to them. Gaining their trust had taken years, and although the scars on their bodies externally had healed much faster than the ones internally, Tabitha didn't doubt that their memories were just as real as before.

Tabitha pulled Cheryl into her arms and held her Rose gently as she did her best to soothe the woman's spirit as much as possible.

"Rose, I'm sorry. I can't change what happened to your family as I can't change what happened to mine. But I can offer you what I have given to Jerome, Isaiah, and Tiffany—

my devotion, love, and protection as long as I am on this Earth. As long as I am here, I won't let you go. And God will always be there, for he will never let you go. As Isaiah says, *we gotchu, Ma!*"

* * *

If Tabitha had imagined Rose's spirit was broken during their conversation, the fire in those sexy brown eyes removed all doubt that the lioness was defeated. Ayda and Tabitha sat in silence as they listened to the gospel diva battle it out with the R&B diva on a call meant to unite them, not divide them. Cheryl and Roxanna had different opinions about how their collaboration would work, and neither seemed interested in meeting the other halfway.

Tabitha was exhausted from her battle with Rose and the whirlwind of activity since the diva had stepped back into her life. Tabitha's life wasn't dull, and it was filled with various responsibilities, but she had to admit none had been as exciting as recent events with Cheryl Rose Campbell. This moment was no exception as she silently watched Ayda attempt to play referee, counselor, and arbitrator with her two clients.

"Roxanna, I think what Cheryl is trying to say is that often, good collaborations are fortified in face-to-face interactions. Having you come to the church or Dymon's music studio to collaborate on the music for the album and the tour would be a great opportunity to bond with your fellow artists."

Roxanna's facial expression or overall attitude wasn't visible from the conference call, but the tone in her voice clearly expressed her feelings without the aid of a visual cue. The young diva wasn't budging.

"Ayda, I'm clear on what sister Cheryl desires, but we all have our individual special needs, and a real collaboration between peers must recognize that collaboration works well in multiple forms. Since finding my higher ground after some time in solitude, and of course with the Rev's guidance, I understand the importance of solitude to do my best work."

Cheryl tried not to cringe at the sound of what she was sure was a not-so-recovered, recovering addict. Whatever Roxanna had found at the rehab facility and in her counseling with Tab hadn't cured what truly ailed the young woman. But she had promised her minister she would work on her temper and ill manners. So, instead of another round of arguments with Roxanna, she allowed Ayda to settle the negotiations.

Ayda did her best to appear less frustrated and more accommodating than Cheryl. But Cheryl knew a poker face, and the talent manager seemed just as weary of Roxanna's peace, love, and harmony routine as Cheryl. The furrowed brow, the tight jawline, and the wringing of her weathered hands were great telltale signs.

Cheryl sighed softly. At least she could rest her fighting spirit in preparation for another more pleasurable tussle with the good minister. The vision of intertwining their bodies in a heated battle brought a devilish grin to her face. As she glanced toward Tabitha, she caught those lusty brown eyes returning a similar expression.

"Alright, Roxanna. Tell us what you need to feel at ease with this arrangement."

The three waited patiently as the silence on the other end of the line prolonged longer than they would have imagined. From the sound of Ayda's voice, the Queenmaker wasn't doing a good job of protecting everyone's vested interests and was caving to the younger diva's demands. When Roxanna finally revealed her terms, it was Tabitha who stepped in to complete the deal.

"It's simple. I don't have the time or the emotional real estate for a more intimate collaboration. But I do have the perfect music to add to this album. I love the concept of speaking life into the spirit of mankind, by the way. It's so prophetic, sisters. And I have the two songs that would be perfect for the album. You heard the first this past Sunday, *Sinner In Me*, and I've recently composed a song dedicated to the almighty and his devotion to his children. It's entitled *My Everything*. I'm sending you the tracks now so you can listen to them and confirm what I strongly believe you'll discover: they're the perfect addition to *The Good News* album."

"And if we don't?"

"Don't what, Tab? I'm not clear on what you mean."

"If we don't agree they're perfect for the album, Roxanna, what then? Will you be willing to agree to an intimate collaboration between the four of us in a place of your choosing? You, me, Rose, and Dymon?"

The silence returned to the other line, but when Roxanna finally uttered her words, they weren't as prophetic as her previous dissertation but more agreeable.

"That's fair, Tab. My spirit tells me that the final decision will be good for all of our spirits. Send me a message after you've heard the tracks. Namaste, sisters. It's time for my mindfulness walk."

* * *

After listening to *Sinner In Me* for the second time and Roxanna's new song, *My Everything*, neither Cheryl nor

Tabitha could deny that Roxanna had been spot on about them being perfect for the album. Now, as they sat with an even different set of youthful spirits and discussed Dymon Stud's contribution, Cheryl felt less resistance from the famous hip-hop artist and a more collaborative nature than their earlier conversation with the temperamental R&B artist.

"So, Ms. Campbell, thank you for wanting to collaborate. I may be more of a bedside Baptist, but I get my praise on, too. And my bae is working on me to pay more visits to her family's church."

Ah, young love!

Cheryl could see the ripeness of their fortified fruit as the popular *Dayla* sat cozy together in the choir room with their future versions of themselves. Cheryl couldn't stop herself from feeling some type of way or just plain old jealous of the freshness of their youth and their relationship. Given time and age, she silently predicted they might not be as sprung on each other.

But then, the looks Tab had been giving her since their last private discussion made her question if the fire would grow cold as the lovers grew old. Either way, they would grow wiser and more cautious in how they expressed their love. For now, she shook off the negativity and allowed herself to enjoy the contagious romantic vibe that the young folks were spreading.

"Dymon, first of all, call me Cheryl. And thank you, too, for elevating the music that we're going to create on this album with your fresh brand of praise. We don't all know the love of God from inside of the church. Our walk with God is individual and personal to our needs."

Dymon and Layla nodded in agreement. Cheryl could tell that Dymon was relieved by her acceptance.

"So, I'm excited to hear your thoughts about these *bars* you've created, and I would be interested to know if you'd like to compose the beats for the song as well."

Dymon's huge grin and eyes grew bigger by the minute as the gospel diva blessed her even more with the opportunity to add the full brand of D-Stud Musik to the album.

"Forreal? Eh, I gotchu, Cheryl. This track is going to be fire! I even started working on a beat just to give me that extra feel while I was thinking about a few bars. It seems God was working in mysterious ways and preparing me to give you the music and some lyrics."

Cheryl smiled brightly. "I couldn't agree more. So let me hear what you got."

"Aight. Just keep in mind that it's just a rough draft. But I'm thinking of something like this:"

VERSE 1
I know he won't do me wrong,
Man, without him, I'd be weak,
But I know he is strong,
Always picking up the pieces when it fall apart,
And he don't ever ask for nothing,

He just wants my heart.

I been going through some things,
Putting all my trust in man,
Yea
Just to see him change,
Yea
I been feeling pain,
So I put it up to God,
And he clapping,
at any weapon formed against me,
And I see the temptation,
Whenever I am tempted.

VERSE 2
Living life without him,
Got the days feeling like a century,
I know that I got God,
Anytime I hear my name,
Is mentioned,
Partly, why I never stressing,
Yea
I gotta give him thanks,
Yea
I been counting blessings,
I know he is my protection,
Know that I ain't perfect,
Yea
I can see it in my reflection,
Life is what you make it,
Yea
It's all about perceptions,
See a chance then take it,

God will give you your direction,
And always make sure that you have good
intentions.

The room was silent for a few moments, and Dymon wondered if God hadn't used her after all to add a powerful message to this album. She glanced at Layla, who didn't seem concerned by the quiet—maybe this was just how church folk processed stuff. Dymon sure hoped that she'd get some feedback soon, even if it was in the form of a clap-back! By now, her bros would have either been giving her fans a sneak peek of the fire bars on the Gram or clowning on her about how whack they were.

Instead, her elders just sat quietly, and then slowly, a smile formed on both of their faces before Cheryl put her out of her misery.

"Well, Dymon, you were absolutely right. God was definitely working with you to bless this album. An hour ago, we acknowledged how God never lets us go and how he works through others to keep us. And that conversation and your music and bars have me truly inspired. I can tell it from my partner in rhyme over here; Tab is feeling it, too."

Tabitha chuckled in agreement. She couldn't hide her pleasure in how well she and Rose were in sync, especially when they got the same inspiration for a song and other rhythmic things.

"Rose is right, Dymon. After those powerful verses, you got my mind working overtime. Maybe we can run through some ideas for Cheryl's verses if you have a little more time."

"Fo'sho! I'm just glad y'all didn't hate it. I was getting worried for a minute. You were so quiet. Right, bae?"

Dymon turned to Layla for confirmation and saw more pride than worry in her woman's eyes.

"Yes, Dymona, I knew you were worried. But I also believe in your music; I know your heart was in those words. I didn't doubt their power wouldn't come through for Rev and Cheryl."

"Aww, bae, that's why you've always been my day one. I love you, Lay. You never let me go, either," Dymon said before leaning over and giving Layla a PG-rated smack on the lips.

"Um, sorry if I broke, um, a church rule, kissing my bae in here. My bad."

Cheryl and Tabitha giggled as if they coveted their own little secret, which they did.

"Dymon, you're fine. We're not here to judge you, and we certainly won't be hypocrites, for that matter."

Dymon's eyebrow raised with curiosity, and before Layla Joy could reign in her nosey lover, the former bad boi got all Taylor Horton on their two elders.

"Oh yeah? I thought I was feeling some hotness from you, too. Wassup, Rev, Cheryl? Are y'all trying to get cuffed up?"

"Dymon! Stop. Sorry, Rev, sorry, Cheryl. She means well, but sometimes Dymon speaks before she thinks."

Dymon laughed. She didn't get offended by Layla's constant censoring of her outbursts. But she wouldn't stop digging until her hot aunties spilled the tea.

"It's okay, Layla. I like your directness, Dymon. I'm pretty direct, too, and I know my counterpart here doesn't always feel as comfortable when I speak my mind, either. But you don't have to be shy around me. As far as us *cuffing up*, I take it that term doesn't actually refer to using hand-cuffs, does it?"

Dymon burst with laughter, and Layla and Tabitha couldn't hide their blushing faces from Cheryl's bold question.

"Nah, not exactly. I guess the term for y'all would be booed up, right?"

Cheryl gave Dymon a sly wink and then turned to Tabitha. "I don't know, are we, Tab, *booed up*?"

Tabitha knew there was no point in resisting what had never stopped existing between them and wouldn't be canceled, no matter how she tried to protect her feelings.

"Yes, we booed up. Rose has been my day one too, and will always be."

* * *

The couples continued to enjoy their collaboration, sharing stories about how each got together in between going over Rose and Tabitha's ideas about the new *He Will Never Let You Go* song. As their time together came to an end, Cheryl realized even more the direction she wanted *The Good News* album to evolve into.

"Dymon, Layla, thank you for hanging out with us today. You know, honestly, when Ayda proposed a new album to me in light of what's happened, I was more focused on a solo project—not that I don't enjoy collaborating with other artists. I saw this project as a burden and penance for my mistakes, which I know you're aware of. But this project has brought me so much more than that. It's returned me to Tab and introduced me to new, powerful young voices like yours that can help me bring light to this project. Thank you for that."

"Nah, it's our pleasure, Cheryl. Bringing diverse sounds together for the same message is fire. It's what I'm doing with my music production company, and with Isaiah. That bro was something else when I first met him, but he's free now, you know from all that darkness and trying to be something that he's not. And his music is more powerful and can reach more people in a positive way than before. No offense, Rev."

Tabitha nodded and then gave Dymon a warm smile. "No, offense is taken Dymon. You're right about my son. He was lost for a while, and I understood his need to hide his true self. Being out and proud in America is not easy, but Rose has recently reminded me it can be even harsher and deadlier in other countries. Giving Isaiah a home here didn't drown the memories of his first home and the price he paid for being a gay man. So, I'm grateful to you for being there for him when he was truly ready for a change."

"Oh fo'sho! Isaiah's another one of my bros."

"Speaking of change. Rev, is Unity planning to participate in the *Jumping for Jesus Jam* this year?"

"Um, no, Layla. I hadn't given that much thought. We typically don't perform at that scale; it's a big competition, and most of the larger congregations in Atlanta, like your uncle's church, have a better chance of winning."

"I agree. Uncle Raymond and the choirs have done well over the past six years, but that doesn't mean Unity wouldn't be just as successful. You've got amazing singers like Jerome, Tiffany, and Isaiah. And a new, less traditional sound that could reach a broader, young audience would be amazing. Right, Dymona?"

"Oh, yeah, fo'sho! And you know, Isaiah and I will help you cook up some fire tracks. Layla's right; you should definitely enter."

Tabitha could feel the heat from Cheryl's attention on her as well. She knew her kids were great singers and songwriters, but going up against the Bishop and other megachurches seemed highly unlikely that they'd even place in the competition. It was super competitive, and the money that larger congregations had would overwhelm their Daniel in the lion's den of megachurches, mega talents, and megamoney!

"I appreciate it, Dymon and Layla, but it's sort of short notice for us to jump into this event. I'm sure the submissions have probably already closed."

"No, they're not. You can go online today and sign up. You have two more days before the final applications and almost four weeks to prepare. Please, Rev, consider it. My uncle and his choir need some fresh competition. And I'd love to be a part of a team that whips them and gives them a run for the gold. It's healthy competition, and my Uncle Raymond would love to bicker with me over who's going to win."

Tabitha and Cheryl were both quite familiar with the overzealous and prideful Bishop Raymond Woodward. He would definitely be peacocking during the entire event, and though Tabitha had no desire to step into the ring with the Bishop, giving her kids a chance to shine whether they win or lose, was starting to sound good to her.

"Come on, Tab. Let's do this. You know I'll help wherever I can. And who knows, maybe this will be an opportunity to create more music for the album and to give this new direction a test drive."

"See, see, that's what I'm talking about. Leggo!"

* * *

After being coerced by her three eager cohorts into signing up the Unity choir for the *Jumping for Jesus Jam* competition,

Tabitha found herself trying to find reasons to linger around Rose. Their day had been long and productive, but her body was aching for some rest and further nourishment.

Would any of that involve Cheryl Rose Campbell? She sure hoped so.

"So, good work today, right, Tab?"

"Yeah, Rose, we did good. Um, I guess you're heading out now?"

"Is there a question in that or just an observation?"

Tabitha could hear the teasing sound in Rose's voice. She wished the woman didn't make her so nervous right now, as if she were asking her out on their first date.

"Maybe."

"Maybe what, Tab? I know Reverand Tabitha Scott can use her words better than that, which is why all the ladies love Tab."

Cheryl couldn't help herself from teasing her minister. She didn't want their time together to come to an end either, although Ayodelle would be pissed with her if she canceled their popcorn and wine date night. It was time for their traditional binge-watch of Shonda Rhymes's *Scandal*. And Olivia Pope and the President needed their undivided attention this evening, along with the sisters' need to do their own bonding.

"I was just going to see if you'd like to get dinner. That's all."

"Is that all? Just dinner, Tab?"

"Rose..."

"I know. I apologize for messing with you. Although I have in the past and do want to in the present, to mess with you. But I can't this evening. Ayodele and I have a girls' night scheduled."

Tabitha couldn't hide her disappointment. Rose had gotten her all warm with her teasing tongue and now she wanted to douse her with a cold shower by declining her invitation.

"Oh, okay, fine. No problem. You have a good evening."

"Tab?"

"What Rose?"

"You know I want to spend time with you, more time, outside of Unity. I just can't tonight. But how about another evening this week?"

"Maybe."

Cheryl laughed softly and then caressed the disappointed minister's arm and was rewarded with that fire in those lusty brown eyes.

"I'll take a maybe. Also, Mitchell and Paul have invited me to go dancing Saturday night. It would seem our old friend, Larisa, is putting on *a grown folks' party*. I'm sure it'll be a lot of fun. It starts at 9 p.m. and will be over by midnight. Care to join us? It'll be just like old times, except I'll be more than legal!"

Tabitha laughed with Cheryl as the memories flooded her mind of the young, mischievous choir girl sneaking into gay clubs with her church boys on a Saturday night and then sliding into a church pew or choir stand early the next morning. Those years seemed so long ago, but Rose was still the same young girl looking for a fun time, especially with her.

"Nope, as much as I enjoyed Larisa's parties, I have different responsibilities now, Rose. I need to work on my sermon for this Sunday, and it just wouldn't be a good look for Unity's minister out in them streets."

"Are you serious? Tab, it's an early party. I'm sure you'll have plenty of time to work on your sermon, Rev. And it's a chance to dance with me again. Don't you want to do that?"

"Rose, stop it. I really can't. But thank you for asking."

"Fine. If you change your mind, just meet us there," Cheryl said dryly as she gathered her things and headed toward the door.

"Rose?"

Cheryl sighed then turned around to face Tabitha's amused face. The smile on that handsome face and the sparkle in those brown eyes made her even more frustrated with Tab but for more good reasons than bad ones.

"Yes, Reverend?"

"If you can play in them streets on Saturday night, make sure you arrive promptly at church on Sunday. You can have a good time wherever you are, and I'm sure the Lord will appreciate your presence at the 9a.m. service. Go with God, Rose."

it hits different

"AYODELE, no, absolutely not! I already told your sister that I'm not stepping foot in that party. As your minister, it is my duty to present a modest life and walk the straight and narrow."

Ayodele cackled at the sound of her good friend and minister's pious display of virtue—when they both knew Tabitha Scott was far from being any sort of *straight,* and there was nothing restricted in the way she wanted Ayodele's baby sister. Those two horny heifers had been mind fucking as soon as Rose strolled into the church the day she was summoned by the Rev!

"I'm serious, Ayodele. There's nothing funny about my walk with God."

"Tabitha Scott, no, you don't go trying to put God amid your drama with my sister. You two are a mess with all this fussing and fighting when we all know what y'all really want to do. But I'm gonna hold my tongue since we are in the Lord's house. What I'm not going to do is let you sit at home sulking over Rose when you know you want to be with her! Also, I'm tired of hearing my little angel whining over you and messing up our girls' night. Do you know I couldn't get through one episode of Ms. Olivia Pope and that handsome little white boy without my sister finding some way to tie in the drama of the president and his mistress to y'all drama?"

For the first time during their debate, Tabitha cracked a smile. She was pleased to know that even during Rose's special time with Ayodele, her woman had been thinking about her. *Her woman?* Tabitha silently chastised herself for claiming Rose when she knew the woman could be a short-term pleasure like the temporary joy of a rose once it faded away.

"Oh, you think that's funny. Well, Kerry Washington and I have a thang, even if it's just through those re-runs and you messing up our thang. So, be ready Rev at 8 this evening. I'm picking you up, and we are going to this party for just a few hours. Then you can get back to your pious ways."

Tabitha prepared to dispute Ayodele's demand, but the statuesque guardian of them all held her hand up to silence any protest. There would be no point in putting up a fight. Ayodele had become the ideal replacement for Ola Agwuegbo upon her mother's death. From the day Deaconess Agwuegbo had been introduced to the much younger Tabitha Scott during her first day at their former church, the woman had taken the new minister under her wings.

Even after Tabitha had come out as a lesbian and Ayodele had informed their Mount Paul the Baptist Church community that she was transitioning as a transwoman, Ola Agwuegbo had stood beside them both. She had protected them from the criticism and removal from their church home and followed them both to the temporary dwelling for Tabitha's new church.

When Ola had taken her last breath on this Earth, it was Ayodele and Tabitha who sat by her side to give her the strength to pass on to higher grounds. It was Reverend Tabitha who presided over Ola's funeral, performed the eulogy, and offered more comfort to Ayodele and Rose. Ola's strong maternal presence was deeply missed by the church community and greatly by her children and the devoted minister.

Tabitha smiled warmly at the thought of Ayodele's strength to carry on Ola's legacy of kindness and love to others and resigned herself to the reality that she didn't want to be anywhere else but in the presence of Ayodele and Rose this evening. Even if she hadn't gone out clubbing in ages, Tabitha didn't doubt that her memory would serve her properly when it came to bumping and grinding with her Rose.

"Alright, Ayodele. As always, you win."

* * *

Cheryl Rose Campbell sat like a sultry soul singer propped up on her pedestal, a barstool at the pop-up club spot on Broad Street in downtown Atlanta. She was all decked out for the party like Black royalty, but sadly, this princess was short of her princess. Mitchell and Paul did their best to entertain their sulking sistah, but Cheryl spent most of their kiki time sweating her watch and cell phone.

Cheryl and her two-man choir boy crew had been at Larisa's party for almost an hour, and there was still no sign of Ayodele or Tabitha. Her sister had promised she'd do whatever was needed to bring the good minister to this party and put Ayodele out of another day of misery, listening to Cheryl lamenting over Tabitha's lack of attention to the diva's needs. It would seem that Ayodele was no more persuasive than Cheryl had been earlier in the week.

"Sistah, come on, gurl. Cheryl, we should be on the dance floor and show these children what time it is! I don't know why Larisa invited all these young kids, but we can show up and show out right, gurl!"

Cheryl was prepared to put up a fight and remain stuck to that barstool with her second Cosmopolitan for another 30 minutes before she made Mitchell and Paul take her home. But the strong arms of her two escorts propelled her to get off her perch and float onto that dance floor like the regal diva she was. Although she had been a little apprehensive about hanging out at the event, none of the young queer children seemed to be disturbed by the scorned singer.

Some were gawking at her, holding up their cell phones, getting a few sizzle-worthy reels, but for the most part, they let her be, except the occasional young ones and some in her age range who flirted from afar. None of them had her full attention like Tab did. Even out of sight, she was definitely not out of her mind. Cheryl did her best to entertain her choir boy crew with their insistence on her partying like it was 1999.

Sandwiched between the two, Cheryl felt like the chocolate center of a confused ice cream sandwich with one dark chocolate cookie on one side and a vanilla cookie on the other—a strange version of a *Neopolitan*.

"Cheryl, gurl, this music is fire! You could do a song like this. Have you ever thought about making a gospel house track? I know it's old school, but it'd be a fantastic revival, don't you think?" Paul whispered in her ear as he did his best not to get too close to that plump booty that was backing up to his lean frame. He was partial to a bodacious butt, which was one of the reasons Mitch had caught his eye, but Paul wasn't trying to stir up no trouble with his man because of his pansexual tendencies.

Cheryl listened to the music more carefully, although she had spent their few minutes on the dancefloor in her private fantasies. Though it had a nice beat and a gospel flavor, the music wasn't as soulful as the gospel house of the 90's. She turned to face Paul and prepared to explain the difference and her indifference to the idea, but his huge, sparkling white tooth grin made her less callous and more cautious in her response.

"Paul, thank you for the idea. But I'm not sure if it's my style or would appeal to my audience."

Paul wasn't deterred by her polite refusal to consider his idea; he wasn't a successful real estate agent in the cutthroat Atlanta market for nothing. Perseverance always paid off, no matter how challenging the buyer or owner could be.

"I feel ya. But don't you think it's time you open yourself up to a new market? This is a great opportunity to mainstream your music and get in both gay and straight clubs. I could also see your music playing internationally, especially the queens across the pond. Just think about it. We can chat about it later. If you're interested, I have some friends who could help you make it happen."

Cheryl nodded and promised she'd think it over. But she'd have other things on her mind for the immediate future, as Ayodele's promise was kept. Her sister and her minister were weaving through the small crowd coming her way. Paul mistook the bright smile on Cheryl's face for enthusiasm over this idea, but when Reverend Tabitha

Scott approached them and pulled Cheryl away from her threesome, the moment was a bit bittersweet for the constant salesman.

"Did you forget something?"

Tabitha held up the missing purse that Cheryl hadn't realized was missing! But the diva hadn't forgotten one other important thing, and obviously, neither had Tabitha, considering she'd decided to make a guest appearance after all. Tab was looking as phyne as fuck in a sexy mauve pants suit and low-cut black blouse that molded to every inch of the minister's voluptuous body. Those thick lips were painted with her signature plum lipstick with an extra hint of shimmer to it, and Cheryl wanted nothing more than to suck that plum off those tempting lips.

Cheryl accepted the extended peace offering, but Tabitha held tight to the other end.

"And what do I get for protecting your bag?"

Before Cheryl could muster up a saucy comeback to Tabitha's teasing, the valiant minister released her hold on the purse and pulled Cheryl into a slow, soft, sweet kiss that intensified as their lips greeted each other like distant lovers who were finally reunited and making up for lost time. Tabitha's tongue teased Cheryl's mouth with tentative stroking, caressing, and sucking that made her Rose whimper in frustration until that tongue plunged into her mouth and fervently stoked the fire burning within.

Tabitha moved Cheryl to the dropped tempo, Larisa's DJ was playing and used her hands to stroke the same rhythm out of those swinging hips. Their private dance was not so private, and Ayodele was tired of the shameless PDA! She pulled them apart and stepped in between the two lovebirds.

"Nah, nah, nah! Sister, get a hold of yourself, and you

too, Tabitha. Now, I brought you two sick puppies together, but we not doing this scandelabra on the dance floor."

Cheryl and Tabitha giggled, but the heat was still present amid their older sister's teasing. Ayodele was relieved to hear the DJ picking up the tempo of the music, and when her favorite gospel house mix came pumping through the wall speakers, her body took on a life of its own.

Cheryl enjoyed seeing her sister express herself openly, and for a moment, she forgot her lusty thoughts of Tabitha Scott and joined Ayodele in dance. Tabitha wasn't about to be outdone by the two pretend pageant divas and joined them in the voguing and praise worshipping, and when the beat transitioned into Jungle House, their bodies swayed to a more tribal rhythm.

Mitchell and Paul were just as eager to join the trio, and their party of five sweated out their perms, weaves, fine attire, bras, and panties for over an hour. The DJ's revival of 90's house music and hip hop transported them back to their early youth and, though shrouded in secrecy, was one of the only times they truly felt free. True, they were all deep in the closet, except for Ayodele, who was thinly accepted as a gay man at the time in the church community. But their youth fooled them into believing they had all the time in the world to be their true selves and have the careers they wanted and the partners they loved without fear of condemnation.

Years later, they'd grown older, wiser, and lonelier. Their youth faded, their careers not as they imagined, and their relationships torn apart. Tabitha was feeling the aging for sure, as her knees ached from all the dancing, and her lower back begged her to sit her old ass down somewhere! She could see the fatigue in Rose's eyes and that sexy body that moved just a tad bit more tenderly during a fast beat.

The six-inch heels were probably punishing those soft, manicured feet, and she wanted to rub them and soothe both of their seasoned bodies as they slouched on her couch at home in each other's arms. A glance at her watch brought her back to the reality of their current world. It was time for her to return to her duties as the leader of the Unity flock and leave tonight as a fond memory until she had another opportunity to give Rose that proper homecoming.

Tabitha gave Ayodele the sign that her chaperone needed to prepare to take the fatigued minister home. Even Ayodele looked relieved as she pointed to an empty barstool and made her way there to wait for Tabitha to say her farewell to Cheryl. Tabitha turned her attention to Cheryl, who held a knowing expression that warned her minister the diva wasn't happy about the abrupt change in plans. Those arms that had wrapped around Tabitha's waist and caressed the sexy minister's needy backside now wrapped around Rose and refused to budge.

"Is that how you gone do me, Rose?"

Damn that sexy ass voice! Rose hated that she loved hearing the deep contralto voice that was smooth as butter and thick as dark chocolate. It wrapped around her senses and made her want to dive into its essence and owner. But she wasn't going to give in that easily.

"Go on, Rev, you clearly have more important things to care for than my needs."

Tabitha tried to hide the fire those words ignited, but she was just as hungry to have her needs taken care of, too —just not tonight.

"Rose, please don't make this harder than it already is. You know I want you in my bed, underneath me, giving me that body the way you know I like to please it. You know I want to hear your sighs of satisfaction, your cries for more, and you speaking in tongue that only I can translate. But I've got another duty to take care of right now. So, do me a favor. Don't hang out in them streets too long. Take your so sexy ass home soon. Ya, feel me?"

Cheryl couldn't help the moistness seeping from her special spot in the thin panties that hid that thang that Tabitha was promising to satisfy. She couldn't hide the naughty twin nipples that pressed against her blouse, aching to get some of what Tabitha promised. She definitely couldn't hide the lust in those eyes and the moan that escaped her lips at the mere thought of Tabitha's devilish descriptions, which would cause her to spend her evening masturbating to the very thought of her minister's expert lovemaking.

Tabitha smiled confidently as she enjoyed unraveling Rose's defenses. The stubborn stance and closed arms dropped to her side and allowed her minister to pull her into a final embrace. The feel of Tabitha's warm body against her own warm, sticky body was welcomed, even though Cheryl knew they both looked a hot mess!

"Be good, Cheryl Rose Campbell. I'll take care of you later. But you and yo boyz better be in church bright and early tomorrow. If you can hang in these streets tonight, you can hang with Jesus tomorrow. Amen?"

As Tabitha and Ayodele walked through the same streets, their bodies ached from years of living. But the cool night air and the remnants of their earlier celebration had them feeling young again. They strolled with a pep in their step, enjoying the 15-minute walk from the club to Ayodele's powder blue 2009 Lincoln Town Car. Despite its age, the car was in excellent condition with only 74,000 miles on it. The exterior and interior were expertly maintained, hiding any signs of wear and tear. As they approached the car, they relished the thought of sinking into the plush leather seats and stretching out their tired limbs in the spacious interior.

But their joy was quickly shattered by a deep voice calling out insults toward them. The slurred voice filled with hatred and aggression released an initial assault against them. Ayodele and Tabitha ignored the young man, not bothering to make eye contact or acknowledge his presence.

The situation escalated as two more young men joined in, surrounding Ayodele and Tabitha with menacing looks and aggressive movements. These boys couldn't have been more than 18 years old, but they were already filled with hate and animosity.

"Hey, tranny! Where the fuck do you think you're going with your fake wannabe woman ass?" The leader of the group sneered at them, his companions laughing and jeering behind him.

The thicker, dark-skinned, mouthy one stepped in front of them. Although he was built of substance, muscular, and menacing in his own right, his stature was shorter than either Ayodele's 6 feet or Tabitha's 5'7". But his bravado was more significant than any predator. Ayodele stepped forward into his face, but Tabitha's hand steadied her, and she moved her body in front of her friend.

"Son, whatever this is, I'm going to ask that you reconsider what you're doing. We don't want any trouble, and I don't think you do either."

As the three teenage boys howled with laughter, one of

them sneered in Tabitha's face and spat a mouthful of warm saliva onto her cheek. She could feel the liquid seeping down her skin, bringing with it a sense of disgust and humiliation.

"Shut up, you fucking cunt!" The boy shouted, his breath hot and smelling strongly of alcohol. "You have no idea what kind of trouble your pussy eating ass is about to be in!"

Before Tabitha could respond, Ayodele sprung into action. She swiftly pulled her out of harm's way before throwing a punch at the bully's eye.

"Ayodele! Stop!" Tabitha cried out, but it was too late. The other two boys with bats in their hands began swinging wildly at Ayodele while Tabitha jumped in to defend her friend.

Despite trying to follow Christian teachings of turning the other cheek, Tabitha felt her anger rising like a dragon's fire. She fought back against the boys as they spat on them, threw bottles, and swung their bats dangerously close to their heads.

Amidst the chaos, bystanders pulled out their phones to capture the violence unfolding before them. A small crowd started to form, but no one stepped in to help. That is until Tabitha heard the voice of her lover—the woman who should have been far away from this brutal battle. The woman she would do anything to protect.

With renewed determination, Tabitha continued to fight alongside Ayodele, using all her strength to defend both herself and her loved one from the attackers' relentless assault.

"Get off me, freak! I'll stick this bat up your freak ass!" One of the boys screamed as Ayodele pushed him to the ground, dropped her entire 250 pounds on him, and grabbed the bat from his hand.

"You messed with the wrong muthafucka today!" Ayodele screamed as she turned that boy over and beat his ass with the same weapon he had used against her.

As Tabitha struggled against the leader of the group, she saw Rose running toward them, her high heels in hand. With a fierce expression on her face, Rose swung her stiletto heel at the attacker on Ayodele's back. When he pushed her to the ground, Ayodele and Tabitha's anger intensified.

"Sister!"

Ayodele flung off her attacker and grabbed the bat, and started swinging at Rose's attacker's head.

"I will kill you, muthafucka!"

Cheryl's heart raced as she scrambled to her feet, dirt smudging her face and clothes. She reached out to grab Ayodele's arm, trying to prevent any further harm from being done, but her sister was too quick. But it was Tabitha's questionable behavior that would create a more deadly situation.

"Get the fuck back, now! If you boys don't get your asses up and be on your way, I swear before God, I will send you to your maker before your time!"

Suddenly the brutal battle ceased and everyone fell into complete silence as they stared at the angry minister with the menacing black 9 mm Glock pistol directly pointed at her attacker.

"Now, I don't want to take a life tonight, but if you try to lay another hand on any of us, it will be the last thing that you do. I tried to reason with you, but you children think life is a fucking game! This ain't yo drive by shoot 'em up video game. This is real, you little muthafuckas! And if I have to show you how real it is, I will. There ain't no do over, you hear me!"

"Tab, please. It's okay, calm down. They hear you," Rose pleaded as she slowly approached the furious minister.

"I got this, Rose. Nothing's going to happen that ain't supposed to happen. I just need to know which road these boys want to take."

"Sister, please, Rose is right. I love you, Tabitha, but we got this. We don't need the gun. This is my fault," Ayodele pleaded.

Tabitha could feel the tears rolling down her face—tears of anger and frustration. Her hand held the gun so tight she could feel the imprint of the cold metal etching an unwanted memory in her skin. But her aim didn't waver. The sounds of Rose, Tabitha, Mitchell, and Paul begging her to stand down and the faces of the now cowardly assailants were distorted by her rage. All she could hear and feel was the pounding of her heart and the need to bring justice for Ayodele, Rose, and her own children.

Tabitha didn't hear the midnight black Hummer SUV pull up to the scene, or the sound of a familiar voice until the strong hand wrapped around hers and that gun commanded her attention.

"Rev, whatchu doin' out here? Let me take care of this, Tab. I gotchu."

"Darcy?"

"Ayyeee, Tab, don't be calling me that. Ain't nobody calling me that but my moms, and she done left this Earth. People know me as the Hammer. Put away this piece, and Imma take care of all this. You hear me, Rev? Go on home with yo fam."

Tabitha could see her crew's pleading eyes and the three boys' fearful eyes. She knew they were no longer afraid of her and that gun, but more fearful of Darcelle Bondrage, her old classmate from back in the day. Even at the age of 12, Darcy was running the streets, doing whatever was needed to take care of his mother and stay out of the way of his alcoholic father.

Despite the dangers of his street hustles, his classmate and neighbor, Tabitha Scott, offered him a sanctuary. She helped him with his school work, fed him when he was hungry, and hid him in her bedroom when he was running from the law or other street hustlers. Now, he was taking care of her mess. The Hammer released his hold on her. Tabitha tucked the gun back into the holder strapped to her waist. Ayodele and Rose moved in quickly and pulled her into their arms.

"Take the Rev home. These fools not gonna be no more trouble. Ya hear me?"

Tabitha moved away from Ayodele and Rose for a moment. She needed to ensure that whatever the Hammer did would lead to a different place than she had planned on taking those boys. She was still mad as hell, but Tabitha knew she wouldn't be able to live with herself if she truly sent those boys to the grave.

"Dar—Hammer, what do you plan on doing with them?"

Hammer flashed his diamond and gold grill then squeezed Tabitha's shoulder. The pressure made her wince. She had put up a good fight, but those boys had gotten the best of her.

"Sorry, there, Rev. That's why you need to get home and let your woman take care of you. Time is running out. The police is going to be here soon. We need to push on. They're going to be alright. Trust me. You need to leave, and me and my crew will clear the scene."

"Alright, Hammer. We'll go. But please come by and see me at the church soon."

"No doubt. I'll swing by. See ya, Rev."

* * *

Tabitha, Ayodele, and Cheryl sat quietly like church mice on the sofa in the rebellious minister's home. They waited patiently to be admonished for their bad behavior and nurtured for the wounds they had incurred from the street fight. And the children prepared to parent their elders weren't going to hold their peace.

Tabitha's children had met them at the door armed with various kitchenware; she assumed they were prepared to use these items in the street fight in her defense. The weaponry was quickly dropped to the ground, and their arms surrounded her with the love she needed at that very moment. Tiffany and Isaiah pulled Ayodele and Rose into the love fest and politely deposited them beside their mother on the sofa.

Now, it was time for their *Come to Jesus* moment. Tiffany knelt in front of Tabitha and started nursing the bruises on her mother's face with their first aid kit. As she soothed the red welts and bruises, the hand that lent aid trembled, as tears trickled down Tiffany's face.

"Tiffany, it's okay, baby. I'm okay. Don't cry."

Although she tried to console her daughter, Tabitha's words only incited a waterfall from those sad brown eyes. Tabitha took the cotton balls and antiseptic and put them on the end table. Then, she pulled her daughter into her arms.

"Please, Tiffany, come on, baby, it's alright. I promise everything is alright now. I don't look that bad, do I?"

Tabitha did her best to lighten the mood just a little bit, but neither Tiffany nor her brothers were going for her deflection.

Ayodele and Cheryl wished they could comfort Tiffany and her brothers, but as much as they wanted to put up a good front, one of their best nights had suddenly turned into one of their darkest moments. In those strong yet young brown eyes, Cheryl wasn't blinded by Jerome's accusatory daggers. Although he had always been cordial to her and supportive of the development of the new album, Cheryl knew Tabitha's eldest child wasn't sold on the singer's redeeming qualities.

At least Isaiah seemed to be in her corner, enough to tend to her wounds. He gently covered the scrapes on her knees with ointment and cleaned off her face and hands from the red Georgia clay that she had fallen into when her assailant had flung her to the ground. Her true attention was focused on Tabitha and Tiffany as she silently wondered how to make this right.

"P-please, Mother, p-please, p-please, don't leave me! I c-can't, I c-can't lose you!"

Tabitha held Tiffany tighter as she tried to will her body to reassure her daughter she wasn't going anywhere, at least without a damn good fight!

"I'm here, Tiffany. Don't worry, baby, I'll always be here."

Tiffany pulled away abruptly from her embrace, and the anger and sadness in those tear-filled eyes surprised the minister.

"No, no, stop lying to me! Stop lying to us! Why? Why did you do this? You put yourself in harm's way, and you know I would die; I would literally die without you! I can't lose you. You're my only Mother. You're the only person who truly loves me. Please don't do this again, promise me!"

Ayodele tried to remain stoic and supportive of both Tabitha and Cheryl. Still, her own guilt over the incident and putting the courageous minister in the situation made her ashamed and regretful. How could she make this right? How could she prevent the hatred that was ever present? How could she protect herself or the people she loved without any casualties?

Ayodele felt the tight grip of her sister's hand on hers, and Cheryl's head fall on her weary, broad shoulders. She was so tired of this never-ending cycle as long as she remained Black and trans, which neither was going to change even on her deathbed.

"Come here, Tiffany, please. Don't pull away from me," Tabitha encouraged.

The young girl returned to Tabitha's arms, and her mother soothed her head with gentle strokes.

"Do you remember, daughter, when you would want my attention in the midst of me chatting on the phone or working on my sermon, and you would cry to me and tell me that I didn't care about you or didn't want to spend time with you? You remember?"

Tiffany held on tightly to Tabitha but nodded her head into her mother's soiled clothes. Tabitha kept stroking her head and reminiscing over the days when the 20-year-old was only 12 and had only been with her for two years. It had taken Tiffany those two years to trust Tabitha, to allow her new parent to touch her, and to reassure her their life together wasn't temporary but now and forever, whether on this Earth or beyond.

"Remember what I said? I would rub your head just like now and promise to always make time for you. I will always be there for you, Jerome, and Isaiah. I will be there when you get married, when you have your own children, and when you won't need me anymore. But I will still be there, always with you, Tiffany. So, I know this is a scary time. Truthfully, it was scary for me, for Ayodele and Rose."

Ayodele and Rose nodded in agreement. Tabitha's affection and words of encouragement to her daughter reminded them of the loss of their mother, Ola. In times like these, Ola would have risked her own life to protect either of her children. She had done it before, and they didn't doubt that Ola would do it again if she were there. Cheryl pulled her sister into her embrace, and they found comfort in their memories and each other.

Tabitha saw the fear and sadness in Jerome and Isaiah and knew it was just as important to comfort her strong boys. They might have been less emotional than Tiffany or honest with their true feelings, but Tabitha knew they needed just as much reassurance.

"Come on, Tiffany. Stand up now. Help your old mother up."

Tabitha gathered her children together in a circle. "I have told you most of your lives that we are no stronger than our weakest member. We uplift each other, no matter when we're weak or strong. I know you're disappointed in me this evening, but I ask you to help lift me up in my time of weakness by doing what you're doing right now—being here for me, Ayodele, and Rose. Things are going to be alright. We are all a family."

Tabitha encouraged Ayodele and Cheryl to join them in their circle and pray with them that they would all find the strength to get through this night and the fallout that would occur later.

* * *

"Rose, may I speak with you for a moment?"

Cheryl didn't hesitate to follow Tabitha to the privacy of the minister's bedroom. Her body was still aching from the night of dancing, and the bruises she'd experienced, but Cheryl wasn't too tired to spend more time with Tabitha. Her mind warned her not to linger any longer in the minister's house and to take her sister home so they could get the rest they needed. But her heart and body wanted Tabitha to console her as she had done for her children, and she wanted to console her minister.

Tabitha gently guided her into the dimly lit room and quickly closed the door behind them before pushing her Rose against the back of the door. Cheryl's eyes sparkled with a pleasant surprise, but her hands automatically wrapped around Tabitha's waist.

"Are you alright, Rose?" Tabitha moved her hand gently across the red, bruised skin of Cheryl's face and brought the heat that her lover needed to feel.

"Better," Cheryl responded with a sigh.

Tabitha smiled and gently ran her lips over the tender, bruised area and Cheryl's lips, which ached for her attention. Her eagerness to have Tabitha made Cheryl less gentle with her minister's bruises. Cheryl responded to the kiss with a deep tongue exploration of Tabitha's mouth, which made the eager minister wince.

"I'm sorry, Tab. Did I hurt you? I'm so sorry." Cheryl gingerly ran her thumb across the cut along the side of Tabitha's mouth and kissed it softly.

"I'm better now," Tabitha replied before leaning in again to those thirsty lips. Despite the pain, she returned an even deeper kiss. Her hands removed Cheryl's from around her waist and lifted them, and held them against the back of the door as she grinded her body to Cheryl's equally needy body.

"Oooh, Tab!"

Tabitha's tongue licked Cheryl's neck, and one hand released Cheryl's pinned arm to focus its attention on her breast, which was eager for the caresses that brought the soft nipple to a stiff erection. Tabitha continued holding Rose's other arm against the door as her lips and hand worked Cheryl into a fantastic frenzy!

When Tabitha took that suspended hand and moved it in between her pants and panties, Cheryl released a deep moan at the feel of her minister's undeniable desire for her.

"I'm hard Rose. So, fucking hard for you. Stay with me tonight. I need you," Tabitha whispered in Rose's ear while instructing those slender fingers to caress her erect clit into a happy ending for the both of them.

Rose could feel a twin desire growing between her legs and her breasts aching to be released from their prison. She wanted nothing more than to lay with Tabitha and fuck her lover just like she needed. Ayodele needed her too, perhaps even more than the two horny women wanted each other.

"Aww, yes, Rose. Fuck me, baby! Please, fuck me! I need you, Rose!"

Tabitha's passionate pleas tore at her heart, and Rose's body was screaming for Tab to win this battle too, but she reluctantly and slowly removed her hand from that thick, rock-hard clit. Rose gently pushed Tabitha away from her body, and the shock and disappointment in those sexy brown eyes made her sigh with mutual disappointment.

"What's wrong, Rose? Did I do something wrong?"

Cheryl's body whimpered at the sound of the sweet plea for forgiveness. Would her body forgive her for what's to come? She ran her hand softly over Tabitha's face and then forced herself to put a slight distance between them.

"You did nothing wrong, Tab. It's me. I want to stay. Please know that with all my heart, I want to be with you. But my family needs me right now like yours needs you."

Cheryl saw the confusion in Tabitha's pleading brown eyes and knew she'd need to try harder to make her lover understand why she'd have to go this time.

"Rose, you and Ayodele are my family, too. You're with family. Why would you want to leave?"

"You're my family too, Tab. But Ayodele needs me, just me right now."

Tabitha pulled Cheryl back into her arms. She wouldn't give up without a fight. She'd have to make Rose see that it made more sense for all of them to be together.

"We need each other, Rose. You and Ayodele can stay here. We have room. I'll even leave you alone tonight if that's what you want. We don't have to *be together*, but just be together, here, under one roof."

Cheryl did her best to free herself from the temptation. Her persuasive minister was so sweet and enticing. Even though Tabitha Scott promised to leave her alone and just be together, Cheryl knew there was no way she'd be able to *be together* with Tabitha and really leave her lover alone.

"Please don't make this harder for me, Tab. You know I want to be here with you, and I want to fuck you so much it hurts. But Ayodele needs my undivided attention right now. If I stayed, I wouldn't be able to do that. I'd be thinking about you and how close you are to me, how much I'd want to end the night in your bed, in your arms. Your children also need time with you too. And you need to rest. I hope you plan on staying home tomorrow."

Tabitha tried to listen without prejudice to Rose's plea,

but the adrenaline from the night's misfortunate events was still running through her veins, and her Rose's nearness made her want to work out the situation on top of or beneath Rose or both. But she couldn't deny the additional turmoil she was putting Rose through because of her selfish need. She released Rose from her tight embrace and tried to give her a sincere smile and acceptance of her own defeat.

"I know you're right, Rose. I'm grateful that you're the more thoughtful of us in this moment. As much as I want you here with me, Ayodele does need you, and I should tend to my family. I also don't want to walk away from my duties for the Unity congregation. I will be there tomorrow to preside over the sermon and to face them for their judgment of my actions. If you stayed tonight, I wouldn't be able to leave you alone either."

Cheryl smiled softly and then ran her hand over Tabitha's face before giving her another gentle kiss. "I never want you to leave me alone, Tab. But I get your point, and Ayodele and I will be by your side tomorrow at church. Like you said, if I can party in them streets, I can certainly show up and show out for Jesus. See ya tomorrow, Rev."

if we care

JEROME WRIGHT quietly assisted Reverend Tabitha Scott with her robe, ensuring he paid close attention to not causing her more pain than she'd already endured the previous night. He was honored to prepare Unity's minister each Sunday morning to preside over the congregation with peace and serenity. But his heart was conflicted by his duty to ensure his Reverend Mother got what she needed versus what she truly wanted.

The bruises were still visible on her face, and the pain she suffered from the stiffness of her arm and what he feared may be a sprained wrist seemed to go unnoticed or at least not taken seriously by the good minister. So, Jerome did his best to arm her with the proper weaponry she would need to get through these most recent events.

"I see Leon is in the house today. Can I assume you've both decided to mix business with pleasure?"

Despite her frustration and disappointment from last night, Tabitha was in a pretty decent mood. If she were honest with herself, she knew her sunny disposition had everything to do with the presence of Cheryl Rose Campbell at the service. She silently prayed they'd be mixing business with pleasure as well soon. Her eldest son's solemn face warned her Jerome wasn't in as good of spirits as she was.

Jerome smoothed down her collar and then stepped slightly away from Tabitha. "Leon isn't here for me. He's here for you."

"For me? Why?"

"Mother, you can't be so blinded by that woman you can't see the potential trouble you're in, that you all are in. I asked Leon to come to service in case we have police presence today and they attempt to pursue charges against you."

Tabitha was quiet for a moment. She had felt Jerome's disappointment in her since last night. Still, she hadn't expected the deep animosity he revealed toward Rose or his maneuvers to avoid any legal or criminal charges on her behalf. A part of her was disturbed by his disregard for her feelings toward Rose. The other part that appreciated her son's love and devotion to care for her was blown away by his adoration.

"Son, you know I appreciate you always looking out for me. I don't think there will be any trouble today because we did nothing illegal. We were attacked, and we defended ourselves."

"Have you gotten so distracted by that woman you don't see what you're saying makes no sense, Mother?"

Tabitha held up her hand to silence Jerome. She understood his frustration, but she had no intention of them continuing down a path that would cause more bruises than healing.

"Jerome, first, let's back up with you giving more respect to Ms. Cheryl Rose Campbell than I'm hearing right now. *That woman*, Rose, has done nothing wrong and is not to blame for what happened last night."

"But isn't she? You wouldn't have even been at that club, in that area where you were attacked, had you not been chasing her. You don't even care about how this has affected us, your children. How it's affected me. I do everything I can to protect and be here for you. But you forget what's important every time *Cheryl Rose Campbell* comes around. You risk everything!"

Tabitha wanted to be angry or deny Jerome's words, but she knew there was some truth in what her son had accused her of. Instead of arguing, she chose to meet him where he was and accept his disappointment in her and his pain and fear. She closed the distance between them and pulled his reluctant, stoic body into her arms.

"Jerome, I'm sorry. Sometimes, I forget that you need me to care for you and protect you the way you do now for me. I know you're grown, son, but I feel your need to be supported better than I have been doing these days. I'm not blinded by my righteous behavior. I know that the police will have questions and may try to find blame with me. But I will handle it, I promise you. And I appreciate you bringing our lawyer in to assist me with that."

Tabitha released Jerome from her arms and then wiped a stubborn tear from his face before her grown son could regain his bravado.

"But I have to insist you not blame Rose for this situation. I'm not blinded by my feelings for her, no matter what you or anyone thinks. I know our relationship hasn't been ideal, and she has hurt me in the past. But none of us is perfect, son. And I haven't given up on her, as I hope you won't give up on me. So, I'm asking you to politely show her some respect and not assume your mother has no backbone or mind of her own. What happens between Rose and I is our business. Just as what happens between you and Leon is yours. Understood?"

"Yes, Mother. I apologize, and I won't make that mistake again."

* * *

As Tabitha stepped into the pulpit, she was shocked by the enormous amount of support she'd never imagined she would have received. The morning devotion service had been the regular crowd, and although there were a few stares and whispers regarding her new badges of honor, no one had dared question the devoted minister's appearance. With the highly publicized brawl on social media, Tabitha knew they were all fully aware of the incident and expected her to address the matter during the larger service.

She wasn't surprised that Rose and Ayodele weren't present for the early devotion. Still, Tabitha couldn't deny her relief seeing them both on the front row, accompanied by Ayda Kohn. Their new warrior women crew of Mikail Rollins, Whitney James, Dymon Stud, Layla Joy, and even Roxanna had decided to put in an appearance.

But the wall-to-wall bodies that filled the sanctuary and spilled out into the foyer and as far as the eye could see outside the church was definitely not the turnout the shocked minister had anticipated. Many of the faces in the congregation were Unity's devoted members, but the over-flow were strangers to Tabitha. Although unfamiliar with the church environment, they were clearly determined to show their allegiance to the three crusaders.

Many representatives from the trans community were present, and the young and old queers from various races were present as well. Intermingled with the crowd were some local politicians looking to capitalize on the situation for campaign purposes, reporters from local news and social media, and their favorite auntie, Taylor Horton, from *Atlanta Alive*, close to the front. Tabitha admired that woman's tenacity and ability to always find a way to be in the thick of things.

Tabitha's eyes continued to scan the church but remained focused on the woman who had kept her promise and showed up to support her. She also didn't miss the police presence, which included the Atlanta Chief of Police and a few detectives she was both friend and minister to.

When Tabitha walked past the podium toward her seat, the sound of movement in the congregation focused her eyes on her judge and jurors, who stood and raised their right arms in the air. She heard the strong voice of someone in the crowd exclaim, "No justice, no peace!"

The rest of the audience responded, "No justice, no peace!"

They continued this call to action four times before Tabitha walked to the podium and raised her hand for them to be seated. She did her best to keep her emotions steady, but the undeniable support of the people throughout the room and outside was overwhelming. She could even see the impact that the solidarity had made on Ayodele and Rose. They were standing for her, too, but also for themselves. The choir stand behind echoed the sentiment.

Tabitha hung her head low and did her best to regroup. She felt Jerome's hand on her shoulder then accepted one of his favorite handkerchiefs to wipe the tears from her eyes.

"Don't cry, Mother. We all stand with you, no matter what. We love you. Don't cry, please. They are here for you and want to hear from you. Hold your head up, Mother; there is nothing to be ashamed of."

Tabitha nodded, quickly wiped the tears away, and faced her congregation. Jerome silently moved away and took the chair to the right of Tabitha's throne.

"Good morning, Unity. In less than 24 hours, I witnessed many things I'd never anticipated. I have to say that this appearance, right here, right now, is one of the most beautiful, touching experiences that makes my heart sing. Please, please have a seat if y'all expect me to get through this day without messing up my mascara and robe."

Tabitha did her best to infuse some humor into her address to the congregation. Her heart was joyful yet moved so deeply that she seriously didn't know how she would get through the service without completely breaking down. She'd done her best last night to keep up a good front with her children, Rose and Ayodele, and even attempted to fool herself. But the reality of that night haunted her even amid this joy. She could still see the angry faces of those young boys, still see herself holding that gun pointing at them and threatening to take their last breath from their young bodies.

It would be hard to erase those memories for her, Rose, and Ayodele, and probably for those who had it on repeat on social media. Tabitha silently prayed this morning's service would be the beginning of their healing. The congregation, lucky enough to have seats, obeyed her command and sat down. Those in the aisles, in the back, and outside stood attentively waiting for her next words.

Tabitha cleared her throat and prayed that God would comfort those harmed by this incident and similar ones of this nature.

"You know, I had no idea what last night would lead to. I had expectations, but nothing like what truly occurred. Truthfully, I was going on a date for the first time in a long time, and I was nervous and excited all at once. Your minister didn't know if she could get her groove back after all these years."

Tabitha heard the laughter and a few catcalls of encouragement for the beautiful, seasoned sistah. "Go head, Rev! You still got it!"

She saw Rose blushing from the front row and Ayodele teasing her sister. She was glad she brought them a little light before her story took a turn.

"I'm trying, y'all. I'm trying. But I say all that to say you never know what can happen along your way toward joy. Sometimes, the road to happiness is paved with a lot of heartache, and sometimes, it just flows like a serene river. Sometimes, to get to joy, you must deal with your past demons to prepare for a better life. And last night, I crossed a path hoping for a wonderful second chance at love and then met the horrors of the past. And I apologize to you for not being the leader you believed me to be in my response to the hell that was placed at my feet last night."

"Rev, nah! That ain't yo fault! Rev, you did what was right! You brave, Rev! No justice, no peace!"

Someone in the crowd was determined to correct Tabitha's interpretation of last night, and the rest of the congregation co-signed the sentiment. Tabitha raised her hand to quiet them down, but they went a little bit longer to reassure the good minister she had nothing to be ashamed of or sorry for.

"I appreciate y'all, I do. And I won't lie to you and say that if the situation ever happened again or I could have the opportunity to do it over, I wouldn't react the same way. In today's world, we are at war, a serious war with a hatred that is born from ignorance and privilege. And often, reasoning is impossible in certain circumstances. I have been a victim of gang violence. I lost my mother and father to a drive-by shooting, and yet God let me live. I have never understood why the Lord saved my life and took theirs."

Tabitha paused for a moment and tried to regroup before forging on. Although her parents' murder had taken place over 40 years ago, that day lived on in her mind and would always be with her forever. It was the rage that dwelled within her that she did her best to extinguish. It would rise and suffocate her often during times of stress and struggles. She cleared her throat and then continued.

"But I do know that if I hadn't been alive and sister Ayodele had been alone last night, we all might have lost another beautiful soul to senseless violence. And I had no intentions of letting Ayodele fight that battle alone, even if it meant my own death. I will never let anyone that I love walk alone until the day I leave this Earth. You are my family; no matter your struggles, I am here for you. I stand with you. I'm blessed to see so many faces I have yet to meet, know, and love here today. If you are seeking a church home, a family that will stand with you, know that Unity, that I am here for you too. No matter what happens in our world, that is not God's plan for us. Amen?"

* * *

Tabitha sat quietly in her office at Unity while she waited for Barbara Jean Rashan, Atlanta Police Chief, to begin her inquisition. Although Barbara was a friend of Unity and also a former member of Mount Paul the Baptist Church, the elected official was determined to present a hard-nosed, crime fighter appearance to the city known for its high crime rates and gangs as much as for its booming music and movie entertainment industry.

Jerome and Leon sat quietly in the back as Barbara and Tabitha sat around the fearless minister's desk. Barbara had promised the three that this was just a friendly conversation, a mere due diligence on her part to ensure no foul play was performed on the good minister's end or that of Rose and Ayodele. But Tabitha's crusaders weren't about to leave her alone without proper legal defense.

As Tabitha waited for Barbara's first question, her mind wandered to Rose and Ayodele waiting in another room for the Police Chief's next interview. She was happy to know that they were also protected by their crusaders, Mikail Rollins and Ayda Kohn. Tabitha would insist that Leon represent them as well. Her time for contemplating the next moves to protect her extended family was over. Barbara was ready for the inquisition.

"Well, Reverend, it's good to see you. It's been a long time. I'm sad to say it's not how I expected we'd spend time together again."

Tabitha blushed but tried to correct her unexpected response to the Barbara's sly flirtation. They'd not only been members of the same church in the past but also had a brief romantic history, which clearly Barbara Jean Rashan wanted to commiserate over during her interrogation.

Was it an intentional distraction to throw the minister off her game?

Tabitha wasn't sure, but she was confident her Rose wouldn't be too pleased by the start of this conversation if she were privy to it.

"Chief, it's good to see you, too. And I agree; I wish it were under different circumstances."

"Unhuh, well, it's not. Do you want to tell me what I don't already know from the social media outtakes?

"What do you need to know? I have nothing to hide, Barbara, you know that."

Barbara's raised eyebrow and smirk might have been a sign of more than the actual incident Barbara came to Unity to discuss with the faithful minister. She did her best to mask her envy of Cheryl Rose Campbell. No matter how long ago the not-so-secret relationship between the two had been on and off again, the woman still had her claws stuck into Tabitha Scott's heart.

Barbara had done her best to persuade Reverend Tabitha toward her bed more times than she cared to remember. As soon as Cheryl paid Tabitha a casual visit, Barbara was a distant memory. Well, today, the two lovesick trainwreck would have to sit up and take notice of her, at least for the time being.

"What happened to those boys, Tabitha? Where are they? And where is the gun that you held them hostage with?"

Leon's deep voice interrupted Tabitha before she could come to her own defense. "Now, Chief, you know better than to try and lead my client in any way to incriminate herself of any wrongdoings. Reverend Scott is willing to assist you in any way that she can. But to imply that she has done harm to three criminals, young or not, is shameful, to say the least, and is a poor attempt at entrapment if we want to get more legal about it."

Tabitha did her best to hide her smile and pleasure at Jerome's boyfriend's tactics. Although Jerome might not be ready and willing to claim the tall, mellow yellow, pretty boy, they looked mighty good together. Jerome quickly signaled her to wipe the smile off her face, straighten her posture, and behave. His papa bear behavior just caused her more joy and warmed her heart. She did her best to pretend to be the serious adult he demanded.

"Now, Leon, I understand your duty to protect your client, but avoiding the behavior that Reverend Scott displayed during this criminal matter will not bode well with me or the court. That is, if there should be any reason we should move this conversation to a more legal environment," Barbara warned.

Leon took the empty seat next to Barbara, leaving Jerome in the back of the room, primed to instruct his disobedient minister from a distance.

"Chief, there's no reason to threaten us with a legal matter. Clearly, from the videos we've all seen, my clients were acting in self-defense. Whatever happened to those boys after they ran away has nothing to do with Reverend Scott, Ayodele Agwuegbo, or Cheryl Rose Campbell. As far as the weapon, we have proof of purchase and license to carry. As you can see from the incident, it was a good thing that Reverend Scott had a way to defend herself. Otherwise, you might not be so lucky as you are today to be sitting here accusing her of foul play."

Barbara's scowl and flared nostrils didn't deter Tabitha's brave defender. He patiently waited for the Chief to calm herself and make her next move to intimidate his client into sharing more about the actual manner in which the boys disappeared into thin air.

"Well, Tabitha, you've got a good one here. I should know better than to try and put one over on him. This boy has been a tornado ever since my sister gave birth to him. But, nephew or not, if I discover that you are helping Reverend Scott hide any misdeeds, I will lock you in the cell right next to her. You hear me, Leon?"

Leon smiled confidently over his victory but nodded with respect to his elder. "Yes, Chief. I hear you loud and clear. So, I assume there's no further need to speak with the Reverend or the others unless you want to take their statements in your pursuit of real justice from their attackers."

Barbara playfully hit Leon over his thick, curly head and gave him a warning glare to not push her too far.

"Leon, you let me do my job, and I'll let you do yours. No, I don't have any further need for Reverend Tabitha, but I still want to question Ayodele and Cheryl Rose Campbell. So, lead the way, and I'll do my best to get out of y'allz hair. I'm sure everybody's ready for Sunday dinner. I know I'm ready for a good meal. Your Uncle Charles is getting some cue ready for the family. You might want to stop by Leon and pay him a visit. It's been a while."

* * *

The room was eerily quiet when Chief Rashan sashayed through the meeting room that held Reverend Tabitha's co-conspirators. A few moments ago, the vibe was much brighter as Ayodele did her best to regale Congresswoman Rollins and Ayda Kohn with childhood memories of her little angel. Even as a child, Ayda silently recognized that the gospel diva had always been a handful.

Although Cheryl playfully denied any truth to her sister's *tall tales*, she was thankful for the fond memories and the support of Ayda and Mikail. During the moments that they had awaited the Chief of Police's interrogation, Mikail had given them more insight into her private life. It hadn't gone unnoticed by Cheryl that whenever the congresswoman mentioned Whitney James, her eyes sparkled with a special adoration for the sexy songstress.

Cheryl didn't want to pry any further, given her previous need to remain private about her relationships and her sexuality. She secretly hoped the two beautiful women weren't merely friends but much more involved than that. They seemed like a perfect fit, even with their distinct uniqueness, and reminded her of a younger version of herself and Tab.

When she met the piercing brown eyes of Barbara Jean Rashan, Cheryl wondered what mysteries that window to the Chief of Police's soul would tell. The statuesque woman seemed indifferent toward the room's occupants except for her laser focus on Cheryl. Somehow Cheryl had the feeling this special attention paid to her had something to do with yet another bitch trying to piss in her backyard.

Cheryl met Barbara's stare with unwavering confidence. If Barbara had any plans to save the popular minister's soul from Cheryl, she'd soon discover the battle had already been won by the gospel diva.

"Afternoon, everyone. I see we have a full house. I don't think we need this much company to have a nice chat. Do you, Cheryl Rose Campbell? Do you feel you need this much backup to deal with the law?"

Barbara's saccharine smile paled in comparison to the sweet southern charm with a hint of acid Cheryl returned in kind. "Now, Barbara Jean, we're neither strangers nor foe. Our friends were simply here to keep us company while we waited for you. I think we all know from these recent events I'm not afraid to fight and protect what is mine."

"Is that right, Cheryl? Well, this conversation is going to be more colorful than the one I had with Tabitha. She seemed less enthused about the situation. I can't wait to hear what you and Ayodele have to say about the incident. Congresswoman Rollins, it's good to see you."

Barbara scanned the room and turned her attention toward Ayda Kohn, sitting near the door. "And I don't think we've met."

Ayda greeted Barbara with a warm smile and a firm handshake but wasn't blinded by the woman's curious infatuation with her client or the tension between the two. She could only imagine this friction derived from their apparent mutual interest in the good Reverend Tabitha Scott.

"Ayda Kohn, Ms. Campbell's manager. It's nice to meet you, Chief Rashan. If there is anything that I can assist you with, please don't hesitate to contact me."

Ayda handed Barbara her card and then quietly took her seat. Barbara looked at the expensive business card and couldn't believe her good fortune to be in the presence of the woman who had cleaned up yet another scandalous singer.

"Ah yes, now I remember you. I knew you looked familiar, Ayda. You seem to be in the business of repairing broken people. How is Roxanna these days? Is she still doing her recovery work? I wouldn't want to have to have one of these conversations with her too, any time soon. I trust you're keeping her on the straight and narrow."

"Chief, these folks have a busy schedule. Why don't we get on with your questions so they can get on their way," Leon interjected.

Leon wasn't sure what his aunt was up to with the snappy commentary, but he could tell by the look in Cheryl Rose Campbell's eyes that the diva was at a boiling point. He didn't want to have to defend her for another assault charge, especially not his mother's baby sister.

"Fine, Leon."

Barbara looked around the room at the unwelcoming

faces and then turned to Leon before sitting at the table with her nemesis.

"*Young folks.* Always in a rush to get to nowhere. But not like us, right Cheryl? We know how to take it nice and slow."

Ayodele touched her sister's hand and gently encouraged her to ignore the crazy-ass Barbara Jean Rashan, as the woman clearly didn't understand her rude behavior was only going to make her sister explode. But perhaps that's what her intentions really were.

"Chief Rashan, my sister, and I are more than willing to give you what you need. What do you want to know?"

Barbara looked Ayodele up and down and then turned her attention briefly to Mikail and Ayda. "Yes, well, I do have a few questions. But I really must request a smaller audience. Congresswoman Rollins, Ayda Kohn, do you mind giving us the room?"

Mikail squeezed Cheryl's other hand and then stood without protest. "Sure, Chief, we'll get out your way. Cheryl, Ayodele, we'll be right outside if you need us."

Mikail and Ayda walked quietly out of the room, and Barbara silently studied the two firestarters. Leon sat beside her at the table, ready to protect and serve his new clients. Although Barbara wished he was on the other side of the law, she silently admired her young nephew's discipline.

"Now, first, I want to say that I'm sorry you experienced this violent behavior in my city, Ayodele. The city of Atlanta doesn't take homophobic violence lightly, and..."

"Transphobic violence," Ayodele corrected.

"Yes, right, transphobic violence. We don't take any violent acts lightly. My goal is to understand the circumstances of last night from both of your points of view and to find your assailants as swiftly as possible. Can you help me do that?"

"Chief, my clients can give you a statement about what they experienced, but as Reverend Scott told you earlier, their attackers fled the scene. So, their whereabouts will have to be determined by the fine Atlanta police force."

Barbara plastered another one of those empty smiles on her face to avoid giving her nephew the business. His constant interception of the ball from her more than capable hands to serve his clients with warning signs to prevent her investigation tested her willpower and family loyalty—something Leonis Jefferson Wilcox didn't seem to know too much about.

Her sister was spot on in naming her nephew Leonis. He was a lion, quick thinker, witty, and highly imaginative, especially when it came to the fiction he was weaving around the innocence of these three. She cleared her throat and then pressed on, praying she wouldn't have to put her much taller and stronger nephew over her knee like she did many years ago and give him a good butt whooping!

"Okay, Leon. Then, Cheryl, let's focus on your side of the story. From what Reverend Tabitha has publically shared with the entire congregation, she was only at this club because of your persuasion. It seems like trouble just seems to follow you, I'm afraid, my dear."

Leon was primed to interject, but Cheryl decided that she was perfectly capable of putting this mouthy bitch in her place. She raised her hand and motioned Leon to step aside and let her respond.

"Barbara, somehow I don't think this conversation is really about the incident but of a more personal matter. So, just between us girls, let me be very clear about my intentions and my *persuasion*. My intentions are permanent, and so is my persuasion when it comes to Tabitha Scott. So, no need to wonder how long this will last or when I'll leave. I'm not going anywhere unless Tab is with me. Now, I won't lie to you and say that I'm sorry things didn't work out between the two of you; that would be a false testimony. But I will thank you for giving her an option so she's clear about what and who she really wants. Now, if there are no further *real questions* about last night's incident, can we all get home to our families and enjoy the rest of this Sunday?"

thank you for your love

WHEN CHERYL and Ayodele stepped out of the room into the hallway, their crusaders spilled into the narrow space. Cheryl was happy to see the good minister in the group. She watched Barbara Rashan grant Tabitha a curt smize and traipsed past the group with Leon in tow, as Cheryl assumed they were finalizing the brief interrogation. She also spotted Whitney James and Jerome, who still seemed displeased with her but stood in solidarity for his mother's sake.

Mikail was the first to approach her with a tight hug. "I trust things went well?"

Cheryl nodded, "Yes, I think Leon will handle his aunt appropriately, with, of course, a bit of guidance from me."

Ayodele cackled at Cheryl's mild description of the read she'd just given the jealous gentile. "Hmph! My sister is way too polite in the *guidance* she gave Ms. Thang! But I think we good now."

Ayodele gave Cheryl a high-five and then made her way toward some of her friends.

"Well, I'm glad you took care of that situation. You

know, I truly admire your ability to weather these storms that have come your way and enjoy your relationship openly. I hope to be as brave one day. Until then, I will look toward your relationship with Reverend Scott as one I will have as well," Mikail said.

Cheryl was about to inquire further about Mikail's confession, but Whitney James interrupted their conversation. She softly touched Mikail on the shoulder before giving Cheryl a huge smile.

"Sorry to interrupt, ladies. Cheryl, keep doing the damn thang. I'll reach out soon to further discuss that song you wanted on your new album. I'm honored to collaborate with you. But I'm afraid I have to steal the Congresswoman Rollins away. My brother is hosting a dinner party and wants his favorite politician present."

"Yes, well, you definitely better get going before Bishop James puts y'all on a prayer list for being tardy," Cheryl teased.

Mikail gave Cheryl a sly wink and a quick hug before turning to Whitney to let her escort her to their next event. Cheryl watched them walk closely together down the hallway, and before turning her attention to her minister, she caught the brief affection Mikail granted Whitney. A slow, tentative hand moved toward Whitney's and held it softly as fingers entwined and pressed home their silent need for each other. Memories of the touch of Tabitha's fingers entwined with hers during their frequent lunches at Denny's flashed before her eyes.

"Rose, are you okay?"

The sound of Tabitha's voice startled Cheryl, but she quickly recovered and focused on her plans for the rest of the day—hopefully, with her minister.

"Yes, sorry. I'm fine. You?"

Tabitha smiled brightly and caressed Cheryl's face softly before briefly running over those wanting lips. "Yes, I'm good now."

Cheryl could feel Tabitha's desire to lean in and kiss her, but the woman's restraint was commendable because her lips were pleading for that kiss!

"Tiffany and Isaiah are making Sunday dinner. *God help us!* But if you're brave enough to try whatever they're making, they've asked me to invite you and Ayodele to dinner. Jerome and Leon will be there, too. It's just a small gathering with family—if you want to come."

Cheryl smiled seductively, then whispered, "The question is, do you want me to come? Because I certainly would like to."

The fire in Tabitha's eyes confirmed Cheryl had hit her mark. It had taken everything in her spirit to will herself to go home with Ayodele last night instead of bedding her sexy minister. Although she was glad for their girl time, Cheryl was ready to recreate that scene in Tabitha's bedroom from last night and much more.

"*Rose.* It's a sin to tease your minister, you know that?"

"Who says I'm teasing? Yes, of course, we'll come to dinner. Afterwards, is up to you? I already know what I want for dessert. Do you?"

Before Tabitha could answer her Rose, the woman was sashaying away to join the rest of the party, preparing to head to the house for dinner. Unfortunately for the frustrated minister, she was left standing in silence to contemplate how she would make this dinner fast food and rush straight to the happy meal she truly desired.

* * *

The aromas wafting from Tabitha's three-story home in downtown Decatur were enough to make her eyes and mouth water. She couldn't believe the heavenly fragrance of sinfully good-smelling soul food coming from her kitchen if her challenged cooks, Tiffany and Isaiah, had anything to do with the meal.

Her entourage was just as eager to get into the house and have their bellies fed with what they hoped would be just as delicious as the aroma. Tabitha felt Cheryl's soft hand, pull the key from her grasp and guide the key to unlock the door. She hadn't forgotten all those years ago when she'd been so frazzled, horny, and eager to get Rose to her bed when her motor skills had failed her to do the simple task of opening the door.

"I see, it's still sticky," Cheryl teased.

"*Rose.*"

"Ayyyeee, everybody! Welcome! Y'all, in for a bomb ass, I mean, a good dinner. Ain't that right, sis?"

The hungry guests were happy to excuse Isaiah's more than exuberant greeting, minus Jerome's brief scowl at his brother's usual overzealous behavior. The dinner table was set beautifully, and the food decorated the 8-seater with various savory meats and vegetables. Tabitha noticed the two had pulled out her fine china, typically reserved for holiday events or Unity's dignitaries. But she wasn't disap-pointed at her children's elaborate presentation, especially since Rose was one of the honored guests.

"Well, Tiffany, Isaiah, this looks and smells wonderful. But what I need to know is where y'all hiding Mama Flo's Soul Food Kitchen containers?"

"Ma! Forreal? We did this all by ourselves, right, sis?"

Tiffany snickered, and those young brown eyes held mischief, which Tabitha knew reflected their deceit. Her youngest child couldn't hold water. So, either Mother Florence had catered this food for them, or they had hired one of Isaiah's former caterers to handle the dinner.

"Sis, come on, back me up?"

Both younguns burst into laughter as their guests looked from one to the other with skepticism.

"Ayyeeee, we never said we were gonna *make the dinner*. We said we were going to *have y'all over for dinner*," Isaiah playfully defended.

Tabitha shot him some side eye, and he burst into more laughter. "Have us over? Son, is there something you want to tell me about your living arrangements? You've been hanging around here more lately than at your crib."

"Ma, come on. Let's sit down and have this good food before it gets cold. Ms. Cheryl, you come on over here and sit next to Ma."

Isaiah continued to direct the seating arrangements. Once he was happy with his setup, he helped Tiffany take their drink orders and continued to entertain them with his usual provocative conversation. By the time everyone was fed and feeling nice from Isaiah's signature punch, he and Ayodele were swapping embarrassing stories about their siblings and daring each other to a dance off of old school and new school moves.

"Come on, little boy, let me show you how real dancing is done."

"Oh, come on, Auntie, you don't wanna challenge me. It won't be pretty for you."

Cheryl was relieved to have the humorous distraction from her body's need to enjoy Tabitha's company. She could still feel her minister's watchful eyes on her as they enjoyed the show between Isaiah and Ayodele. She was also aware of Jerome's gaze on her, even though it was clear that

Leon wanted his full attention. Cheryl knew they would have to have a serious discussion before the evening was over. She respected his concern for his mother, but she'd need to have a gentler conversation with Jerome than she had with Barbara to inform him that she'd be a permanent fixture in all of their lives.

For now? She decided to join the fun and recruit Tabitha into her mischief.

"Shall, we show them our skillz, Rev?"

Tabitha's eyes lit up with amusement and a bit of trepidation, considering they'd all taken quite a beating of their old bones last night from the dance floor to the street fight. But those sexy brown eyes and that soft hand that beckoned her to the dance floor would not be denied.

"Alright, Rose. But you better tend to my injuries if I break more than a sweat."

Cheryl attempted to recruit another couple before they took to the floor. "Jerome, Leon, how about you show us what you got?"

Leon's eyes lit up, and he was ready to grab his dance partner, but Jerome shook his head and declined. Lucky for Leon, his second favorite dance partner, Tiffany, tapped in for her sulking brother and grabbed Leon's hand. "Come on, Leon, I gotchu!"

"Bro! Ayyyeee, if you not gonna dance, you be deejay. Get on over there and put on some beats, bro!"

Jerome obeyed his brother's request, and before long, he was swept up in his deejay duties. He used his collection of hip-hop tunes from the 80s to the 2000s to turn Tabitha's living room into a present-day Soul Train dance floor. Isaiah and Tiffany were in their element as self-proclaimed professional dancers. Leon did his best to keep up with the middle kid's erratic changes in his dance routine.

Cheryl and Tabitha did their best to imitate the young ones. Ayodele was in her own world and twirled around Isaiah with African moves that were tribal, sexy, and unfamiliar to her competitor. After a few minutes of torture trying to compete with Isaiah at his game, Cheryl decided it was time for the OGs to take the helm and force the children to follow their lead.

"Okay, you proved your point, Isaiah. Let's see you copy our style of dancing," Cheryl challenged.

"Come on, Tab, Ayodele, let's show 'em what we working with! Cabbage Patch."

The trifecta happily went into an homage to the 90s dance routine. They kicked off with the Cabbage Patch, then moved into Laughy Taffy, Tootsie Roll, and Soldier Boy before their backs and knees warned these seasoned sistahs to sit their behinds down!

"Ayyeeee, Cheryl, Ma, you workin' that cake! I see why Ma trying to cuff that thang!" Isaiah exclaimed as he cut in between Cheryl and Tabitha and started dancing with the diva.

"Watch your mouth, son! Nobody should be talking about Rose *thang* but me," Tabitha teased.

The exhausted dancers, young and old, burst into laughter but kept on dancing, a tad bit slower but still determined to ride out Jerome's vibe. When their deejay slowed the pace and hit them with some 90's slow jamz, they were all grateful for the reprieve from the faster beats. Tabitha cut in on Cheryl and Isaiah and reclaimed her dance partner, who was more than happy to have the good minister's hands rubbing on her cake!

Cheryl could feel those eager fingers squeezing her bottom and impressing upon her the restrained desire that needed to be unleashed. Although her body was heated and moist from those dance moves, she knew the slowly rising reaction to Tabitha's foreplay was the real reason she was getting so hot and bothered.

"I hope I wasn't too presumptuous in my warning to Isaiah."

Cheryl's quizzical expression alerted Tabitha to her confusion.

"Your thang, being mine. If I'm mistaken, forgive the assumption."

The tight squeeze against her needy bottom punctuated Tabitha's words and made Cheryl drip with anticipation of living up to the promise to claim her *thang*.

"Stop teasing me, Tab. I don't think I can take the games right now. I need you as soon as possible. Come home with me, please," Cheryl whispered into her ears.

The look in Tabitha's lust-filled eyes confirmed that her minister was definitely game for the invite. Just for clarity, she leaned down and gave those plump lips a deep, longing kiss that sent a shiver from Cheryl's spine to her special spot that was greedy and ready to be fed to its heart's desire.

"I'll be right back. I need to use your restroom," Cheryl uttered breathlessly as she removed Tabitha's grip and escaped to the hall bathroom.

Tabitha couldn't hide the disappointment in Cheryl's response from the onlookers, who didn't make their prying eyes less noticeable. She covered her long face by doing clean-up duties that were much needed in the kitchen. Ayodele and Tiffany followed her. Tabitha did her best not to stand at the bathroom door, awaiting Cheryl's response.

* * *

When Cheryl did get the courage to return from her hiding place, she was met with the curious eyes of Jerome Wright standing near the bathroom.

"Oh, sorry, Jerome. I didn't mean to take so long."

"I'm not waiting for the bathroom. I'm waiting for you. Can we talk?"

Cheryl wanted to sort things out with Jerome, but she hadn't imagined that, at this moment, they would have to engage in a meeting of the minds. Her nervousness to take things further with Tabitha, although she wanted to so much it hurt, made her somewhat eager to stall a few more minutes with Jerome as a distraction.

"Sure, of course."

Jerome led her to Tabitha's office at the end of the hall and closed the door behind them. He turned on the overhead light, and Cheryl adjusted her eyes to the sudden brightness. Jerome's solemn face and piercing brown eyes were illuminated in the bright light. Cheryl took a deep breath and silently promised to be patient and kind and not lose her cool, no matter what came out of the boy's mouth.

"I wanted to talk with you because since you've been back, my mother's life has changed—her behavior as well. I know you're not blind to the fact that she feels deeply for you."

"Yes, I'm aware, and I feel deeply for her, too, Jerome."

"Do you, Ms. Campbell? Because my mother's heart is something I won't allow anyone to play with. She may be falling for you again, but I'm not falling for your routine that has happened over and over when you've returned to her life."

"Jerome, I understand your concern. I respect your love and need to protect Tabitha. She is blessed to have you, Isaiah, and Tiffany in her life to care for her as she cares for you. I know you haven't seen the best of me over the years or even recently, but I won't lie or provide you with empty promises."

Cheryl didn't miss Jerome's scowl or the accusing eyes aiming daggers at her.

"I will tell you the truth and what I have told your mother. I love Tabitha, and I've never stopped loving her. I wasn't ready in the past to be open about my sexuality and, therefore, not open about my relationship with her. I've been scared most of my life that if I came out, my father would track us down in America and hurt Ayodele or my mother. Even when I learned of his death, I was still afraid of the consequences of being openly lesbian."

Jerome wanted to discredit Cheryl's fear, but he couldn't deny the truth in her words. His asylum in America and the home Tabitha had offered him hadn't been accepted easily. For years, he worried that he would be forced to return to Nigeria or that he, too, would be tracked down by his family and murdered.

Even now, as he enjoyed the freedom of asylum, he found it hard to be completely vulnerable with his feelings, especially when it came to Leon. Even though his lover spent most nights at Jerome's townhome, and his clothes took up half of the closet, his toothbrush was firmly planted in the bathroom along with his razor and other toiletries, Jerome had found it difficult to share his living arrangement with even Tabitha.

"I know you probably think because I was outed that I had no choice but to be honest now. But I could have denied it and repented for *my sins* to save my status within the church and with my fans. Honestly, I needed that push because it gave me the freedom to be myself and to return to Tabitha, a woman I love with all my heart. I've wanted her since I first met her at church, and promise you, I have never stopped loving her, and I won't stop whether you or anyone else disapproves."

Cheryl patiently waited for Jerome's response, which she anticipated would be more combative. But the serious demeanor didn't reflect his next words.

"I'm in love with Leon Wilcox, and we've been living together for the past two years. Mother doesn't know; no one knows."

Cheryl didn't know what quite to say in response to that revelation. But her heart felt that Jerome's confession was a sign he would become more friend than foe from now on.

"Are you afraid, too?"

Jerome nodded. "Yes. I guess you think I'm a hypocrite."

Cheryl softly stroked Jerome's arm then granted him a warm smile. "Not at all. Coming out to anyone, within or outside our community or family, can be scary. But what has prevented you from sharing this with Tabitha, if you don't mind me asking?"

Jerome exhaled a deep sigh. "What if it doesn't work out? I care for him deeply, but I am a man of certainty. I live my life in a way that ensures my success. Mother counts on me to be strong and a leader. She has since Isaiah and Tiffany came to live with us. I want to be her support. I love her, and she has given me everything. If this relationship I have with Leon doesn't work out, what will she think of me?"

"That you tried and that you will survive with or without Leon. You can't believe Tabitha would judge you, especially given our on-and-off again relationship. I don't believe it's Tabitha that you're concerned with, but more your own standards. I resonate with perfectionism. I'm like that in my music and sometimes in relationships, but that's draining and hard to keep up as you age, trust me. Trust your heart, Jerome. That's my advice to you. If I'm willing to risk putting myself out there with Tabitha, knowing she could reject me and would have every right to, I challenge you to do the same. You and Leon are a handsome couple, and honestly, Jerome, we all can feel the energy between you."

Jerome snorted and then allowed his handsome face to wear a bright smile.

"You make good points, Cheryl Rose Campbell. I will do my best to take your advice. I will also take my mother's advice, focus on my own affairs, stay out of your business, and give you the proper respect that you deserve."

Cheryl's raised eyebrow and smize reflected her amusement. She was happy that the determined minister had stood up for her but just as pleased that Jerome would give her another chance. She extended her hand to him to seal the deal with a handshake, but Jerome pulled her into a quick, strong embrace before leading her back to the others.

Cheryl soon discovered that she was in for another pleasant surprise. The rest of their dinner party was busy grabbing their coats and personal items, preparing to head out. Tabitha was quick to clear up Cheryl and Jerome's confusion.

"It would seem everybody is planning to go to the movies. Tiffany, Isaiah, and Leon are going to see some action flick, and your sister has a movie date with a mystery person, who she refuses to share with us."

"*Really, Ayodele?* This is news to me, too."

Ayodele cackled. "Sister, you can't know all the tea. Some things have to remain a mystery. I trust you'll be okay if I take the car and get to stepping? Tabitha has agreed to take you home."

"Ayyyye, bro, you need to come on with us too. We got a deal on some tickets: buy one, get one free. So, Tiffany and me, and you and Leon, if you are cool with hanging with all of us?"

Jerome nodded, gave Tabitha a kiss and hug, and extended the same to Cheryl before gathering his things to join the three. Cheryl didn't miss the surprise in Tabitha's eyes in response to Jerome's new expression of kindness toward her.

"I'll explain later," she whispered.

i'm coming back

"SO, are you ready for me to take you home? Or..."

Cheryl admired Tabitha's chivalrous behavior as her sweet minister did her best to do the right thing, or so she pretended. They both knew that escorting Cheryl to her condo wasn't the first order of business for either one of them. They had waited way too long for this night, and Cheryl wasn't about to delay having her after-dinner treat for a 30-minute drive to her Buckhead home.

"Or. I'm ready for that, Tab. Aren't you?"

Cheryl leaned in for a kiss and could feel the faint hint of Isaiah's special punch on her lover's breath. Tabitha's hands instinctively wrapped around Cheryl's waist, pulling her closer as their lips reconnected for the first time since their last kiss earlier in the day. The softness of Cheryl's lips against hers was like a slow seduction, building and building until it became too hot to bear. Tabitha could feel herself breaking out into a light sweat, unsure if it was from the intense kiss or from her familiar menopausal symptoms.

Any thoughts of hot flashes were quickly pushed aside

as Tabitha's hands roamed down Cheryl's body, eliciting moans and gasps from her lover. She traced her fingers over the thin fabric of Cheryl's skirt, feeling that plump cake before sliding them further down to caress the soft skin between her thighs. When her fingers slid in between Cheryl's butt crack and dipped inside the soft fabric and stroked that hungry pussy, her Rose bloomed under the powerful nourishment.

"Ooh, Tab! Keep touching me, just like that. Deeper, baby, please, touch me deeper!"

Cheryl's encouragement made Tabitha more adventurous. She removed her fingers momentarily and pulled her Rose to the sofa, where she laid her woman down. Tabitha sat between Cheryl's open legs and removed the sexy black stilettos from her lover's feet, then pulled the moist panties from her sweet treasure and prepared herself to slowly enjoy the special dessert prepared just for her. Cheryl's hand stopped her from proceeding with her mission.

"Tab, what if the kids come back? Can we at least go to your bedroom?"

Tabitha felt ashamed for acting impulsively without considering the consequences, but Cheryl quickly alleviated her embarrassment. She took Tabitha's hand and placed it against her silkiness, guiding her fingers to pleasure her just the way she liked for a brief moment.

"You wouldn't want me to demonstrate my octave range to your children, would you? I want you to make love to me, Tab, just not here in the open. Don't be embarrassed. I want this just as much as you do. Now take me to bed, Rev!"

Tabitha's eyes sparkled with amusement and desire, and she eagerly followed Cheryl's lead. "Yes, Rose. Follow me."

Tabitha and Cheryl made their way to the master bedroom. Cheryl couldn't help but notice that Tabitha's new home included some upgrades in her decor. The queen-sized bed had been replaced with a California king in a spacious and beautifully decorated private suite. Cheryl couldn't wait to experience all the amazing things she wanted to do to Tabitha in that bed—and all the things she desperately craved for Tabitha to do to her there.

Tabitha attempted to guide her, but Cheryl took control and moved them both toward the bed. With a gentle push from Cheryl, Tabitha sat down on the edge of the mattress. The excited minister couldn't help but watch with admiration as Cheryl slowly undressed in front of her. The mature body before her was just as alluring as she remembered, if not more so. It had curves that were still sexy and feminine but also showed signs of age with a bit of extra weight around the midsection and a keloid scar from an appendix removal. Tabitha could relate, having her own abdominal scarring from a hysterectomy.

Despite any imperfections or scars, Cheryl's beauty shone through just as strongly as when they first met 25 years ago. She was still breathtakingly stunning, and Tabitha couldn't resist pulling her close to feel her soft curves, the raised keloid markings, and the extra fullness around her waist.

Cheryl couldn't help but feel self-conscious as Tabitha's hands explored every part of her body.

"Tab, please stop. Don't touch my ugly scar or fat rolls. I want to turn you on, not off," she pleaded with shame for her perceived flaws.

"Rose, no, you're beautiful just the way you are. Every inch of your body is beautiful to me. You're my woman, right? *Right?*" Tabitha reassured her, continuing to caress every imperfection with love and adoration.

Cheryl fought against the urge to pull away as Tabitha's hands persisted. "Yes, I'm yours—scars, wrinkles and all. If you want me."

Tabitha's lips conveyed their desire to Cheryl as they kissed and licked her belly and then delved deeper into her smooth, shaven pussy. Any doubts or hesitations Cheryl might have had about her lover's thorough exploration were quickly erased by the pleasure she was experiencing.

"Oh, Tabitha, that feels so good. You can touch me wherever you want; just don't stop."

Cheryl could feel the smile on Tabitha's lips as they continued to please her. Tabitha's hands pulled her closer until she was straddling her lover, and her mouth lavished attention on her breasts with skillful mastery. Her nipples responded eagerly under this treatment, and Cheryl let out a moan of pure bliss.

With one hand stimulating her between her legs, Tabitha's mouth worked wonders on Cheryl's breasts until they were both aching for more. When Cheryl broke away from their kiss, Tabitha felt a momentary disappointment.

"Tab, take off your clothes. I want to see you, touch you, fuck you! You can't have all the fun."

Tabitha laughed nervously but followed Cheryl's instructions. Cheryl switched places with Tabitha—eager to see the body she hadn't laid eyes on in a very long time. As each piece of clothing was removed, Cheryl grew more and more aroused. Tabitha's teasing pace was making her hornier and hornier, and she didn't hesitate to lend a hand. Together, they slowly unveiled an older body that pleased Cheryl just as much as hers had pleased her lover.

Cheryl scooted back on the bed and used her finger to beckon Tabitha to join her, but her lover hesitated.

"What's wrong, Tab? I need you now," Cheryl pleaded.

"Before we continue, Rose, there are some things you need to know about me. It's not about you at all, please don't think that. It's just something that has changed for me."

Curiosity and concern formed on Cheryl's face. "What do you mean, it's not me but you? What's wrong?"

"I want you just as much as you want me right now, but my body might not show it without some assistance. It's not like before. Do you understand?"

Cheryl had an idea of what Tabitha was referring to, but she didn't want to make an assumption or make her woman even more uncomfortable than she already appeared to be.

"Show me what you mean, Tab. Whatever it is, I have no doubt that we can work it out together. I want you right now so bad, and I will do whatever you want me to, need me to. Show me, please."

Tabitha smiled softly, then moved to the nightstand, pulled out a bottle, and presented the lubricant to Cheryl as if she were handing her a bottle of the finest champagne. Cheryl took the bottle in one hand, took Tabitha's in the other, and guided her onto the bed next to her.

"Ever since the hysterectomy and menopause, I've not been the same. No more super wet for me, or as the children say, no more WAP for me."

Cheryl smiled softly and then moved her hand to Tabitha's face. She leaned in and kissed her deeply before pushing her lover back onto the pillows.

"Now, that's where I disagree. It doesn't matter how you achieve that wet ass pussy, as long as it's with me and only me. I may be a tad bit younger than you, Tab, but our bodies have changed, and I appreciate a little help in that department, too. So, there's nothing to be ashamed of or worry about. I gotchu, Ma!"

Tabitha laughed as Cheryl gave her best impression of Isaiah. She was also relieved to know she wouldn't disappoint her Rose. The feel of those soft hands rubbing her breasts gently and then with much more vigor and Cheryl's sweet mouth tongue fucking her made her body come alive with even more excitement.

When those lips traveled further down south and caressed her lower lips with just as much intensity, Tabitha's body hummed with the beginning of an infrequent orgasm. She opened her body wide for her lover's expert manipulation of her instrument. And when her Rose lathered both of their bodies with the smooth silkiness of the lubricant, then intertwined their lower halves into a scissoring fucking good time, Tabitha exploded under her Rose's thrusting, humping, and bumping motions.

They bucked and grinded, moaned and screamed, clinched and released, circled around and around, up and down, and rode the wave of the most amazing orgasm that shook them into a delicious climax.

"Rose! Fuck me, baby! Fuck me!"

"Oooh, Tab, baby, ooh, hold on, just a little bit more! Oooh, yesss! Tab!"

With a deep sigh, Cheryl fell into Tabitha's embrace and shuddered as the final wave of her climax washed over her unexpectedly. Tabitha hugged her close, soothing them both into a more relaxed state. Cheryl could feel Tabitha's heartbeat against her cheek, and she reveled in the slow rhythm as they came down from their blissful high. She snuggled closer into Tabitha's arms, feeling at home.

"Are you okay, Rose?"

Cheryl lifted her head with a smile. "More than okay. I'm home."

Tabitha returned her smile. "Yes, you are. I'm glad you found your way home."

"Me too, Tab."

"Do you feel tired?"

Cheryl raised an eyebrow, wondering what other surprises the mischievous minister might have up her sleeve.

"I'm good, not tired enough for bed yet. What's going on, Rev?"

Tabitha giggled. "I was wondering if you'd like to try some new things? Unless you're scurred?"

Cheryl playfully side-eyed Tabitha, remembering all the times she had used that same line on her years ago.

"You know I'm not scurred of anything. What did you have in mind?"

Tabitha's eyes lit up with mischief, and the next hour would be spent exploring new desires and fulfilling fantasies beyond Cheryl's imagination. She relished in the evolution of their sex life and the freedom of expression they shared together.

iconic god

TABITHA DID her best to focus on the energetic chatter between the children who should have had her undivided attention as she sat in the headquarters of D-Stud Musik, but her mind often wandered to the where-abouts of her partner—business partner that is, and perhaps part-time lover? For the past two weeks, she had been knocking them boots with her Rose minus yesterday and the day before that.

Rose had gotten her libido raging, something that she didn't think was possible all these years of adjusting to the side effects of menopause and old age. But the fire was reignited. Thoughts of Rose's sweet lips, soft, womanly curves, sexy smile, deep moans, and that octave range that threatened to bring the cops a knocking as her Rose unabashedly enjoyed their lovemaking kept her stead on Cheryl Rose Campbell!

Through prayer and much preparation, Tabitha could give and receive pleasure beyond her imagination. And Rose just kept finding ways to make the extra measures fun and sexy, which made her eager minister completely addicted to her will and her way!

Now, as Tabitha sat trying not to sulk under the watchful gaze of her eldest son, her baby boy's teasing glances, and her empathetic daughter's concerned eyes, Tabitha did her best to appear engaged in the Gen Z discussion about some reality show or another or where they wanted to order takeout, or how they were going to spend Dymon's earnings from her new album.

Tabitha tried to hide her amusement at how quickly Layla Joy got Dymon's *bros*, including Isaiah, in check about trying to dip into the young talented hip-hop artist's coffers. The spirited and beautiful young woman reminded Tabitha of her Rose in their younger days. But she couldn't deny that the mature and refined Rose was just as captivating, if not even more.

"Dymon Stud, this is a maze you have here. If it wasn't for your head of maintenance, *Mr. J*, I'm not sure if I could have found you. I would have been here sooner, but Mr. J was eager to regale me with a medley of songs from my latest album. It would seem he's a fan. But I'm here now and have to give it to you. You have a magnificent studio. I love the aesthetics, and the equipment is top-of-the-line. I'm impressed, Dymon Stud."

Cheryl Rose Campbell's voice quickly switched the conversation and focus to the sexy diva who sashayed into the lounge dressed in a black and white Kimona-inspired dress that molded to her curves and accented that bountiful bottom that Tabitha loved to adore so very much. The sexy black stilettos, Tabitha's favorite shoes on those beautifully pedicured feet, gave femme fatale vibes, and her minister loved every minute of Rose's grand entrance.

"Wassup, Cheryl Rose Campbell. I'm glad you like my

spot. I got a lot to show you and the Rev. We've been working on that track with the stems you and Rev sent over. I think you're going to really like how we put the song together."

"Yeah, Rose, you know I gotchu. I been in here day and night helping D make that track fire! Plus, we got some surprises for you and Ma, too. We been working on our own songs like you asked us to, right Rome, Tiff?"

Jerome and Tiffany gave each other a knowing look but didn't rat out their brother, allowing him to take full credit for coordinating the entire project. As the middle kid, Isaiah had always struggled to figure out his role in the family. He alternated between trying to be the leader and usurping Jerome's natural role as the eldest. Other times, he enjoyed being spoiled like the baby of the family when the youngest of the siblings, Tiffany, wasn't spoiled at all. She was the empath who worried about and nurtured every member of their family, even when she was a child.

"Yo, bro, stop capping! You know Romey Rome and Tiff been in here every evening laying down dem tracks. But Isaiah is right, Ms. Campbell, they fire!" Kenyatta Carter, Dymon's right hand, interjected before taking a quick puff on a fatty.

"Ayyeee, Kenny, c'mon," Dymon reprimanded, trying her best not to lose control of her squad.

Working with Reverend Tabitha Scott and Cheryl Rose Campbell had been much more fun and less *religious* than Dymon imagined when Ayda Kohn first approached her with the project. Still, she hadn't forgotten who her new collaborators were, including the low-key minister's children. Clearly, Layla's long lecture from the night before with Kenny, Sam, and Dre had either been forgotten or wasn't as effective as her bae had intended.

"Uh, oh, um, sorry, Rev, Ms. Campbell. I'll take this outside," Kenny apologized before pulling her stout body into a standing position and moving out to the patio with Sam and Dre following.

Tabitha could see the embarrassment in Dymon Stud's eyes and the irritation in Layla Joy's. But the three amigos were just as entertaining and mischievous as Isaiah could be. She was more than used to their young antics, and not much surprised her these days after raising and continuing to *occasionally house* her grown son.

"Dymon, it's all good. We're not here to judge or expect you to behave differently because of our presence. Although I'm a minister, I am also a woman with my own needs and desires. So, please, don't censor your family or yourself for us. I'm enjoying getting to know you, and since *Ms. Campbell* has chosen to make an appearance, I think we can get started."

Tabitha shot Cheryl Rose Campbell a disapproving glance. Though she might not be judging the D-Stud Musik family, she was definitely throwing some shade toward her distant lover. Cheryl didn't let Tabitha's prickly disposition distract her or deter her from enjoying her minister's company without an argument.

What was distracting was said minister's gorgeous face and body. She had put herself through a timeout with Tabitha Scott, but she was aching to get up close and personal in a more private setting. Cheryl wasn't blinded by the mutual horniness in Tabitha's tensed body and testy behavior toward her. She silently promised she'd give them both what they needed tonight. Two nights without being underneath her minister was two nights too long.

Cheryl ignored the watchful eyes as everyone, including her moody minister, waited for her to respond to Tabitha's saucy words. Instead, she claimed the empty space next to Tabitha and sandwiched their bodies together, leaving no room for the imaginary wedge Tabitha pretended to drive between them.

"You know you could have rode with us. You didn't have to drive yourself."

Cheryl slid her hand over Tabitha's thigh and gently rubbed the smooth cashmere material of her minister's black slacks. "Now, Tab, you know I'm perfectly capable of driving myself."

Tabitha tried not to be swayed by that more than tempting hand, but her body was heating up at each slow caress. Cheryl pushed her wanting thigh closer to her lover's body. Tabitha moved slightly to passively encourage that teasing appendage to give her some space so she could think clearly with her head and not with her heart. But her Rose didn't pay any mind to Tabitha's weak attempt at distracting her from soothing her minister's body.

"Well, I guess that explains your MIA behavior for the past two days—you needed your space to do things your way." Tabitha continued to bait her.

Tabitha knew she was creating a scene amongst her younger colleagues and family. Cheryl had not only brought the lust back into her life, she had ignited the minister's possessiveness toward her Rose. Tabitha had done her best to calm her territorial tendencies, but the two-day waiting game had caused her to unravel.

It didn't help that Cheryl's hypnotic fragrance was getting her higher than any Gunga could, including that strong blunt that young Kenyatta Carter had perfumed the small room with. All Tabitha could smell, think, or see was Rose.

"Well, you know what they say—why buy the heifer if

you can get the sweetness for free," Cheryl retorted in a sassy tone.

"Oh, shit! Cheryl, that's true, that's true, and y'all been giving it up a lot. Dem walls are thin!" Isaiah exclaimed.

"Isaiah, language!" Tabitha and Cheryl shouted in unison.

Their audience of five burst into laughter at the comic relief of the ever TMI Isaiah. The rest of their group couldn't deny that the Rev and Cheryl were giving just as many details, if not more, than Isaiah was. Dymon and Layla gave each other a knowing look as they silently identified with their older aunties. Their relationship hadn't always been as smooth as it was now. Both women were strong-minded and enjoyed a good battle of wits.

Jerome and Tiffany remained silent as they watched their mother attempt to roast Cheryl Rose Campbell. They had their own secret opinions of the new couple, but both promised to let grown folks handle grown folks' business. Although both were rooting for the two to stay together this time, they weren't blinded by their mother being a little cranky the days Cheryl was absent. Still, they enjoyed this new side of her as well.

Tabitha Scott seemed filled with joy and more free to be vulnerable than they'd ever seen before. Even now, as they witnessed her temper tantrum over the diva's behavior, they enjoyed seeing her focus more on her happiness rather than that of her family and congregation.

"Well, what if I want to give my milk away for free?" Tabitha whispered in Cheryl's ear.

Cheryl enjoyed the brief feel of those lips grazing her earlobe, and she couldn't hold out any longer from rewarding her determined minister. She turned toward those pleading lips and gave her lover the deserving kiss they both wanted. They could hear Isaiah cheering them on in the background, but their bodies only registered the beat of their hearts and their twin desire for more.

When Cheryl finally released Tabitha's lips with a deep moan, she clarified her real feelings for Tab. "I miss you too, Rev. So, stop being mad at me. I promise to make it up to you tonight and going forward."

"See, see, that's what I'm talking about. Ma and Cheryl be making dem movies!"

"Okay, enough, brother. Why don't we focus on what we came here for? Dymon, if you don't mind, can you play the *He Will Never Let You Go* track so the Rev and Cheryl can hear the latest version?"

Jerome finally decided it was time to step in and course-correct his brother's usual antics and playfulness—and his elders' inability to focus on the professional before the personal. The look in Dymon Stud's eyes expressed the artist's gratitude to Jerome for redirecting their focus.

"Sure, Jerome. So, Rev, Rose, we think we got the final mix, but my feelings won't be bruised if you want to rework it until you're satisfied."

Cheryl and Tabitha did their best to be as attentive as possible, but the heat between them was still ever present. Cheryl decided to give Tabitha some space, but when she motioned to separate their bodies, she found her sexy minister's hand holding her steady in place.

"Stay right where you are," Tabitha whispered.

The sound of that sexy voice did a number on her lady-parts, and Cheryl prayed she'd regain her composure and concentration. As Dymon played the track, the music and the collaborative performance between Dymon and Cheryl switched their vibe up.

Dymon nervously waited to get their feedback. Layla gave her a quick, confident smile and sexy wink to soothe her good girl's anxiety. This project was becoming increasingly meaningful to Dymona, and Layla knew that the approval of Reverend Tabitha Scott and Cheryl Rose Campbell meant more to her than just her ego. The contemporary gospel music they created was much different from Dymon's usual hip-hop tracks. This project brought her closer to the memories of her grandmother and her childhood attending church with G-Ma.

"Kenyatta was right, Dymon. This is fire! I love it. It's more than I could have envisioned, and it's a perfect blend of both of our styles. And thank you, Jerome, for helping us with the lyrics."

Dymon beamed with pride. The former bad boi was happy that her new attitude and walk in life could be expressed in this music. "Thanks, Ms. Campbell..."

"Cheryl, Dymon Stud. We're family now."

"Fo'sho. Thanks, Cheryl. I appreciate knowing you liked the track. What about you, Rev?"

Tabitha's face lit up with humor. "Oh, so you want to know what I think, huh? This y'allz thing, you and Rose. You don't need my input," Tabitha teased.

"Ayyeee, c'mon, Rev. You know I respect your opinion just as much. You're the reason we had the original melody. Jerome told me you and Cheryl vibed and came up with the initial lyrics. So c'mon, whatchu think?"

"Oh, alright. I'm just kidding you, Dymon. Of course, I agree with Rose. This track is fire! I say this honestly; I can see this being one of many hits off the album. Thank you for adding your flavor to the music."

"Oh, that ain't all we got, Ma! Wait until you hear your fam's tracks," Isaiah interjected.

"Alright, son, you know we want to hear your music. C'mon on with it."

"Um, wait. I have a question before we get started," Cheryl chimed in.

With such a serious expression on her face, her captive audience had no idea what would come out of that sassy mouth. Cheryl wasn't as extreme as the provocative commentary of Isaiah, but you never knew what either would say.

"*Dymon Stud*, I know that's your artist name because I've noticed that Layla Joy always refers to you as Dymona. So, I'm curious, why the name *Dymon Stud*?"

Everyone seemed to breathe a sigh of relief except for Isaiah, who was, as usual, amused by most things.

"Oh yeah, sure. My real name is Dymona Alexander, and that's what Laylanna has called me since day one when we first met 20 years ago. But my Ma used to always say when I got big one day, she wanted me to shower her with diamonds for spitting out my big behind! She used to watch dem old Marilyn Monroe movies all the time, and that one, *Gentlemen Prefer Blondes*, she'd watch over and over. You know, the one where Marilyn Monroe sings, *Diamonds Are a Girl's Best Friend*?'

Cheryl and Tabitha nodded in recognition of the 1953 classic. They were more than familiar with the iconic movie and Madonna's *Material Girl* song and music video, inspired by Marilyn Monroe and the film.

"Ma said that the only way she'd get that type of ice would be from me one day. She always believed in my skillz, you know. And *Stud*, well..."

Dymon flexed her muscles and playfully did a body-builder pose, then shot a sexy gaze toward her aunties. Her playfulness was rewarded with laughter from the group.

"Got it. It fits you," Cheryl complimented.

"Thanks, Cheryl. I gotta a question for you."

"Yes, Dymon?"

"Your name, is it your real name? I know Rev always calls you Rose. Is that your real name?"

Cheryl and Tabitha shot each other sheepish grins before the diva explained her chosen artist's name. Before she could begin explaining and hoping that her younger audience would understand her references, Dymon's bros returned to the lounge and sat quietly, waiting to be clued in on the chatter.

"No, it's not completely my real name. You may be too young to remember this old crime drama, *Charlie's Angels*."

"Oh, yeah, we know that movie. You talking 'bout that hot bae, Kristin Stewart, right? I've seen all her *Twilight* movies on Netflix. She my dream bae!" Sam interjected.

Cheryl and Tabitha were quickly reminded that they were in the company of babes—not that they had truly forgotten. She smiled politely and then gently corrected young Samantha's assumption. The cute little baby dyke was so proud of her response that Cheryl hated to correct her.

"Not exactly. That was a reboot of the original that came out in 1976, but Cheryl Ladd didn't actually become a part of the cast until the second season when she replaced Farah Fawcett."

"1976? I wasn't even born then!"

"Sam, c'mon?"

"Oops, sorry, Ms. Campbell. I meant no disrespect. Forreal."

"It's okay, Sam, I understand. That was a very long time ago. I get it."

"But you still a hot auntie, Ms. Campbell. No cap. You fire!"

Cheryl blushed and appreciated the youngster's compliment, but she didn't miss Dymon's frown or Layla's scowl. The children were going to get it later on. Cheryl had no doubt about it.

"Well, thank you, Sam. That is very kind of you. So, Cheryl Ladd and her character Kris Munroe were my favorite on the show. On the other hand, my mother was a huge fan of actress Jacklyn Smith and her character Kelly Garrett."

"Oh, okay, got it. So, what about the rest of your name?" Dymon was becoming more intrigued by her elder's choice of names, which fit the diva perfectly.

"Rose Agwuegbo is my real name. My family is of Nigerian descent, and after my mother and sister came to the States for asylum, she decided to retain my father's surname but wanted to give me a less-than-Nigerian first name. She always said I was her beautiful flower—her Rose. For years, my family was very poor when I was growing up. Leaving her home and her career in Nigeria forced my mother to take lower-paying jobs in America. Often, we didn't have much to eat, but out of the food we did have, for some reason, I loved Campbell's Oodles of Noodles, hence the surname, Campbell."

"That's a perfect mashup of names, and it has star power, just like you, Ms. Campbell—I mean, Rose."

Cheryl smiled brightly. She could see why the ladies loved Dymon Stud. The reformed bad boi was a charmer, just like her Rev.

"Why, thank you, Dymon. I appreciate the compliment. Like Layla, Tab has known me for over 25 years. When we first met, I was not Cheryl Rose Campbell, the singer, but choir girl, Rose Agwuegbo, meeting our new Minister of Music, Reverend Tabitha Scott."

Cheryl and Tabitha looked into the dreamy eyes of their young audience and were surprised by their appreciation of their elders' herstory. Although the temperature in the room was less erratic than before, given Isaiah's high energy, Cheryl felt the need to redirect the energy to something less personal.

"Okay, you all. I think it's time for you to let us hear the new fire music that Isaiah has single-handedly orchestrated," Cheryl teased.

Mission accomplished. The added humor renewed the excitement, and Isaiah went into his routine of directing their listening party. By the time Tabitha's children had premiered a set of six tracks, each writing and performing two songs of the six, Cheryl and Tabitha were amazed and speechless.

Jerome's love songs to the heavenly Father were breathtaking. At moments, they were somber but also filled with adoration and hope for a better world in homage to God's blessings bestowed upon his children. Isaiah's songs were more combative toward a society that abused religion and used God as a weapon against those they refused to understand or accept. Tiffany's music was more praise and worship and eloquently spoke to our lack of appreciation for God's sacrifices for us and our fascination with social media and materialism.

Three sets of eyes remained glued to Cheryl and Tabitha, patiently waiting for their reaction. The two were so overwhelmed by the musical worship that they weren't quite sure how to put it all into words. Their silence encouraged the three to begin explaining the method behind their music.

"Ayyeee, Cheryl, I was inspired by your interview with that sexy auntie, Taylor Horton, a month ago. You know, when you said that people used God as a nemesis. And you were right about dat. There's so much real hate and harm being done in this world in the name of the Father, but all people want to look at is condemning love just because it's love of the same gender. So, I wrote *God as a Nemesis*, and then that flowed into *It Hits Different* because loving the Lord ain't what folks are preaching about, and D just brought that fire with the beat for that one! Ya, feel me?"

Tifffany chimed in before Cheryl and Tabitha could respond.

"And *Iconic God* continued with that thought of how people place their energy on the wrong things. Social media is one of the most dangerous and hateful places sometimes; it's where people go to judge and condemn others, including themselves, by spending more time comparing themselves to false idols. *I Love to Call His Name* was a tribute to God's love and encouragement to focus on God as the true influencer."

Cheryl and Tabitha remained quiet as they waited for Jerome to explain the creation of his music. But the unexpected input from Sam and Dre from Dymon's squad changed the spiritual vibe into a heated argument that neither anticipated.

"Ayyyeee, speaking of dat, y'all, we gotta share sumtin' with y'all. That biyah, I mean, that gurl, Cartier is on the Gram right now. She up to it again, now she begging folks to save her dirty ass, I mean, to bail her out," Sam explained as she watched the reel and read the comments.

"Sam, this ain't the time for that. Whatever's going on with Cartier, that noise none of us want to hear," Dymon discouraged further discussion.

But it was Cheryl who countered the request with her own interest in learning more about what her nemesis was up to now.

"Dymon, if you don't mind, I'd like to know what's happening."

Cheryl could feel Tabitha's eyes burning a hole in her neck. She didn't have to look into those curious brown eyes to know that her minister wasn't too pleased by her interest in a young woman Cheryl professed she had no sexual relationship with.

"Sure, Cheryl. Go ahead, Sam."

"She not slamming you, D or Ms. Cheryl, forreal, dis all about her situation with her tuition. She's begging people to help her get a few bags to stay in the country. She is scared she's going to be deported back to Nigeria. But I think that's what her dirty ass, I mean, that's was she deserves."

"I couldn't agree with you more, Sam. Galatians 6:7-9, *A man reaps what he sows. Whoever sows to please their flesh, from the flesh, will reap destruction.* It would seem that Cartier is beginning her reaping stage, and we should leave her to it."

Cheryl could hear Tabitha's voice warning her woman to leave the matter, and particularly Cartier, alone. Despite Tabitha's valid feelings, Cheryl couldn't ignore the potential danger that Cartier would encounter if she were to return to Nigeria and its laws.

"Tab, Psalms 103:10-12 also says," *As high as the sky is above the Earth, so great is his love for those who respect him. He has taken our sins away from us as far as the Earth is from the West.* God is a forgiving father, and you know that. I'm not condoning her past behavior or who she still is, but she can't return to Nigeria. We can't let that happen."

"*We can't?* Rose, what are you saying? This *innocent*, as you're making her out to be, destroyed your career. She used you and thought nothing of how she would tear your world down. Now, you want to feel empathy for her? What really happened between the two of you?"

As the words rolled out of her mouth with the venom she felt, Tabitha couldn't deny the hurt that appeared in her Rose's eyes or the shock from the deathly silence from their audience. Although she regretted her inappropriate response and the harshness in her words, Tabitha was confused and frustrated with Rose's behavior toward someone who supposedly created false accusations against the former celebrated star.

"Mother, let us temper our words. This is not a black-and-white situation. I don't believe that Rose's concern is solely for Cartier, but what she will face after being publicly known as a lesbian in America and a celebrity here. No matter how small her reach is, it's never too small not to get back to Nigeria. How would you feel if Isaiah had to return there after his public outing?"

Jerome did his best to be gentle with his Reverend Mother. He knew Tabitha's emotions had nothing to do with her ministry and more with her feelings toward Cheryl. He also knew it was his duty to rescue his mother from destroying what was starting to feel like a very fragile relationship with Cheryl Rose Campbell.

The look in those determined brown eyes forewarned Jerome that Tabitha Scott wouldn't back down as easily as he prayed she would.

"Son, I know you mean well, but this is different. Isaiah hasn't purposely hurt anyone or tried to destroy their lives. She doesn't deserve your empathy, Jerome."

"Ma, c'mon, you know dat ain't true, and it ain't what

you taught us. You know I did a lot of harm my entire career as Lit G2G. I was the worst kind of fuckboi. Excuse the language, but it's true. If it hadn't been for D, I would continue to do that shit like before, even though I was tired of pretending to be somebody I wasn't. When I came home, you didn't judge me. You forgave me, helped me, loved me, and you kept loving me even when I was away doing all that bad stuff."

Tabitha didn't like the truth that her kids were forcing her to see the error of her ways. As much as she wanted to sulk in her jealousy, she had taught her children too well to minister to those who are angry and judgemental by *speaking the very words of God.*

Tiffany was the last to employ her to see this situation in a different light. "Mother, we don't know what life Cartier has experienced before coming here. But I do know that if you hadn't saved me when I was 10 years old from the nightmare that I lived every day, I don't know what type of woman I would be today. God gave you to me as my new mother, Jerome, and Isaiah as my brothers, and you all protected and loved me. We can't let her go back there. Please, Mother."

"Tabitha, we need to talk privately. Please, everyone, excuse us for a moment."

Cheryl didn't wait for Tabitha to agree to her command. She stood on firm ground and walked with her head held high and backside to her minister as she walked briskly toward the studio's exit. She could hear Tabitha's footsteps behind her and Tabitha's voice calling out to her, but she kept on walking. Cheryl was heated, not with passion but with the hurt of a woman who had been publicly embarrassed yet again by someone she deeply cared for and never would have expected to do such a thing.

Her fast pace wasn't something her inactive body was used to, but she kept going until she finally reached the parking lot and her car. Tabitha was right behind her, and now, as they stood face to face, Cheryl had no empathy but anger for her minister.

"Rose..."

"No, don't say another word. I think you've said all that I needed to hear. I thought we were done with your need to hurt me, judge me, and dredge up the past. I also thought you believed me when I said I didn't sleep with Cartier. But clearly, everything I say to you is a lie in your mind."

"Rose, that's not true. I just don't understand why you're defending her. She hurt you, and because I do care about you, I don't want her to use you or hurt you again."

"No, Tab, it's not because you care about me. You're jealous, and you don't trust me. You've been pissy ever since I walked through the door. I know it's scary for you to trust me, to give me another chance. Believe it or not, it's scary for me too. I was getting too comfortable with us, the routine we just fell into. I was scared you'd grow tired of me."

Tabitha attempted to reach out to Cheryl, but her angry Rose withdrew from her intentions.

"No, Tab, don't touch me right now. I'm mad at you! I'm hurt by you. You don't get to just say you're sorry and then pull me into your arms. I'm not a child, and I don't need you reprimanding me. You don't understand why I'd be concerned about Cartier? Then you haven't heard a thing that I've said about my mother and Ayodele and what your own children have said about their former lives before you. You take for granted the so-called freedom we have here in the States. I would have done the same had I not grown up listening to my mother's stories or seen how Ayodele has been treated even here in the States. No matter what Cartier has done to me, she doesn't deserve the punishment she might receive returning to Nigeria."

Tabitha couldn't argue with Cheryl's truth or her children's painful memories and experiences. She had been selfish and jealous of Cheryl's response to the news of Cartier's distress. Tabitha had let her temper get the best of her. She looked at Cheryl with pleading brown eyes and silently promised she'd do better.

"Rose, I am truly sorry. What can I do to fix this?"

Cheryl hated that her body had a weakness for this minister's sweetness. That docile and apologetic mannerism was charming, like a misbehaving puppy pleading for pissing on his mother's favorite rug. She did her best to quiet the impulse to melt into those eager arms that waited by Tabitha's side for any opportunity to surround Cheryl.

"You can arrange to have Cartier's tuition paid for on my behalf."

"What!" Tabitha wasn't expecting that request and couldn't hide her disbelief at Cheryl Rose Campbell's generosity.

"You said you wanted to fix what you've broken between us. If you want me to believe that, Tab, you'll do what I ask. I'll transfer the money to your charity for the tuition. And I want you to have Mikail Rollins deliver the scholarship to Cartier without informing her that I donated the money. This needs to remain just between the three of us. Understood?"

"Rose, this makes no sense. Fine, you want to bail her out. I disagree with it, but I will stand by your decision. But not letting Cartier know that you're her benefactor is not right. She needs to know that despite what she did to you,

you cared enough about her situation to bail her out. It's the right thing to do."

Cheryl braved a brief moment of affection with Tabitha. She stroked her frustrated minister's arm softly, then that brooding beautiful face before she returned her hand to a safe space beside her leg.

"Tab, as much as I know you still doubt me and are angry with me, I know you still care about me. I also know that despite the distance between us and all of the disappointment that I brought into your life over the years, you came to the rescue when I was recently at my lowest. You didn't have to enlist Ayda Kohn to help me, bring me back to the church, create this project for me to work on, and surround me with wonderful supporters like Mikail, Dymon, Whitney, and Roxanna. You cared about me despite my sins and gave me an opportunity for redemption. I am merely paying it forward and giving someone else a chance."

Tabitha wanted to deny the truth in Cheryl's words, but the woman who stood before her was not the same selfish diva of the past. Cheryl Rose Campbell had grown over the years and not just during their most recent time together. Tabitha had noticed it from the moment she laid eyes on her again at church that first Sunday and as they continued to spend time together. Honestly, she couldn't give herself the credit for Cheryl's growth—that was all her Rose's work with the help of God, not her minister.

"You're right, Rose. I can't argue with that—as much as I want to. I will do what you ask."

For the first time in the past few moments, Cheryl granted her minister a soft smile. "Thank you, Rev. Oh, and one other favor, please?"

Tabitha's raised eyebrow signaled she was slightly leery

of the subsequent request, but she nodded complacently. Whatever she needed to do to make amends, she was willing and able to do, or so she thought.

"Please let everyone know that I have to leave. You can tell them I don't feel well or whatever you like."

"Rose, wait, why?"

Tabitha saw the sadness return in Cheryl's eyes, and she already knew the answer to her question.

"Because you hurt me, Tab. I just need some time away. Please understand that. I'm not trying to end things with us, but I need to deal with how I feel—alone."

Tabitha steadied herself and tried with all her might not to reach out to her Rose or beg her to forgive her on the spot. She resigned herself to lie in the bed she had made with her own misdeeds.

"I'm sorry, Rose. I never meant to hurt you. But I also understand your need for time and space. I will handle the arrangements for Cartier and give you your space. I will wait for your return to my arms. I'll always be here for you, you know that."

Cheryl's defenses crumbled momentarily. She moved toward those regretful, sweet lips and gave her minister a deep kiss before returning to her car.

"I'll see ya later, Rev."

brand new

"THANK YOU, Ms. Rollins, thank you, Reverend Scott! I don't know how to thank you enough! I can't believe you're doing this for me. You saved my life. How can I repay you? I promise I will. I'll repay every cent once I get my first big contract. I promise!"

Tabitha sat silently beside Congresswoman Mikail Rollins at the roundtable in the District 5 headquarters. She studied the young, animated woman who had caused so much chaos in Cheryl Rose Campbell's life. She did her best to restrain her desire to punish Cartier for her misdeeds. Cheryl didn't want retribution, and Tabitha had promised she'd be the good minister her Rose needed.

Tabitha couldn't resist the need to give a little extra guidance to the wayward troublemaker. Cartier was about the same age as Tiffany but a complete contrast in her behavior to her kind and forgiving daughter. Although Tiffany had gone through her own horrible experiences in her former home, Tabitha's daughter had risen above the trauma. She healed and returned love, not hate, from her tragic upbringing. Tabitha would like to think that her love and guidance for her daughter had played a role in Tiffany's walk in life. So, she decided to do her best to set this young woman on the right path, whether her Rose had approved her methods or not.

"Why delay what you can do today?"

Cartier's surprised expression announced her confusion and fear of the former silent minister staring so hard at her as if she were peering into Cartier's soul. Cartier wasn't unaware of Reverend Tabitha's reputation, even before the social media viral of her valiant efforts along with Cheryl Rose Campbell and her sister, Ayodele. During her brief moment with Cheryl, she had listened to the diva praise the minister's name in an awake state and call out to the minister in her sleep.

Cartier really had no idea why Reverend Scott would have anything to do with saving her ass, considering the fallout between Cartier and Cheryl. By the look in those serious brown eyes and the minister's rigid posture, Cartier could feel the intensity rising in Reverend Scott. She didn't doubt the fearless minister was prepared to do battle again if needed to protect Cheryl Rose Campbell.

"Sorry, Reverend, what do you mean? What can I do? I will do anything to repay you and Ms. Rollins's generosity."

Tabitha's raised eyebrow warned Cartier that whatever the determined minister wanted would be more challenging to deliver than her empty promises.

"Good, Cartier, I'm glad you asked for clarification. Proverbs 27:1 tells us to *not boast about tomorrow, for you do not know what a day may bring forth*. I'm sure you wouldn't want to delay what you could rectify now for some undefined time in the future. You may be young and feel you have all the time in the world, but tomorrow isn't promised to us. *Ya, feel me?*"

Cartier nodded with a cagey expression. Mikail did her best to mask her own expression of amusement. The young troublemaker might not have fully understood where Reverend Tab was leading her, but the congress-woman was more than aware of the valiant minister's intent. Reverend Scott was stead on seeking retribution for Cheryl Rose Campbell. Mikail couldn't blame Tabitha for wanting to fight for her lover's honor—she would do the same and had for Whitney. So, Mikail refrained from inter-vening and allowed the good minister to handle her business.

"Good, Cartier. I'm glad we see eye-to-eye. You should know that the person you really need to thank for this scholarship is Ms. Cheryl Rose Campbell. The source of this money didn't come from the True Colors Foundation, but directly from Ms. Campbell."

"Cheryl! Cheryl did this for me?"

"*Ms. Campbell* did this for you, Cartier," Tabitha quickly corrected.

Cartier lowered her gaze and reigned in her high energy. She couldn't believe that the diva had done such a generous thing. For a moment, Cartier fantasized that perhaps it was because the beautiful woman really did have feelings for her. She couldn't deny she secretly held feelings for the older woman. Cartier hadn't meant to hurt Cheryl, no matter what the stern minister might think or say. She had to explain herself and let both of the women who stared at her with judgemental eyes know that she wasn't as horrible as they saw her.

"Yes, Reverend, sorry, Ms. Campbell. Why would she do such a wonderful thing for me? I know I haven't been the best person toward her, and I regret my behavior. But to know that she would do this for me..."

"Exactly my point, Cartier. Such a great gift from a benevolent woman like Ms. Campbell shouldn't be taken lightly. You should know that she requested the scholarship be donated to you anonymously through the foundation. She didn't want you to feel obligated to her in any way."

Cartier looked at Mikail for clarification as if she needed an interpreter for the foreign language the minister was speaking. Such generosity that Reverend Scott was testifying on behalf of Cheryl Rose Campbell was utterly foreign to Cartier. In her former life in Nigeria, Abidemi had only known transactional feelings. With her father absent from the home, her mother had used her own body to survive— and when the men's eyes wandered to ten-year-old Abidemi, she had given her little one as an offering more than Cartier would care to remember.

Throughout her life, Cartier had grown to accept transactional love. When she met Cheryl Rose Campbell, it felt different. The celebrated diva, the beautiful, sexy songstress, offered her warmth, kindness, and laughter and even promised future opportunities to help her with her singing career. Cartier had believed she had found a new home in the mature arms of a lover. *How could she have been so wrong?*

"I don't know what to say. This is truly very generous and kind of Cheryl, I mean, Ms. Campbell. What can I do to show my gratitude?"

"Cartier, there are many things that you can do to show your appreciation. Understand that this is not coming from Ms. Campbell but from me. Although she might empathize with your situation, my main concern is for the woman you did your best to destroy. As much as I have questioned why she wants to do such a benevolent thing for you, I do not believe that she is paying out blood money to cover her own sins. With that said, I am here to clarify what really happened between the two of you and how you can help repair this misconception. And let me be clear, I am not asking from the perspective of Ms. Campbell's minister. Cheryl Rose Campbell is my woman and always has been and always will be. Understand?"

Mikail feigned a cough to hide her shock and amusement at the feisty minister's bold statements. She had to give it to Reverend Tab; the woman didn't mince words, and she didn't come to play; she came to slay the devil and the dirty deeds that had been done. If she could have given Tabitha Scott a high-five and a few snaps of her fingers, Mikail would have broken character in a heartbeat. But the congresswoman was a professional politician, and she knew decorum and perception were more crucial during such matters than showing her true sisterhood in the presence of the young nemesis.

"Yes, Reverend Scott. I feel ya. You have every right to be angry with me, and so does Ms. Campbell. I regret that I caused her harm. Please believe me. I was confused."

"*Confused?* Is that what you were, Cartier? *Confused?* You seemed pretty confident in your attack against Ms. Campbell on social media. What were you confused about? Did you misinterpret her intentions toward you?"

Cartier tried to conceal her rising temper and jealousy. Reverend Scott was really coming on strong with this pissing contest she was challenging her with. Though it was obvious the bold minister had succeeded in regaining Cheryl's heart, she didn't have to rub salt in Cartier's open wound. Instead of retaliating or giving a false testament yet again, Cartier decided to do the right thing for once in her life. She would tell the whole truth and nothing but the truth.

"My life hasn't been easy, Reverend Scott. I say this as no excuse for my actions. Nigeria, my mother, wasn't kind to me. I guess I didn't learn to be too kind to others, either. That night, Ms. Campbell talked to me like a real person, not a commodity, and I liked how she made me feel. She made me feel like a real person, with feelings, dreams, and promises."

Tabitha sat quietly and listened patiently as Cartier revealed the events of that night. As the young woman described the impact Cheryl Rose Campbell had made in her life in that brief moment in time, Tabitha couldn't deny that her Rose had always had a way of making people feel special including her minister.

"I wanted more of that feeling. We were drinking, and I was having so much fun, and I kept pushing to go with her when she said she was going home. She had declined my request multiple times, but then she seemed like she was unsure of herself. She probably had more drinks than she needed to, so I offered to make sure she got home okay, and my last attempt was successful."

Cartier paused and did her best to gather her thoughts. Although it hadn't been that long ago, she wanted to tell the truth and get the facts right—not retell the story based on her fantastical version of the truth. It was hard to keep the reality straight from the fantasy because she had thought about Cheryl since that night and hoped they'd one day reconcile. But the truth was staring back at her with determined brown eyes and a stance that warned Cartier to relay just the facts.

"When we got to her hotel room, she ordered food and more drinks, but shortly after the food arrived, she went to the bathroom, and she was in there for a long time. I heard her talking at one point, I thought to herself. When I went to the door and opened it, she was on the phone. She didn't even really look at me before she was telling me to go back out. By then, I had gotten comfortable—you know what I mean? I just had my bra and panties on, and she looked at me, but not really."

Tabitha's jaw started to ache from her familiar unwanted signs of TMJ. Cartier describing how she paraded that young body in sexy lingerie in front of her Rose's eyes that night was making her condition worse. She tried not to grind her teeth or clinch down on the sensitive molars. But Cartier had better speed up her sordid details before she used those sharpened teeth to bite the young woman's head off!

"So, what happened after that, Cartier—and feel free to skip the intricate details."

"Yes, yes, right, Reverend. We did end up in bed together, but not like I said. Cheryl went to bed, and I sat up for a while, but I got in bed with her when I knew she was asleep. I tried to wake her to do something, but at first, she was sound asleep. She was dreaming, and I could hear her call out..."

Cartier hesitated and wondered if the feisty minister really wanted to know that Cheryl was dreaming about her —of course, she did. Cartier begrudgingly thought to omit this information. Those sharp eyes and that body posture of the minister looked as if Reverend Scott was about to lunge at her like a ferocious lioness, which made her rethink, skipping the details.

"She was calling your name, Reverend Tabitha. She was dreaming about you. I shook her, and she finally woke up. When I offered to fill her dreams with someone else—with me, she did her best to be nice and declined my offer. She asked me to leave, said she would have a driver take me home, and apologized. Said this had been a mistake. But all I heard was that I was a mistake, something I've heard all my life. So, I was angry with her, and I argued with her, but she never threatened me; she just kept apologizing. I hated the fact she was so nice, so fucking; I mean, she seemed like she felt sorry for me. So, I left. You already know what I did next."

Tabitha had mixed emotions about Cartier's reveal. Her heart was lighter now that she knew her Rose had been telling the truth and had never stopped loving her minister. There was also a mixture of anger and empathy for Cartier, who clearly struggled with her own baggage. Tabitha's children had done their best to help her understand Cartier's plight well after Cheryl had abandoned her at Dymon's studio. Although they were true in their defense, Tabitha knew her jealousy clouded her judgment and heart.

"Thank you, Cartier. I know that was hard for you to share, and as much as I disapprove of your behavior, none of us are without being judged for our sins. We all make mistakes, but what we learn from those mistakes and the path we choose to take after them is what builds character. Are you ready to be your best self?"

Cartier looked Tabitha straight in the eyes and didn't waver when she responded. "Yes, Reverend Scott, I am. What do you need me to do?"

* * *

Tabitha was ready to start her day with a song in her heart. Although she hadn't spoken to Cheryl in almost a week, she was content to wait for her woman to forgive her. With the

Cartier situation put to bed—no pun intended, Tabitha felt even more hopeful that she could build a more permanent relationship with her Rose. She just had to be patient, which was the same advice she had given young Rose Aguwegbo many years ago and many times after that.

As she headed toward her kitchen and the familiar sounds of her not-so-empty nest, Tabitha looked forward to sharing her morning coffee and a quick bite with her three children. When she spotted Jerome's number flashing across her cell phone, the good minister soon learned that their daily routine would be taking a slight detour.

"Jerome, is everything alright? I thought you were at the house already being entertained by your brother's loud raucous."

"Sorry, Mother, but I've run into a problem. My car won't start, and I've tried to get a jump, but that didn't work. Don't worry, I've taken care of your transportation. I hired a car service to pick you up this morning. They should probably be arriving in a few minutes."

Tabitha continued to walk toward the loud chatter and laughter with a confused expression. Why Jerome decided she needed a car service when she was fully capable of driving her own car to the church didn't make sense to her foggy brain, which was in desperate need of her favorite fresh-brewed coffee that her son always had in hand, ready to serve her. Instead, the sheepish faces of her younger, mischievous children had all eyes on her with weird little smirks on their faces.

Was she being punked by the three amigos? Something was definitely afoot in this *Tabitha Scott* unexpected drama.

She met their amused eyes with suspicious brown eyes but kept her ears sharp to detect just what Jerome was up to.

"Son, you know I could have driven myself around today. You shouldn't have troubled yourself to hire a driver. I enjoy our time riding together not as a necessity but as something I look forward to doing with you. You know that."

"I know, Mother. And I enjoy being with you every morning, too. But it's done now. Please, don't turn the driver away. I'll see you as soon as I can once I get this situation straightened out."

Tabitha was about to continue protesting the necessity of the car service when the sound of the doorbell interrupted her rebuttal. She glanced at Tiffany and Isaiah, who didn't seem in the mood to budge from their seats, and quickly realized that if someone was going to get the door, it would be her.

"Fine, Jerome. I think your car service is here already. I'll see you later. You let me know if I need to pick you up, or maybe you can call Leon. He might be able to come by and give you a ride."

Tabitha didn't miss Jerome's long pause before responding with a lack of comment regarding the potential aid their lawyer, Leon, could offer him. As much as her eldest had kept his interest in Leon a secret, Tabitha understood the looks and energy they shared around each other —it was just as familiar and real as hers and Rose's whenever they were together. But she wouldn't push her son to confess his true feelings. In time, Tabitha hoped he would trust her with his secret.

For now, her focus would be preoccupied with the woman standing at her front door, looking just as tempting as ever, with that beautiful smile and feminine essence oozing from her body as if her Rose hadn't put her in a timeout for almost a week.

"*Reverend Tabitha Scott, is it?* I'm Cheryl Rose Campbell, your Uber driver for today. Are you ready for your first destination?"

Tabitha could hear Isaiah and Tiffany snickering in the background, but the beat of her heart was overpouring the sounds of their antics. She had truly missed that beautiful face, those deep brown eyes, and those sweet, plump lips. She wanted to pull her woman into her arms, plant a kiss of longing on her mouth, and then drag her Rose upstairs to the privacy of the bedroom and show her just how much she had missed her.

Instead, the excited minister tried to play it cool and remain calm. Tabitha Scott wasn't about to show Cheryl Rose Campbell just how thirsty she really was.

"Hello, Rose. So, you're in the transportation business these days, I see. Although it's news to me, I have a feeling my children knew all about it. Why I was left in the dark, I'll be discussing with them later," Tabitha said, ensuring her voice was a stage whisper both children heard loud and clear.

Cheryl smiled sweetly and did her best to feign innocence, but she couldn't hide her excitement over seeing her good minister. It had been way too long since she'd decided to take some time away from Tabitha—and she was definitely missing her woman. Tabitha was looking such like a woman-in-charge with her sophisticated swagger in the tailored gray business suit with her perfectly coifed pixie haircut, and those full lips painted in a dark berry just made Cheryl want to devour them right then and there!

But they had business to attend to, and she willed her libido to settle down, which was hard of hearing with all that purring going on from her pussycat!

"Don't blame your children for this surprise. I asked

them to help me, and they complied because they knew how much I missed you and needed to see you. I hope that you missed me too. I will try to understand if you don't want me—don't want to see me."

Tabitha was well aware Cheryl was toying with her, and those teasing words made her body hum with a different tune than a few moments ago. *Did she want her?* Cheryl Rose Campbell had been all she could really think about while the distraught minister was in exile from her woman. Words could not convey just how much she missed her Rose, so she let her lips do all the talking.

Tabitha pulled Cheryl into her arms and ran thirsty lips over wanton lips. Tabitha's hand roamed over Cheryl's ample bottom, and the memories of the distance that had been placed between them faded away. Their bodies moved together in perfect harmony. Every taste from welcoming lips and tongues, every caress from determined hands made them want even more, both lost in the moment. Their soft moans and sighs of pleasure increased their desire. But the sounds of their spectators reminded them that they weren't behind closed doors but out in the open for all eyes to see, including Tabitha's neighbors in the modest community.

Tabitha reluctantly pulled away from Cheryl, but those bruised lips from her expert manipulation made her want to dive back in. Cheryl's eyes spoke the same language, and for a moment, Tabitha considered evicting her kids from the house and spending the day in bed with her woman.

"Um, Ma, you and Cheryl gotta big day. You might wanna make dat that movie somewhere more private," Isaiah shamelessly teased them.

Tabitha and Cheryl turned toward his playful eyes. They did their best to display expressions of disapproval, but secretly they wished for the time and place to be the stars in their own private movie.

"Boy, stay out of grown folks' business. But one thing you're right about, we do need to be headed on our way. Tiffany, don't let your brother take all the food out of the fridge like he did last time. Isaiah, you have to leave the house when Tiffany heads to class. Understood?"

Isaiah granted Tabitha a playful frown then nodded in agreement. Cheryl gently grabbed her customer's hand and pulled Tabitha toward her car. It was time they got their show on the road before downtown traffic delayed them for her chosen destination. As they rode through the streets of Atlanta headed toward Cheryl's Buckhead condo, a comfortable silence fell between them, but not for long.

"You know I could have driven myself to work," Tabitha teased as she recited Cheryl's previous declaration of independence when she chose to meet everyone at D-Stud Musik instead of coming with Tabitha and her family.

"You're so right, Rev, but then you'd miss out on my surprise for you. I don't think you want to miss this. I thought we could have breakfast together like old times."

"You mean at *Denny's*?"

Cheryl giggled. The rise in Tabitha's voice told her that their old stomp and ground was no longer a crowd pleaser for her. Truth be told, it was also the last place on Earth that she'd want to dine with her mature palette.

"No, Tab, not Denny's. I'm taking you to my place for breakfast. Unless you'd rather eat somewhere else."

Tabitha refrained from speaking her mind, but her soul was on fire with the thought of enjoying eating at her Rose's most bountiful table.

"Yes, that sounds good," Tabitha mumbled.

A satisfied smile covered Cheryl's face as she enjoyed

teasing her minister and bringing the usually more articulate Reverend Tabitha Scott to a more mild and meek state. She silently promised she'd reawaken the fire deep inside Tabitha much later after they enjoyed their meal and a much-needed conversation.

* * *

Cheryl's condo serenaded them with the delicious aroma of fresh buttery baked bread, savory, peppery bacon, cheesy, creamy scrambled eggs, and a delightful array of juicy fruits. Tabitha's stomach was pleased with the tasteful array of food prepared just for the two of them. Her hostess didn't hide the caterer's containers from Tabitha's sight. Cheryl knew her hard work would be more appreciated under different circumstances.

As they sat at her dining room table overlooking the busy morning of the Buckhead community, Cheryl silently debated how she would initiate the conversation about their recent disagreement. Tabitha must have sensed a change in her mood, and the good minister decided to remove the heavy silence between them. But the chirping noise from Cheryl's cell phone beat Tabitha to the punch.

Tabitha watched patiently in silence as Cheryl checked her texts. She noticed the bright smile and sparkle in her Rose's eyes that should have been meant for her be shared with someone else—and suddenly, the perturbed minister wasn't so eager to be in the begging mood. *Keith Sweat, she was not!*

When Cheryl put the phone down for a second, Tabitha seized the opportunity to jump right in.

"Rose, this food is much better than our old Denny's

specials. Thank you for inviting me to your home. It's been a while since I've been here and since I've seen you."

Cheryl granted her a smile, but not as bright and beautiful as the one she bestowed upon her cell phone admirer. Tabitha decided to forge on with her discourse when the damn texting started up again, and her rude hostess put her full attention on the scrolling words from Tabitha's nemesis!

Enough was enough for the impatient minister!

"Rose, do you think I could garner a little bit of your attention without your *friend* interrupting me at every second?"

Tabitha knew she sounded just as jealous as she did the night at Dymon's studio, but she didn't give a damn. She needed her moment in the spotlight for once. Hadn't she been the good minister and did the dutiful thing Cheryl had asked her to do? It was time she was rewarded for her efforts. She looked into those bright brown eyes filled with amusement and knew her Rose wasn't in the mood for a battle with her. Tabitha felt a little childish for her behavior, but she wasn't prepared to back down from her stance.

"Who are you talking to anyway?"

"Tab, are we really going to go there again?"

"Where would that be, Rose? I haven't seen you for almost two weeks, counting the first week of isolation and then the second one for the misdemeanor you accused me of."

Cheryl couldn't contain her playful energy. As much as she knew Tabitha was serious about her lack of attention on her minister, Cheryl's body was way more attentive than she needed it to be if they were going to have a real discussion before she took said minister to bed. The texts were a distraction—rude, yes, but a needed one to keep her head moving in the right direction.

"Tabitha, it's Tiffany. I'm sorry for the interruptions, but she needed me."

"*Tiffany?* What is going on with you and my children? When did Tiffany become your chat buddy? And why?"

Rose shrugged then put the phone down to give her full attention to her salty minister. "It's just girl talk. She needed a woman's perspective on a few things, and I was happy to help her—that's all."

"*That's all? Am I not a woman?* What do you mean she needed girl talk from a woman's perspective?"

"Tab, don't get offended. You know your children love you, and Tiffany respects and needs your guidance. I approached her first about my feelings for you. Then, the conversation naturally gravitated to the young woman she was interested in. We bonded, that's all."

Tabitha tried to hear the truth in Cheryl's words, but she still felt some type of way about her children not coming to her first with their concerns. Partly, Tabitha worried that she had offended them too when she was so careless with her words about Cartier's former circumstances in Nigeria. Maybe they identified more with Cheryl and Ayodele now than with her.

Tabitha felt Cheryl's hand gently caress hers, and those tempting fingers stroked a desire that was already lit within her aching body.

"Tab, I'm sorry if I interfered in some way. It wasn't intentional. I was happy for the opportunity to get to know your children. Especially since I plan on seeing more of them—more of you."

"Is that right? You were so quiet earlier. I didn't know if

this was a *welcome back into my life* breakfast or a *so-long loser* meal."

"Tab, you know I could never let you go. I just wanted to give you time to enjoy breakfast before we talked. You know it's rude to talk with your mouth full?"

Tabitha's jealousy and concern dissipated at the sound of those teasing words and that teasing touch that was getting more intense by the minute, and so were her ladyparts!

"You're right about that. When my mouth is full of you, I can't speak a word but just mumble, *Mmm, Mmm!*"

"Reverend Tabitha Scott, watch your language!"

"All I'll promise to do is watch you. You're all I've been thinking about since the day you came home. Look, I know it's my fault that we've been apart recently, and I truly regret my behavior at Dymon's studio. I never meant to hurt you or to disrespect you. I..."

Tabitha was having her moment when the chirping ass cellphone interrupted her apology attempt yet again. But this time, her Rose paid it no mind. She just granted Tabitha that sexy smile and brown eyes, which encouraged her remorseful minister to proceed with the current tune that was winning back her Rose's heart.

"Rose, I also understand you needed your time away. As much as I wanted to try to force my way back into your life, I did my best to stay away. But I missed you every day."

"Tab, I missed you too. I didn't really want to be away from you either. I..."

Cheryl's and Tabitha's phones began to sound an alarm that neither could ignore. The rampant texts and calls forced them to pay attention to the culprits. Cheryl and Tabitha scrolled through their messages. Ayda Kohn was more persistent than Tiffany or Isaiah and decided to call her. As she accepted the call, Cheryl noticed that Tabitha had decided to take a call from Isaiah. Something must be pretty serious if both of their cell phones were blowing up.

"Hi, Ayda. Sorry for not responding to your text. I just saw it. I'm in the middle of having breakfast with Reverend Scott, and..."

"Yes, yes, Cheryl, that's fine. It's important that I speak to you now, please."

Cheryl had never heard this much excitement in the Queenmaker's voice, and the urgency in her nature made her fear another scandal had broken. God forbid it had anything to do with her—especially as she was just getting to a place of acceptance being open about her sexuality and her reconciliation with her sexy minister.

"Yes, of course. What's wrong, Ayda?"

"Perhaps, do you mind including Reverend Scott in this conversation, Cheryl?"

Cheryl glanced at Tabitha, who was deep in conversation with Isaiah and thought twice about disturbing her, but Ayda seemed desperate to share the news with the both of them.

"One second, Ayda."

Cheryl gently touched Tabitha's hand to get her attention. "Sorry, Tab. But Ayda needs to speak with us. Should I tell her to call later?"

Tabitha shook her head and then briefly turned her attention to Isaiah. "Son, let me call you back. Thank you for being so persistent in getting me this info. I'll handle it from now on. We'll talk later. And Isaiah—stay out of the fridge. Later, son."

"Sorry, Rose. Go ahead, put Ayda on speaker, please."

Cheryl and Tabitha listened quietly as Ayda Kohn further explained what Isaiah had already given Tabitha the good news about. Would Cheryl Rose Campbell think the same about this unexpected revelation?

"I take it you both haven't heard about Cartier's social media explosion. It's been all over Instagram, and we've been receiving calls in the office from news outlets and other organizations that wanted to hear from you, Cheryl."

Cheryl's heart dropped at the sound of the young woman's name again intermingled with hers and more drama on social media. She couldn't look at Tabitha for fear she'd see disappointment or anger in those sweet brown eyes. *What had Cartier accused her of now?* It was the good minister who responded first.

"Yes, Ayda, I'm aware of the situation. Isaiah was able to get to me and give me some of the details. Honestly, I'm glad to hear that this young woman has found the courage to come forth and tell the truth."

Cheryl was shocked by Tabitha's revelation and the soft hand that caressed hers to reassure her that everything would be alright after all.

"But please, Ayda, continue to update us. I haven't had a chance to tell Rose, so this will be her first time hearing about it."

"Yes, yes, of course. Cheryl, another video was released from Cartier confessing that her accusations against you were all lies. She also publicly thanked you for not returning the favor and being mean to her, but instead of saving her from deportation and granting her the scholarship money needed to continue her education."

Those eyes that were once surprised by Tabitha's continuous loyalty and affection were now shocked by her minister's betrayal. How would Cartier have known she was the benefactor of the scholarship money if Tabitha hadn't told the young woman? She pulled her hand from Tabitha's caress and focused on Ayda's further updates.

Tabitha already knew the ice was beginning to extinguish the heat between them. Regardless of Cheryl's momentary displeasure with her behavior, Tabitha didn't regret setting the record straight with Cartier, and she would continue to defend her whether her woman wanted it or not.

"Since this revelation, several interested news shows, including Taylor Horton, want a response from you, Cheryl."

"No. No, Ayda. I will not go on program yet again and revisit this incident. It's done now, and I just want to move on with my life as it is now and as I want it to be for the future."

"Cheryl, yes, I understand. But the publicity could be wonderful for your current and new album. It's an opportunity to promote and receive the apologies you greatly deserve. Please reconsider."

"Thank you, Ayda. I know you mean well, but there's nothing to reconsider. Cartier should have never known where the scholarship money came from, but I'll handle that mistake later. Revisiting one of the most embarrassing moments of my life is not something I want to take a walk down memory lane for. We don't need the publicity; despite this incident, my current album is doing quite well, and so are the royalty payments. The new one will be just as successful without another TMI moment."

Cheryl and Tabitha could hear the disappointment in Ayda's voice, but the shrewd manager didn't push the subject. She continued with her updates, which became more important to them, and had the ability to heal the divide that was beginning to form between the two lovers.

"There's one other thing. We received news from the *Jumping for Jesus Jam* organizers, who informed us that they don't want you all to participate in the competition for this year's event."

"What? Why not?" Tabitha interjected.

She had done her best to remain silent and patient, given she was the reason for Cheryl's rising temper. If the organizers of the annual gospel competition were black-balling them because of this situation with Cartier, she would pick up her sword again and do battle without a doubt.

"No, sorry, Reverend Scott. Let me explain. They don't want you all to compete because they want Cheryl, as a headliner, to perform a 30-minute set of whatever performance she'd like to create to close out the event. They want to honor her work, and they stand with you, Cheryl. Isn't this wonderful?"

Cheryl was just as relieved as the relief she saw in Tabitha's eyes. The thought that her actions would destroy an opportunity for Tabitha and her children would have been difficult to deal with right now, among all the other news.

"Yes, Ayda, this is wonderful news. Except, I won't do it without including everyone that's a part of the album. This is the publicity opportunity that we need to focus on rather than a tell-all expose, don't you think?

Cheryl and Tabitha waited for Ayda's response, and the Queenmaker didn't disappoint in the least.

"Yes, Cheryl, perfect idea. I'll let the organizers know and leave you two to your meal. I have plenty of work here to keep me busy, ensuring this event, your promotions for the new album, and other opportunities run smoothly for you. I'll be in touch soon."

* * *

"So, do you want to tell me why you didn't obey my request that the scholarship remain anonymous? Were you that jealous Tab that you'd betray me?"

Tabitha watched Cheryl in silence as her hostess angrily cleared the table and put away the leftovers without any assistance from her guest, the disobedient minister. As Rose stood at the sink and rinsed the dishes, Tabitha couldn't resist pressing her body against that tensed but voluptuous frame.

"Rose, I know you're angry with me, and I accept that. But I'm not going to apologize for defending my woman. You hear me?"

Cheryl heard that possessive praise, but her body was more intuned to the worship that her teasing minister was paying to her backside. She could feel Tabitha's body caress her with deliberate intent to make her weak in the knees, and her unapologetic behavior was working wonders!

"Yessss...I hear you," Cheryl moaned as Tabitha's hands continued their bold exploration. Those hips that didn't lie about their intentions were moving them to the beat of the dance they both wanted to perform.

"Good, 'cause nobody is going to fuck with you but me. I made it very clear to young Cartier that her antics were unacceptable to me. Irregardless of your ability to forgive and forget, I was there to make her reap what she sowed. Now, I know that's not what you asked me to do, but don't you think we're better together?"

To punctuate her true meaning, Tabitha moved Cheryl's body to their private dance with music that only they could hear from the rhythm of their swaying hips, bumping thighs, bouncing bottoms, and singing yonis!

"Yesss, we do, Tab. Mmmm, we do!"

Cheryl could hear the smile in Tabitha's voice, and knew her minister was more than amused. Tabitha's power to make her Rose bloom under her expert guidance pleased her. Tabitha had every right to be proud of her skills because the moisture seeping from her panties and those throbbing nipples poking from underneath her blouse were definite signs that the talented minister had an even better game in the bedroom than on the basketball court!

"Good, baby. So, let me fuck you now, please, and then I can repent later?"

Tabitha gently pulled Cheryl's hand away from the soapy dishes. She led her down the hallway to the bedroom she hadn't frequented in years. But the path to bed her Rose wasn't something she had ever forgotten. As soon as they entered the bedroom, Tabitha wrapped her arms around Cheryl and let her lips create a path of apologies along that soft skin, from her forehead to her neck and collarbone, and in between the soft texture of the silk blouse.

Tabitha's hands found easy access to those breasts that were screaming for release with the help of the good minister's teasing tongue and frisky fingers. Her hands roamed over Cheryl's body, finding familiar curves and dips that she knew would bring her Rose immediate pleasure. Cheryl put in that teamwork that Tabitha raved about to remove her clothing. Tabitha untucked the silk blouse from Cheryl's skirt. Cheryl reached behind her back to unclasp her bra, releasing her full breasts to Tabitha's eager gaze. Next came the pencil skirt and lacy panties, and then Cheryl quickly stepped out of her heels and presented the beautiful womanly body that brought unspeakable joy to Tabitha. There were no words to truly express how much she desired, needed, hungered, and loved this woman.

Cheryl blushed then smiled softly under Tabitha's appreciative gaze. *Her Rose wasn't being modest, was she?* There was nothing for Rose Aguwegbo to be shy of, especially not the sweetness she presented to her most appreciative admirer. Tabitha pulled her woman to the bed and laid her down. Then she slowly began removing her own clothes, revealing every inch of her sexy seasoned body.

Tabitha was more than ready to shower her Rose with lips that knew how to make her body vibrate with desire, with a tongue that tantalized her senses and made her cream with the horniness of a much younger woman, and with fingers that teased and stroked a ravenous craving for Tabitha to fuck her so good that her body would explode into a million particles of ethereal orgasms!

The thought of what Tabitha would give her during this early morning love making made her moan with the need for the delicious fucking to begin. Tabitha enjoyed those previously bashful eyes worshiping her with their praise for what she came to offer to only Rose Aguwegbo.

Tabitha joined Cheryl on the bed. She slowly moved on top of Cheryl and showered Cheryl's plump lips with slow, deep kisses. The slow tongue action stroked, sucked, and fucked Cheryl's mouth until they were both panting and gasping for air. But Tabitha wasn't done giving her Rose just what she deserved. Her mouth praised those beautiful ripe breasts, then traveled to her belly and lingered along her curves until they reached the ultimate destination of that sweet, warm honeypot ready for equal worship. Cheryl opened her thighs wide, and Tabitha's mouth dipped inside and extended the love that she had preserved for Rose Aguwegbo for over 25 years.

"Mmm, Tab, p-please," Cheryl moaned.

"Not yet, baby. Hold on a little while longer. I'm not ready for you to cum. Hold on for me, please, baby."

"Oooh, God, yes, Tab! Hold on for you. Yesss, I'll try Tab. I'll try!"

Tabitha could hear the need for her Rose to bloom. Praise and worship are what Tabitha would give her Rose until that body trembled with a climatic rush that propelled her into deep pelvic thrusts. Screams of satisfaction from the masterful minister's lips and finger fucking actions brought her one of the most intense orgasms, Rose Aguwegbo had ever experienced.

"Tabitha! Tabitha! Tabitha, yessss! Oooh, God, yesss, Tabitha!" Cheryl's screams of passion sounded like a chant that eventually drifted into a soft whimper. The beautiful flower blushed a bright red and glowed under her lover's dedication and attention.

"Mmmm, Tab. I think you've broken me. You know that?"

Tabitha lifted her head to peer at her woman over those thick thighs that were beckoning her to put in some more work. Tabitha wanted nothing more than to do just that. But Cheryl's hands beckoned to relieve her from her pussy patrol and guard her entire body with the warmth of Tabitha's.

"Did you hear me, Tabitha Scott? I'm broken because of you."

Tabitha held Cheryl tightly. "I heard you, Rose. But what do you mean by that?"

Cheryl snuggled further into Tabitha's protective embrace. "I'll never want or love anyone else as long as I live but you, Tabitha Scott. You've taken my heart, and there's no one on this Earth other than you that would be able to change it."

Tabitha's heart swelled with just as much love as her Rose professed for her. Tabitha understood clearly how she felt because Rose Aguwegbo had broken her the first day she'd laid eyes on her. Tabitha couldn't and wouldn't love another woman either but her Rose.

"You've broken me too, Rose. Together, our broken pieces make a whole, and you complete me; you always have."

As they lay in bed enjoying the warmth of their bodies and lingering in the aftermath of their much-needed love-making before returning to the day, Cheryl couldn't stop herself from teasing her very talented minister.

"Tab, I need you to do me another favor."

Tabitha adjusted her hold on Cheryl's waist and snuggled closer. "Yes, I think my body is up for another round. Tell me what you want me to do, baby."

Cheryl giggled. She was far from being a youngster, but Tabitha made her feel like young Rose Aguwegbo again with the minister's macking skills.

"I want that too...again, but I wasn't talking about you being of service in that way. Since you're so good at giving young Cartier her marching orders, I want you to ask her to do one other thing."

Tabitha tightened her hold even more, but not in a possessive manner. She was prepared and ready to slay the dragon again if needed.

"What do you want me to do?"

"I want you to invite Cartier to write a song for the album. Despite what she's done, she is a talented singer, and I know this will be a good opportunity for her as much as it would be for your children. So, please give her the opportunity to start over with all of us. Please, Tab."

Tabitha leaned in and kissed Cheryl before allowing her

hands to enjoy the feel of her Rose's sweet body. She could feel the rise in those soft breasts and the call from her yoni and knew it would only be a matter of time before her Rose would bloom like only she could make her.

"Yes, Rose, I will do that for you. You know I will always do whatever you need—be whomever you need."

i will praise your name

"MS. CAMPBELL, Reverend Scott, please come this way. Thank you so much for blessing the *Jumping for Jesus Jam* with your holy presence!"

"Thank you, Bishop Walker, for having us. We're all so thankful for the opportunity to praise the Lord this fine day," Tabitha interjected as she escorted Cheryl Rose Campbell through the crowded auditorium to the Green Room provided for their special entourage.

"I couldn't agree more with Reverend Scott. We are truly thankful for being here today. I'm sure our family will give an excellent performance. We've all been working quite diligently to ensure we give you the performance you expect of all the wonderful performers here today and in the past."

Bishop Walker, one of the main organizers, beamed with joy. It had become evident to Cheryl and Tabitha the Fellowship and Worship organization that created and produced this popular annual event within the Christian community was excited to have the gospel diva's presence at this auspicious event.

Cheryl and Tabitha also knew this warm Christian reception wouldn't have been possible a few months ago—even with the phenomenal sales of Cheryl's latest album. Cartier's reveal of her deceptive measures to retaliate against the very innocent Cheryl Rose Campbell and the outcry from both straight and LGBTIQA+ communities after the cruel attack against one of their beloved ministers had also shined an unpleasant light on the organization's lack of brotherly and sisterly love toward members of their same faith.

As they walked through the auditorium, their entourage of infamous and famous singers trailed behind them as if they were walking in an inaugural procession. The crowd assembled in the audience stood and cheered them with much fanfare as if, indeed, the president and her first lady had entered the building. Tabitha was no longer hiding her claim to Cheryl since their previous private time and commitment to each other to pursue a more serious relationship.

The hand that softly grazed her backside punctuated just what sort of claim the good minister had placed on Cheryl. Although she enjoyed the feeling of that most skillful appendage, Cheryl politely redirected Tabitha's hand to a safer and more respectable position within her own hand. With their free hands, they waved to the crowd and smiled brightly as the love paid to them was sincerely felt in their hearts.

Tabitha glanced at their family and wasn't surprised that Isaiah relished the attention. If he could have stopped to give autographs to the younger audience members, he would have most definitely delayed their group's arrival at their final destination. Tabitha threw him a quick side eye when he motioned to step forward and take a picture with a young admirer, and like a scolded little child, he pouted but stepped back in place with the rest.

When they finally made it backstage to the Green Room, Tabitha and Cheryl were met with more admirers—a few neither one was pleased to see.

"Hello, Babygirl! It's good seeing you here in the house of the Lord. How you been, Cheryl? By the looks of you, you being doing just fine, Babygirl," Bishop Raymond Woodward greeted as he approached Cheryl and Tabitha.

"Babygirl?"

Cheryl tightened her grip on Tabitha's hand. She knew when she laid eyes on Bishop Raymond Woodward that he would stir up some trouble. Raymond starting his usual mess wouldn't sit well with the possessive minister.

"Bishop, it's good to see you too. How have you been?"

Bishop Woodward's devilish eyes grew wide with amusement. He didn't miss the salty expression on Reverend Tabitha Scott's face. The woman was never good at keeping her true feelings close to her heart. She always had to share what was on her mind—and if anyone asked him, some things just didn't need to be said or displayed, like them holding hands like two young lovebirds sitting in a tree. God forbid they started kissing out here in public on holy ground!

"You know me, Babygirl. I'm just blessed and highly favored. Come on over here and show your Bishop a little Christian love," Raymond replied with arms open wide.

Cheryl motioned to do the polite Christian thing and greet the Bishop with a platonic hug. But it was Tabitha's hand that kept her stead on her minister.

"No. First of all, I'm not sure why you think it's proper to be less than formal with Ms. Campbell, Bishop, but there will be no Christian loving or anything of the such happening between y'all," Tabitha warned.

Cheryl and Tabitha could hear their younger family members cackling behind them. Cheryl did her best not to break character, but even she wanted to join them in their playful amusement, especially with the surprised expression displayed on Raymond's face. Before Cheryl could referee the two in their pissing contest, the Bishop responded.

"Now, here you go, Tabitha..."

"Reverend Scott, Bishop."

"Yes, okay, *Reverend Scott*, I don't know why y'all get so riled up about nothing. As Proverbs 29:22 says, *A man of wrath stirs up strife, and one given to anger causes much transgression.* Now, we don't need none of that fighting and carrying on you did in the streets a few months ago up here in the house of the Lord. I was merely welcoming an old friend back to the fold. We go way back, don't we, Baby...I mean, Cheryl?"

Tabitha was about to step into the ring again and give the Bishop a knockout punch, but Cheryl restrained her and intervened.

"Yes, Bishop, we do. And there's no trouble to start. We are all here to give praise today. It's good seeing you, and Reverend Scott and I look forward to hearing and *judging* your choir in the competition today."

Bishop Raymond's eyes grew as wide as a saucer. "Judging? Y'all judging the competition? I thought you were in the competition."

Tabitha enjoyed the shocked and nervous expression on the lewd Bishop's face. That's right, his precious choir would be in the palm of her hands, and she took pleasure in making him squirm, knowing that it would be his abilities being scrutinized, not hers, as he often did.

"Yes, we were asked by Bishop Walker to sit as guest judges and perform with our family for a special closing event," Cheryl explained patiently, hoping to end the battle between the baffled Bishop and her mischievous minister.

"Oh really? Hmph, I didn't know that. And I see you don't have just all your *family*, but you got mine too. Layla Joy, Dymona, good seeing y'all here, considering you been spending more time at Unity than in my congregation. But at least you in church somewhere. I guess I should get on back to my people. I doubt y'all have a difficult time judging my choir, as they have been the grand prize winners for five years in a row."

Bishop Woodward didn't wait for confirmation from Cheryl or Tabitha. He strutted on back to his church members, leaving a heavy air of unanswered questions from Tabitha to her Rose.

"You gonna tell me about this *Babygirl* shit?"

"Tab, watch your language. Don't start, it's nothing. Trust me, *lil Raymond* is nothing to worry about, and it's in the past."

"In the past? What's in the past?"

Cheryl gave Tabitha a stern look and did her best to put this jealous rant to bed before their group became even more restless while waiting for their leaders to squash their disagreement. *Mother and Mommy* arguing in front of the other performers from various churches wasn't a good look, and watchful eyes were directly focused on them.

"Tab, it's what I said, the past. There's is nothing for you to worry about concerning *lil Raymond*, and I do mean *little*. Now, are we going to go down that road again where you let jealousy cloud your judgment and belief in me?"

Tabitha still wanted to remain on defense, but Cheryl's reminder of her past mistake when it came to trusting her Rose caused her to reconsider the stubborn approach. Plus, she would have some explaining to do of her own. Eloise Montgomery, the minister's faithful organizer of the *Woman Thou Art Walking* challenge for the Unity congregation, came waltzing backstage with determined eyes on her *Tabby*.

"Oh my good, Lord, Tabby! I'm so sorry for being so late. But you know I wouldn't miss being here by your side for nothing! It looks like I'm the only one that wasn't here. Please forgive me, Tabby."

Tabitha could feel Cheryl's watchful eyes on her, and the heat from her Rose was burning a hole in her neck. Unlike her previous behavior, Cheryl didn't hold onto her possessively but relinquished her hand and stood quietly as she allowed Reverend Tabitha Scott to correct her church member's behavior.

"Eloise, it's alright. You didn't miss a thing. We were just getting settled."

Tabitha looked around and did her best to avoid eye contact with the very determined Cheryl Rose Campbell. She knew that if she didn't put some limitations on Eloise with a quickness, the gospel diva was going to do it for her. But in taking a headcount of their group, Tabitha became more aware that they were missing one other member.

"Actually, you're not the only one missing, Eloise. Has anyone seen Cartier?"

Everyone held the same surprised expression. None of them had realized their most infamous group member was MIA. Cheryl was also concerned about the young woman's absence, and for the moment reserved her reprimand of both Tabitha and Eloise.

Ever since Tabitha offered Cartier the opportunity to write and perform music for the album, Cartier had been a permanent fixture at their rehearsals and meetings for the album and this event. She had also personally apologized to Cheryl and remained respectful in her interactions with the previous object of her desire with the help of the watchful minister's eyes.

"Jerome, can you call Cartier and check on her? And Isaiah, go outside and see if she's stuck in the crowd," Tabitha ordered.

Tabitha's sons quickly jumped to her request in their hunt for Cartier. But Eloise was still an issue. Although Cheryl was concerned about their missing member, she was still focused on Tabitha handling her business with Eloise Montgomery. Eloise's soft caress of Tabitha's arm reminded the good minister that she'd better handle said business.

"Oh, I do hope young Cartier is alright. You are such a forgiving soul, Tabby, to even allow her in your presence, given those unfortunate circumstances," Eloise crooned.

"*Look, Elaine,* don't start this mess up in here again. Get your hand off Tab. She's your minister, but she's my woman. Don't pretend you don't understand what I mean. Now, things are going to change around here. First, you can stop the *Tabby* shit and address her as Reverend Tabitha, and don't ever try and disrespect me again," Cheryl interjected.

Eloise's hand slid from Tabitha's shoulder, and their minister did her best not to burst into laughter. As much as Cheryl's display was publicly noticed by their family and the rest of the performers waiting in the Green Room, she had to give her Rose props for setting the record straight. Now, she knew it was only fitting to co-sign what her woman said—claiming Tabitha as hers was gospel!

Eloise's shocked brown eyes filled with fake tears, and she did her best to present a woman of contrition. Cheryl and Tabitha knew the minister's admirer was far from repenting for her behavior.

"Oh, Cheryl, first of all, I think we got off on the wrong foot. It was never my intention to threaten your place with Reverend Tabitha. I'm sorry you felt that way."

"Threatened? Evelyn, you are no threat!"

"Oh, okay, Rose. I think that's enough. We should all take a beat and settle down. Folks are watching, and this is not what Unity represents. But I apologize. This is my fault."

Eloise wiped her fake tears away and then nodded in agreement. Cheryl stood back and waited to hear Tabitha out but never took her eyes off her nemesis.

"Sister Eloise, I appreciate your genuine concern for Unity and your minister. But Rose is correct. We are a couple, and I love her with all my heart. I've never stopped loving this woman, and she is going to be a permanent fixture around my home and Unity. I know that we all want *unity* in our fellowship with each other. So, please refrain from addressing me as Tabby. And Rose, you know, Eloise's proper name. Let us all behave as Ephesians 4:32 advises: *Be kind and compassionate to one another, forgiving each other, just as in Christ God has forgiven you.*"

Both women silently agreed with Tabitha to at least pretend they were in agreement with their minister's request. But there was no more time for an intervention. Jerome and Isaiah were both escorting Cartier back to the group as if they were bodyguards for the frazzled-looking young woman.

"Cartier, what happened? Are you alright?"

Cartier wasn't deaf or blind to the whispers and stares of the people in the crowded space, but she was grateful for Cheryl Rose Campbell's concern and maybe even a little bit of concern from the minister's watchful gaze.

"No, it'll be fine. I just had a little problem..."

"Yo, Ma, Cheryl, folks outside were giving Cartier a hard time. They still salty about everythang. But you know, I handled it."

Jerome gave his mother a knowing stare but remained silent. He allowed Isaiah, as usual, to take credit for the good deed.

Cheryl softly touched Cartier's arm. "Did anyone hurt you? Are you sure you're okay?"

Cartier enjoyed the feel of Cheryl's hand on her. Then she removed any thoughts of anything other than the woman being kind to her, as she had been from the start.

"Yes, Cheryl, I mean Ms. Campbell. I understand their anger. I was wrong, and I have to be punished for my sins. Maybe I should just leave. It's probably better for everyone if I just left."

"No, Cartier, it's not best for everyone if you leave. You belong here like we all do."

Even Cheryl was surprised by her minister's encouragement to Cartier. Tabitha's willingness to forgive Cartier as she had done just made her love Tabitha even more.

"We are a family now, all of us, and we will celebrate this day like all the other performers. So, Jerome and Isaiah continue to ensure nobody causes any issues for Cartier. Rose and I have to go to the judges' section, but we'll be back for the closing ceremony. Everybody be good, and make us proud."

Tabitha took Cheryl's hand and led her to the location

Bishop Walker had instructed them to go for the judges. On their way to the reserved area, they passed by their friends, the Gospel Girls. Dot and Cleo were busy bragging about how they were both going to win the Best Gospel Old Ship of Zion singer award. Dot had won it four times in a row, and Cleo won the coveted prize last year. Still, neither was willing to accept their crowns might be overthrown by a new, younger competitor, Sashanna Regan from Carlotta's choir. The phenomenal artist had recently signed a contract with Patricia's record label, Gospel Slam Records. Although she hadn't had as stellar of a career as either Dot or Cleo, she was definitely a rising star and crowd-pleaser from her record sales and concerts.

The two bickering secret friends stopped their chatter long enough to give Cheryl and Tabitha a cursory glance before returning to their pretense. Neither Cheryl nor Tabitha took offense to the cold shoulder either gave them. Their elders were still deeply rooted in the closet and had no intentions of walking in the light. Cheryl and Tabitha respected their decision and had a more authentic, although brief, greeting with Carlotta and Patricia, who embraced them with open arms.

"Y'all looking so good together, Rose, Tab. Go on out there and make us proud," Reverend Carlotta praised as she gave them a tight hug and kiss.

"Carlotta is right, divas. You are looking mighty good. Show 'em what gospel royalty indeed looks like," Patricia chimed in.

* * *

Although Cheryl and Tabitha had encountered a few bumps in the road to this place of harmony, they couldn't hide their enjoyment of each other's company. As they sat with the other gospel royalty in the judges section, they spent the three hours of the competition enjoying some of Georgia's best gospel singers and choirs.

Their hearts were filled with reverence over the abundant talent and a feeling of melancholy as they reminisced about their former days as Minister of Music and the lead singer in their old choir. By the time the majority of the performers were done, it was clear to them who stood out the most, even in Dot and Cleo's category. Neither wanted to break it to their dear old friends, but Sashanna Regan was the obvious crowd-pleaser. Even as Cheryl and Tabitha looked at their fellow judges' expressions, it seemed unanimous that she would be crowned this year's Best Gospel Old Ship of Zion singer award winner.

What wasn't a complete consensus amongst the judges was awarding Bishop Raymond Woodward's choir with the Best Gospel Choir award for this year. Neither Cheryl nor Tabitha agreed that Mt. Bethelview on the Rock of Gibraltar Missionary Baptist Church was so outstanding that it overshadowed what the gospel diva and her minister believed to be the better performers. They debated with their fellow judges for some time whether Reverend Carlotta Williams's Better Days Ministry choir was the actual winner.

Unfortunately for their friend, Carlotta's choir would not take home a second award this time. Bishop Raymond's peacock posture was in full effect as he accepted the award instead of his Minister of Music. He then spent 10 minutes giving less of an acceptance speech but more of a mini-sermon until Bishop Walker had their sound manager turn the microphone off.

When Cleo and Dot discovered they weren't the winners in their category and Sashanna was this year's award recipient, they didn't handle the defeat gracefully. However, Sashanna's award speech paid homage to the gospel greats, and minus handing over the award to them, she supplied them with the consolation prize they needed: high praise.

Now, the time had arrived for Cheryl's 30-minute showcase of the wonderful music and hard work her family had created over the past two months. Tabitha squeezed her hand briefly before they stood up from the judges' section and joined their family in the Green Room.

"As Isaiah would say, *I gotchu Ma*. Don't worry; our family will deliver."

Cheryl smiled with as much confidence as she could muster. She wasn't worried about the rest of their family but her own performance. It had been a while since she'd taken to the stage amongst her peers and church folks. But her faithful minister's prediction of the success of their performance was far from what she'd expected. Fusing old-school and new-school praise and worship music was the perfect blend for success. Their music appealed to Cheryl's current fan base and new fans she had unknowingly acquired from Dymona, Roxanna, Whitney, and Isaiah.

Ayda Kohn was not only brilliant, but she was spot on in devising this plan for redemption through a new album and tour. The crowd enjoyed Cheryl, Roxanna, and Dymon's solo performances. They also loved the medley performed by the three and Whitney of some old and new greats. Isaiah, Jerome, and Tiffany were just as well received as a triple threat. They took to the stage together and performed their new singles while harmonizing and backing each other up like they'd always done as Reverend Tabitha Scott's children.

Tabitha stood on the side of the stage. She watched

with pride as her children performed with confidence and natural star power. She felt Cheryl's hand grab hers and hold it tightly as Tabitha tried to contain the emotions that threatened to overflow. Ayodele stood on her opposite side. The three crusaders were now stronger, undefeatable, and devoted to protecting the family they had created by any means possible.

They watched quietly as Dymon and Cartier joined the three on stage. They silently prayed that the audience would be just as benevolent to young Cartier as they had received Isaiah and Dymon's return to the church. A few sounds of disapproval were heard. Tabitha motioned to step in and rescue Cartier, but Ayodele held her back.

"Wait, sister. Let them handle this on their own. Give it a moment."

"Okay, Ayodele. I'll do as you wish, but if they don't settle down sooner than later, I'll handle it," Tabitha promised.

"No, you won't. This is the mess that I created, Tab. I'll handle it if it doesn't get better," Cheryl interjected.

The three crusaders soon discovered their white hats weren't needed, and the younger generation would handle their own problems. Jerome sat at the piano and started to play *Great Is Your Mercy*, and Tiffany started to sing the lyrics. Soon, Isaiah and Cartier were singing in unison with Tiffany and Jerome. Then Dymon joined them at the end with a freestyle rap. This time, the crowd went wild for all of them, giving high praise to the young Ministers of Music!

"See, sisters. God worked it out. There's no need to worry. Everything's gonna be alright."

Cheryl and Tabitha had to admit Ayodele's faith was stronger than either of them. She grabbed both of their hands and walked them onto the stage, and Whitney and Roxanna followed suit.

Now, if only Ayodele had the hindsight to know what would occur as the audience stood and gave them a standing ovation. Even Ayda Kohn and Congresswoman Mikail Rollins were beaming with pride from their front-row seats. As the cheers subsided, a different type of music was heard from the rear of the auditorium. It was a sound like no other—high-pitched, off-key sopranos, and the lyrics bellowing from the choir of voices were displeasing to the ears.

When one of the ushers opened the doors, the mystery performers were revealed. Cheryl and Tabitha were speechless at the sight of the Gospel Girls, Dot, and Cleo, battling it out with Bishop Raymond and the First Mother, Cecelia Woodward. Cheryl and Tabitha recognized the younger woman caught in the middle of the battle as Dot's secret 30-year-old lover, Shirley. Without even hearing the entire argument, Cheryl had a feeling she already knew what the raucous was all about.

Lil Raymond strikes again!

"Raymond, if you don't go get yo ass on away from Shirley, I swear before God I'm gonna pistol whip yo nasty ass!" Dot screamed at the top of her contralto voice.

"Look here, Dot, you can't blame Babygirl for wanting a real man, even if you got them bull daggar ways!" Bishop Woodward spat at his competition for sweet Shirley's affection.

"Raymond, shut yo nasty mouth, boy before I shut it for you!" Cleo threatened.

Cecelia looked like she'd had enough of Dot and Cleo threatening her favorite son. She threw off her beautiful creme-colored hat and grabbed her purse.

"Now, you don't want to go there, Cleopatra, or you, neither Dorothy. Don't you dare think you gonna lay hands on my boy without getting an ass whooping from his mama!"

Cleo and Dot looked at each other and then back at Cecelila with amusement before roaring with laughter. But there was no real joy or humor in their dispositions or in the following words Dot uttered. She grabbed her purse then looked Layla Joy's grandmother dead in the face.

"Look here, Cecelia, you ain't got enough power in that Gucci bag to lay me out. But I promise you before God that if I open this purse, you and your boy will see Jesus before you are ready! That's your problem, always protecting his childish ass, and his problem is always sticking his dick into candy that don't belong to him!"

By the time the purses and the threats were being waved around, Cheryl's and Tabitha's family were racing to break up the heated battle. Layla, Dymon, and Isaiah were the first to get to the sprawling five, and only Shirley looked like she was relieved for the assist. The other much-senior adults looked like they'd take on the Gen Zs, too, if needed.

But it was Bishop Walker's threat to call the police on their rabble-rousers that got them to straighten up and fly right.

"Y'all should be ashamed of yourselves. We are in the house of the Lord, and y'all are behaving like you have lost every ounce of Christian spirit in your bodies. Acting like Sinners more than Saints! Whatever is going on between you all, please take this somewhere else, or we will have no choice but to call the police on some of our most respected servants in our Christian community."

Bishop Walker ended his threat by shutting all the doors of the auditorium. Ayda Kohn and Congresswoman

Mikail Rollins squeezed out the door before the Bishop locked the area down.

"Dot, what on Earth were you thinking bringing a gun to the church," Tabitha gently scolded her elder.

Dot looked into Tabitha's concerned eyes with the fierceness of a mad Black woman who was not to be played with. She opened the purse, and those around her braced themselves in fear she might just put a cap in one of their asses. Dot slowly brought out a joint and lit it with the lighter Cleo was happy to provide from her purse. She took a few puffs without concern for her shocked audience.

"I would have done what you did, Tab, and took care of my own. Raymond and Cecelia better watch their step if they don't want me to put a full round of bullets in their high faluting asses!"

"Oh, Dot, come on, please, put the joint away and calm down. We can't present ourselves like this in front of the children," Carlotta encouraged.

Dot wasn't one to be persuaded otherwise. She looked at young Isaiah, who was cheesing all over the place, and gave him a quick wink, then extended the joint to his more than receptive hands. Isaiah reached for the joint, but Cheryl swatted his hand away.

"Unuh, Isaiah. We don't need any more trouble than my big sister is causing. Dot, we all need to leave now before Bishop Walker or someone else does call the police on us, and you know the Atlanta Police won't be as kind as Bishop Walker with a mere warning."

"Let's head to my house. Ayodele and I were going to cook dinner for everybody anyway. We can sort this stuff out over a good meal," Tabitha suggested.

"I know you don't think we gonna break bread with

that heathen over there!" Cleo shouted where the First Mother and Bishop could hear her loud and clear.

"No, I didn't, Cleo. This invitation is just for the family standing right here. Now, please, let's all get a move on before it's too late," Tabitha warned.

Their group agreed, including the firestarters, Dot and Cleo, and started heading toward the parking lot. Ayda Kohn was the only one with a different plan. She pulled Cheryl to the side.

"Cheryl, I'm sorry. I know you want to head to the dinner, but I have some important news for you."

Cheryl tried to concentrate on her manager's words, but her eyes wandered to Tabitha's questioning brown eyes. She definitely wanted to be wherever her minister was going to be, but Ayda's voice sounded serious enough to force her to pay attention to the Queenmaker. She encouraged Tabitha to go home and promised to follow after her meeting with Ayda.

"Yes, Ayda. What's wrong?"

Ayda smiled brightly, but Cheryl could tell by the stiffness in her posture that the facial expression of happiness wasn't necessarily her manager's true emotion.

"Nothing's wrong, Cheryl. I just have a bit of news from your former manager and record label. They are really impressed by your progress and would like to make you an offer."

Cheryl heard the words coming out of Ayda's pursed lips, but she didn't understand what Ben Castrelli or Monument Records would have to offer her that would make her delay being with her eager minister. As far as Cheryl was concerned, her time with either traitor was done except for the continuous receipt of royalty payments for her previous record deal.

"I don't understand. Ben made it perfectly clear that Monument Records didn't want anything to do with me since the *incident*. Why now? What are they up to?"

"Yes, Cheryl, I understand your concern. But they've had a change of heart, that is, Monument Records has, and they've presented me with an extremely generous offer to share with you. The call came in on my way here to the concert, and they emailed me the offer right before the start of the show. We can go to my office and talk more about the opportunity, or we can set up a meeting next week to discuss it in detail.

Cheryl's curiosity got the best of her. As much as she didn't see herself returning to either Ben Castrelli's management or Monument Records' artist roster, she wanted to know what her absolution was worth.

"Go ahead, Ayda, tell me what the devil is willing to offer me for my penitence."

when i rise

WHEN CHERYL and Ayda arrived at Tabitha's home, the place was overflowing with chatter and laughter. The aroma of a savory supper that was more than familiar to Cheryl's perceptive olfactory skills serenaded them into the crowded living space. Her minister and sister might have been hosting this family gathering, but Cheryl knew without a doubt that they had definitely done the bait and switch Isaiah and Tiffany had done some time ago and gotten the *Soul Food Saint*, Mother Florence, to prepare this festive feast!

Cheryl wasn't surprised to see Dot and Cleo cackling and drinking as their hi-ball glasses were filled with their favorite Jim Beam bourbon whiskey. The absence of the woman who had been the center of the most unexpected cat and dog fight Cheryl had ever witnessed filled those deep brown eyes with curiosity. Dot's girlfriend, Shirley, was either tucked away in the bathroom or had skipped any further scrutiny from their rambunctious family.

Tabitha threw her a sexy gaze and a nod to silently plea

for her woman's attention. But the Gospel Girls had other plans for Cheryl Rose Campbell.

"Rose, I'm glad you finally made it. I know you agree with me; young pussy is off-limits for us more sophisticated palettes. Ain't no way Dot should have been fooling around with that young tail! Right, Rose?"

"Cleo, come on now. We might need to reserve this conversation for a smaller group later on. Don't you think?" Tabitha did her best to discourage the awkward situation.

Cartier was more than aware that all eyes averted to her and then moved back and forth from the present young pussy to the former object of her desire.

"Oh, alright, Tab. You know I don't mean no harm. I'm just saying Dot is in this mess 'cause she won't keep her eyes focused on a full-grown woman instead of hunting somebody's *baby girl*," Cleo half-teased.

Their family might have been enjoying Mother Florence's food, but the tea their elders were spilling was just as tasty! Everybody's eyes were on Cleo, including Dot, who was hearing a different tune from the competitive crooner. The sound of Cleo's words was laced with a mutual feeling that in the 40 years they'd known each other, Dot had not dared to consider or act upon.

Cheryl made a quick pit stop at the Gospel Girls' prime seating area at Tabitha's dining room table. She looked at Cleo and Dot with a motherly stare as if preparing to scold her elders for their misbehaving ways. Instead, she gave each one a kiss on the cheek.

"Cleo, Dot, I see y'all couldn't wait to get started without me. Did you, at least, leave me a taste of that Jim Bean?"

Cheryl's elders roared with laughter. They, too, had feared their little sister would be less than pleased with them for bringing up the diva's past in front of mixed company.

"Reverend Carlotta, why aren't you helping my minister reign these two in? I didn't expect Pat to be the referee, but you, Carlotta..."

Cheryl giggled, then moved to her other sisters and extended them hugs and kisses.

"Rose, you know very well that we can't keep these two in check without some backup. So, we're glad you're finally here," Carlotta teased.

"Yeah, Rose, what took you and Ayda here so long? Whatch'all been up to?"

Curious eyes other than Cleo's blatant interrogation were definitely on Cheryl and her manager. But her news was for Tabitha's lips only. She couldn't wait until they were finally alone so she could give her a piece of her mind and more.

"Just business, nothing as interesting as what's been happening here."

Cheryl escorted Ayda to the kitchen, where Tabitha and Ayodele were patiently waiting for her to come see about them. She first greeted Ayodele, who looked as if she'd been having a few sips or more while repurposing Mother Florence's food as her own.

"Sister, I hope you didn't forget me and Ayda and left some food for us," Cheryl teased.

Ayodele gave her a huge, tight hug, and the smell of her sister's favorite rum teased her nostrils with merriment.

"My angel has arrived. And, of course, I saved you both a plate. These greedy children though of Tabitha's they almost got it though. But you know I always take care of my angel," Ayodele slurred.

"Well, from the looks and sound of it, I might need to

take care of you. Tab, what do you have to say for yourself—letting my sister get all tipsy?"

Tabitha's smile brightened, and she granted her Rose an apology sealed with a kiss. The room full of onlookers enjoyed the PDA and rewarded them with playful commentary and applause. But Cheryl's mind and body were caught up in the rapture of that most excellent kiss that made promises she would ensure Tabitha delivered on.

"Well, if you put it like that, I'll forgive you—this time. Whatchu been up to, Rev?"

Tabitha smiled sheepishly, but unlike her elders, she kept her comments PG. "Just been waiting for you to get here."

Cheryl loved the sound of that sexy contralto voice putting the mack on her like a smooth operator. It made her feel like hearing the sounds of some Sade rather than Sly & The Family Stone's *Family Affair* as their current soundtrack. But she pulled herself together and remembered Ayda was patiently waiting by her side, while the nosey onlookers were enjoying their passionate playfulness.

"Ayda, you ready to get you some good food in your belly? You do eat soul food, don't ya? You know—collard greens, mac and cheese, smoked turkey legs. Can you eat that?" Ayodelle interjected, bringing Cheryl and Tabitha's tender moment to an abrupt trainwreck.

Cheryl didn't know how to repair the potential insult to their good friend and only Jewish caucasian guest, but the Queenmaker didn't need an assist. Ayda smiled warmly and nodded in agreement.

"Yes, Ayodele, I do enjoy soul food. I'm a foodie, you know, and I enjoy many exotic delicacies."

Well not the best recovery as Cheryl had hoped. Ayodele didn't hide her amusement at Ayda Kohn's unexpected response. But it was Dot's, and Cleo's cackles and stage whispers that Tabitha quickly tried to get in check before the Queenmaker was offended. Ayda didn't seem too disturbed or even aware of her faux pas.

"Okay, Ayda. Well, let me fix you a plate, then."

"Actually, if you don't mind Ayodele, could I take your lovely meal with me? I have a few other appointments and wanted to ensure Cheryl was returned to her family since I took up some of her time."

"You got it, Ayda. One plate coming up. You be sure to tell me what you think after you have your dinner."

Ayda smiled brightly, and the aroma wafting from the uncovered pots of savory dishes made her stomach beg to be satisfied. She was sure she'd enjoy the meal more than her friends might think.

"I'll be sure to let you know what I already know I will enjoy. Thank you, Ayodele, for the hospitality."

* * *

Ayda Kohn wasn't the only one enjoying the decadent, lip-smacking soul food dinner. Cheryl savored the last bit of rum-laced sweet potato pie, and it was even more enjoyable being hand-fed to her by her minister. Those teasing brown eyes and plump lips promised to give her even more joy than Mother Florence's delicious dessert!

"Alright, alright, y'all break it up! Since you are all out and proud now, Rose, we know you just want to strut your stuff. But that's the blessing you young folks got in this day and age. We couldn't be like that if we wanted to keep our livelihood or our Jesus," Dot interjected.

Their audience had reduced in size after Ayda left to attend work. Cartier trailed behind her, although Cheryl encouraged the young woman not to flee. Soon, Carlotta and Patricia followed to attend to either work or family affairs. Tabitha's and Cheryl's family were still hanging around enjoying, the varied discussions and desserts. And all eyes were now averted from the playfulness of one set of elders to the stories of another.

"Tell 'em, Dot. They don't know how good they have it. Y'all parading around in your underwear on TV, in these parades, the children partying with straight folks coming to the clubs. Our clubs and bars were ours, and it was where we could be as free as possible without the watchful eyes of straight folks. Now, everybody just mingling together," Cleo chimed in.

"But that's fire, right? We are free to be ourselves. And now, you are free to be yourselves. It's still tough, though. I didn't think I could have a career without hiding, still. But I got tired of hiding, and like Cheryl, I found some fam still loyal to me and some new fam."

Isaiah chuckled after all eyes turned to him with surprised expressions. He knew they were shocked that he hadn't said something scandalous or made some crude joke. But he wanted his elders to see the struggle was still there for acceptance, no matter how *free* it might seem on social media and in these streets. Isaiah understood it could all be taken away, and it wasn't *free to be me* everywhere.

"What? Y'all thought I didn't have no brain or sumtin'?"

Isaiah felt Jerome's firm hand on his shoulder. His big brother gave him a tight squeeze and a warm smile. "Isaiah, you are never without wisdom, brother."

"Thanks, Bro. I'm just sayin' Auntie Dot, you and Cleo can be yourselves now. Ya, feel me?"

"We hear you, boy, but this ain't how somebody my age wanted to be remembered for; it ain't that easy. All those years of hiding, hiding my feelings, pretending to not care about somebody, but really caring too much," Dot responded.

Her voice trailed off at the utterance of her confession. Her mature brown eyes wandered to those of her old friend and rival, Cleo, and the confirmation was received by their mutual expressions. Cheryl softly rubbed her big sister's arm and granted her a smile of encouragement.

"Dot, you know I understand more than ever now. But I don't regret what this situation has brought to me—something, someone that I've always wanted."

Just in case Tabitha didn't get the whole picture, Cheryl turned to her minister with loving brown eyes, and Tabitha's body hummed with desire. The thought of kicking everybody out of her home except her woman and spending the rest of the day in Rose's arms came to mind. Lucky for the two lovers, their silent prayers would be answered sooner rather than later.

"You're right, Rose. Sometimes, you just have to take the lemons and make a lemoncella! I think that's what I'm going to do when I get home. I've stayed long enough, and I'm not about to overstay my welcome."

"Dot, you know you could never overstay your welcome. My home is your home," Tabitha interjected.

Although Cheryl appreciated the benevolent minister's kind heart, she silently prayed that Dot or the rest of their family wouldn't take Tabitha up on that offer. Dot shook her head and then grabbed her church hat and stood.

"Nah, Tab, it's time for me to hit the road. But I'll be in touch. We need to have another gathering at my place. This time, bring these children. It's time they start spending time with their elders more and learning of our ways, as much as we can learn from them."

Isaiah stood up quickly and carefully grabbed Dot's fur coat and placed it around her shoulders like she was British royalty. His elder smiled brightly at her younger partner in crime and then slipped him a joint from her purse before heading toward the front door.

All eyes watched their grand diva make her exit. Tabitha left Cheryl's side to walk Dot to her car, but their sister turned back briefly and aimed those big brown eyes at Cleo.

"Cleo, you coming?"

Cleo's eyes sparkled with excitement, and the 60-year-old sprung from her seat like a young teen smitten for the first time with her older crush.

"Yes, Dot. I'm coming with ya."

Soon, Ayodele followed after announcing she was having her fourth date with her new admirer. Cheryl was still disappointed that her sister hadn't shared this special someone in her life with her little angel. But she did her best to respect Ayodele's privacy. On the opposite front, Tabitha wasn't as patient with her children.

"Alright, here you go. For you, and you, and you," Tabitha announced as she passed dollar bills to each of her adult children.

The three sat with questionable expressions, but Tabitha quickly cleared up any confusion.

"I think it's time y'all take in another movie, don't you? Perfect after a good meal. So, see ya much later, right? Well see you, Tiffany, later on this evening. Jerome, I expect my coffee and company tomorrow for the ride to work. And Isaiah..."

Isaiah's face lit up with mischievousness. He was already prepared to have his mother give him the talk about his insistence on crashing at her home.

"Isaiah, see you later tonight with Tiffany," Tabitha

rewarded her middle kid with a warm smile and confirmed that his home would always be with her if that's what he wanted.

The three took their orders without much fuss. Tiffany and Isaiah were the first to leave together. Jerome lagged behind for a few moments. He returned the money Tabitha had given to him and gave her a gift instead.

"I won't be needing the money. I'm headed home to Leon—to our home."

Jerome silently waited for his mother's reprimand or approval. He wasn't sure which one she'd give. Cheryl gave him a sly wink and then remained silent as they both anticipated Tabitha's response.

"That sounds like a plan, son. I'm glad to hear that you found someone that you love. Leon's a good man, and you're both blessed to have each other."

Jerome's smile held a huge sense of relief. For the first time, he felt more than happy with his relationship with Leon; he felt worthy of it.

"Thank you, Mother. I'll leave you and Cheryl to the rest of your evening. See you in the morning."

Jerome gave Tabitha and Cheryl his customary kiss and hug. Then he left the two in the peaceful silence of Tabitha's home. Although the array of dirty dishes, pots, and pans felt more like chaos, there was nothing but peace between them. Cheryl headed toward the kitchen to help Tabitha clear up the mess, but her woman's gentle tug at her hand delayed kitchen duty.

"That can wait, but this can't."

Tabitha's eager lips found her Rose's sweet lips, and their mouths hummed a melody of lust, longing, and love. Their bodies were well overdue for coupling, but Tabitha did her best to quiet the need to take her Rose straight to bed. Once their lips had been temporarily satisfied, she pulled Cheryl to the sofa. Her hand still had a mind of its own, and it stroked that beautiful face, slid across those pouty lips, caressed that slender neck, and ignited the fire that Cheryl wanted her woman to tend to pronto!

When the caresses stopped, and those inquisitive brown eyes stared into her soul, Cheryl knew that bumping and grinding weren't the only things on Tabitha's mind.

"What's wrong, Tab?"

"Nothing. I was just wondering before I forgot or stopped caring to even know what your absence was about if I should keep it cool between us until we talk. That's all."

Cheryl enjoyed the lusty declaration, and her body screamed for Tabitha to skip the recap and take what she wanted from her Rose. But that was clearly not her woman's plan, even though Cheryl could tell Tabitha Scott was doing her best to fight her desires. The frustration and heat coming from that body just turned Cheryl on even more. Alright, they would have that discussion, but it would be quick because she had no intentions of spending the rest of their night in an upright position!

"Okay, Tab. Let's talk. What do you want to know?"

"What happened with Ayda? Why did she ask you to wait around? Is it something I should know?"

Cheryl could also hear a sense of alarm and maybe suspicion in Tabitha's voice. She tried not to be offended by the lack of trust she felt her woman was displaying and moved the conversation alone.

"She wanted me to know that Monument Records and my former manager were pleased by the damage control Ayda had done. More importantly, their greedy behinds were happy over the record sales and the media attention we've all been getting. They wanted me to consider another record deal and management with them."

If Cheryl hadn't seen the disappointment in Tabitha's eyes, she definitely felt it in her woman's body language. Tabitha moved her body slightly from Cheryl and did her best to keep a level head as she prepared herself to learn her Rose wouldn't be her Rose anymore. Cheryl Rose Campbell was back in the limelight, and Tabitha had no doubt this would just be considered a longer pit stop before she was back to her *real life*.

"I see. So, I guess you're leaving, as usual. I'm sure you don't want to miss out on something that big—something that can't be offered to you here."

Cheryl grabbed Tabitha's hand and ran it across her face and neck, as Tabitha had willingly done only a few moments before.

"You guessed wrong. I have everything I need and want right here, Tab. I'm not going anywhere. I want to be where I should have been—where I've always wanted to be since the day you sat at the piano and moved me with your music —with you. I love you, Tab. I want to be with you, Ayodele, Jerome, Tiffany, and Isaiah. I want to be with our family. And I..."

Before Cheryl could say another word, her woman's lips sealed that request with a deep, sweet kiss that left them both breathless and ready for that pillow talk they had been thinking about all day. Tabitha stood and pulled Cheryl with her as she headed for their private sanctuary, but she felt Cheryl's hand pull her back. A lusty expression met her playful brown eyes.

"What's wrong, Rose?"

"So, you're still trying to get that free milk from this heifer, I see."

Tabitha exhaled a deep sigh of relief and then granted Cheryl a lustful gaze that spoke volumes.

"I'm sorry I didn't make myself clear. I want you too, Rose. I love you, and I want all of you."

Cheryl stopped the playfulness long enough to grant her woman another deep kiss.

"So, are you asking me to be the minister's wife?"

say their names

THE FOLLOWING transwomen of color have been victims of transphobic violence and murder:

- Kylie Monali
- Caelee Love-Light
- Destiny Howard
- Diamond Jackson-McDonald
- Tiffany Banks
- Acey Morrison
- Regina Allen was known as Mya
- Dede Ricks
- Maddie Hofmann
- Kandii Redd
- Hayden Davis
- Marisela Castro
- Keshia Chanel Geter
- Martasia Richmond
- Kitty Monroe
- Shawmaynè Giselle Marie

- Brazil Johnson
- Sasha Mason
- Chanelika Y'Ella Dior Hemingway
- Nedra Sequence Morris
- Fern Feather
- Ariyanna Mitchell
- Miia Love Parker
- Kenyatta Webster
- Kathryn "Katie" Newhouse
- Tatiana Labelle
- Paloma Vazquez
- Naomie Skinner
- Cypress Ramos
- Duval Princess
- Amariey Lei
- Amber Minor
- Savannah Ryan Williams
- Amiri Reid
- LaKendra Andrews
- London Price
- Lisa Love
- A'nee Johnson
- Sherlyn Marjorie
- Chyna Long
- DéVonnie J'Rae Johnson
- Chanell Perez Ortiz
- Ashia, also spelled Asia, Davis
- Koko Da Doll
- Ashley Burton
- Tasiyah Woodland, also known as Siyah
- Cashay Henderson
- Maria Jose Rivera Rivera
- Zachee Imanitwitaho

- Jasmine "Star" Mack
- Kitty Monroe
- Samantha Gómez Fonseca
- Miriam Nohemí Ríos
- Gaby Ortíz

the good news soundtrack

CAN'T GET ENOUGH of this melodic masquerade? No worries. Check out the soundtrack created specifically for this story with music written and performed for the characters. The entire soundtrack is available on download streaming services near you.

Song Titles and Artists

The Good News Intro - The Master of Ceremony
Shining My Light - Cheryl Rose Campbell
Speak Life - Ayodelle
I Love to Call His Name - Tiffany Scott
Thank You for Your Love - Jerome Wright
God as a Nemesis - Isaiah
Sinner in Me - Roxanna
When I Rise - Cheryl Rose Campbell
I Will Praise Your Name - Ayodelle
For You - Whitney James
He Will Never Let Me Go - Cheryl Rose Campbell and
Dymon Stud
Iconic God - Tiffany Scott
If We Care - Jerome Wright
My Everything - Roxanna
Brand New - Cartier
It Hits Different - Isaiah
Let the Living Praise the Lord - Cheryl Rose Campbell

SEVENTEEN

the excerpt

AN EXCLUSIVE EXCERPT

KISS AND TELL

LAYLA WAS ABOUT to be late for her date. The last thing she needed was an intruder to contend with. What else could it be but someone trying to disturb her peace while she scrambled to get her hair in place, cute fit straight, and bag loaded with all the necessities?

The sound of Grandma Bee's voice narrated the thoughts rambling in her head. She contemplated ignoring the persistent knocker like Bee used to do whenever the Jehovah's Witness came around.

Layla knew a confrontation was inevitable when the familiar but unwanted sound of Deshawn Darby's voice swapped places with his incessant pounding on her apartment door. Unless she wanted that young bitch downstairs in 4B to call the leasing office again about the imaginary noise she constantly heard from Layla's apartment. Never mind the late-night visitors partying, loud beats bumping, and weed smoke filtering into Layla's apartment most weekends till the wee hours of the morning!

Every time that light-skinned bitch batted her eyelashes at the apartment manager or the maintenance crew, her infractions seemed to vaporize into thin air like confiscated contraband. But not the trump charges she placed on Layla Joy. Layla was a model citizen compared to the *Only Fans hoe*, Trina, in the garden apartment beneath her.

"What, Deshawn! Chelle isn't here!" Layla screamed at the tall, dark chocolate Hawks basketball superstar. His lean, muscular frame took up the entire space of her apartment door.

Deshawn squinted his eyes, sizing up Layla and then resting on her forehead. The new Hawks point guard towered above her petite frame. Deshawn tried to use his big man status to persuade Layla to loosen her lips and reveal her ex-roomie's whereabouts.

But his slick ball-handling and long-range shooting were evident only on the court. He may have had a game, but he lacked any real mental game. From what Chelle said, his dick wasn't slapping either when using his athletic prowess in the bedroom.

Layla tried to be patient while the time slipped away, but she quickly decided to take point on the situation standing before her.

"Deshawn, I've been trying to tell you, like a million times, Chelle doesn't live here anymore. I don't know where she is; if I did, I'd be chasing her for half the three months' rent she owes me. I'm sorry, but I can't help you."

Deshawn's puzzled expression didn't change much.

"Who are you? And what are you talking about? Where's Michelle Dixon?"

Layla was convinced Deshawn enjoyed making her feel small. But the same old feeling crept over her as she looked into his wide, confused brown eyes. Layla was reminded that she wasn't immune to the infection of his melanin amnesia.

Had the incredible opportunity awaiting her blinded her from her invisible life?

When Trina from 4B sashayed to her door, Layla felt even more defeated. She couldn't take on both of these clowns. But Trina was a blessing in disguise that she never saw coming. Trina looked like she had just stepped off the set of a Lit G2G music video—her makeup was beat to perfection. That bodysuit clung to her like it was sprayed on, with all the stripper's assets on display.

Layla wasn't the only one getting a full view of what Trina was selling. She was a rich dick's magnet, and Deshawn's attention was glued to the bitch in 4B.

"Oh, excuse me, *Lorna*. I don't mean to interrupt. I was just wondering if you could let me borrow your charger. I think I may have misplaced mine last night at Queen Bey's concert."

Layla rolled her eyes and prepared to clap back at Trina with her overpriced Spelman College vocabulary. But Deshawn swooped in all superhero-like in the nasty hoe's defense.

"Hey, bae, my name is DeShawn Darby, and um, maybe I can help you out."

DeShawn flashed a bright white-toothy grin toward Trina that, at one time, her roomie swooned over. By the looks of the sparkle in those money-green contact lenses, Trina was succumbing to his boyish swag.

"Oh, I know who you is, Double D. Who wouldn't know, yo phyne ass!"

Trina's loud ass cackle had Layla feeling some type of way. But DeShawn was living for it—like rich Alfredo sauce sliding down his throat.

"Oh, I'm sorry. I didn't mean to interrupt you and yo bae's conversation. Let me get out of y'allz way."

DeShawn grabbed Trina's arm with the speed he was known for on the basketball court and gently rubbed her caramel latte skin like it was the softest thing he'd ever touched.

"*Bae?* Hell, nah! She ain't no Black Barbie! Look, let me help you out. We can go to my whip, get my charger, and get you straight. Aight?"

Trina batted her long Lena Lashes and gave DeShawn a sensual caress up and down his hairy muscular arm.

"Well, ain't you a gentleman. Thank you, Double D. You so *sweeeet.*"

The two future fuck buddies casually ignored Layla standing in the doorway, dumbfounded by a connection that had been created faster than swiping right on Tinder! Trina locked arms with her new bae and made a beeline for the elevator. As they stepped inside, those Insta-famous lashes swept over Layla one more time.

"See ya, *Lorna!*"

"Layla! My name is Layla!"

The elevator rattled to a close, punctuating Layla's last words, and the window of opportunity was closing just as fast. She snatched up her bag and secured the apartment door. She flew down the stairs, hustling to her ride—a decade-old Hyundai Elantra, ready to take Layla Joy to her ball!

* * *

Layla sat across from Ayda Kohn as the older woman with kind eyes finished what sounded like a pretty important conversation with an artist Layla adored. When Ayda's assistant contacted her for this meeting, she had been less informed about the Queenmaker's reputation, more so than the talent she represented.

After Layla confirmed this wasn't a spam call, she did her background check on Ms. Kohn. She learned that the sixty-year-old talent agent represented some of the biggest and brightest musicians, like R&B singer Roxanna, contemporary Christian Jazz singer Whitney James, and a host of filmmakers, actors, and literary geniuses.

What Layla didn't understand, but she hoped this wasn't a prank, was why Ms. Kohn had reached out to an aspiring actress who had barely scratched the surface of social media success. With just 1k followers on the Gram and a measly 500 for TikTok, she was far from being an icon or influencer like the talent agent's notable clientele.

Layla felt her right foot tapping underneath the table at Rumi's Kitchen. The Persian restaurant was packed on a Saturday afternoon. Although it was one of Layla's favorite places to indulge when her money was right, her stomach was so nervous she didn't think she'd be able to eat a thing or impress Ms. Kohn.

"Apologies for the interruption, Layla Joy. My manners were not my best. Thank you for taking the time to meet with me this afternoon. I know it's a beautiful Shabbos. I'm sure you'd rather spend time with your peers somewhere fun than chatting with this old lady."

Layla shook her head and prepared herself to convince Ayda Kohn that she wanted to be nowhere else but with the woman who could make her dreams come true. But Ayda's mouth moved faster than the speed of light, and she was on to her next topic.

"Layla Joy, are you hungry? I'm famished. What about you? Oh, and what should I call you—just Layla or Layla Joy?'

Ayda took a deep breath and paused long enough to allow Layla to respond to either or both of her questions. Her gentle expression encouraged Layla and reminded her of how her Grandma Bee always reassured her when she was uncertain.

"Layla is fine, Ms. Kohn."

"Ayda. No need for formalities with me, Layla, unless that's what you prefer."

Ayda's eyes searched for confirmation, and Layla approved with a gentle nod.

"Good, now that we've gotten that out of the way—are you a fan of Persian food, or were you just acting on your Instagram? I love your videos on reconstructing gourmet food on a budget. You're such a good cook and engaging. You've got chutzpah, you know that? I was ready to knock on your door and ask for a serving of that last dish you made. What was it? Lemme think. Samosas, right?"

Layla couldn't believe that Ayda had taken such a serious interest in her background to study her meager posts on the Gram. But as Ayda recalled Layla's favorite food hacks, the Jai Ho Indian Kitchen's Lamb Samosa and Madras Fish Curry, she knew Ayda was both a foodie like herself and serious about the details of her potential clients.

The food hacks had been her most popular reels if an average of 80 likes and a handful of comments were compared to her usual two to five likes and no comments.

Watching the vegan influencers for @makeitdairyfree inspired her to post the hacks on cost-effective, delicious meals on a budget.

After Chelle abandoned her with the expensive lease on their two-bedroom apartment in Brookhaven, Layla got pretty creative with her paycheck to satisfy her need to pay the bills and enjoy great-tasting food.

"Thank you, Ms. Kohn, I mean Ayda, for the feedback. To answer your question, I do enjoy Persian food. This is one of my favorite restaurants when I want to celebrate. I do the food hacks because, as you've guessed, I'm a foodie but on a budget. And if I work hard, I should be able to enjoy my money for more than paying bills, within reason.

"From your lips to G_d's ears, Layla. And you make thrifty quite trendy."

Ayda's amusement was hard to disguise, not that she was attempting to be sheepish. She was already enjoying the lovely young woman who sat before her as a potential new client. The innocent brown eyes, flawless ebony skin, and polite mannerisms, with just a hint of the humor and star power Layla had revealed on her social media, reinforced Ayda's suspicions.

Layla would be the perfect unknown to turn into a star. Although Layla's voice often wavered on the insecure side, Ayda sensed a more confident warrior underneath the shy persona.

"Well, I'm glad to know this is a place of celebration for you, Layla. If our conversation goes as planned, I think we'll have lots to celebrate today."

Layla tried to quiet that nervous tapping, which was the telltale to her racing heart. The sound of her foot marching against the bottom of the table and floor reverberated in her ears. Ayda seemed none the wiser as she studied the menu and asked Layla for suggestions. Layla smoothed the imaginary wrinkles in the bottom of her dress and pressed down on the jumpy leg, hoping to silence its fear.

She could barely hear herself describe some of the popular items on the menu. The tapping noise of her foot, the beating of her heart, and her nerves overpowered what sounded like a muffled voice in her ears. Ayda's expression never indicated that she was aware of the drama going on between her mind and body.

Layla was more starstruck than nervous when Ayda finished sharing fun stories of her collaborations with other clients as they waited for their food to arrive. Filling the silence afterward with the beautifully prepared dishes from Rumi's Kitchen also helped to remove her discomfort.

As she enjoyed the last morsel of the rich lamb ribs with the savory grape molasses glaze and kohlrabi salad, Layla could tell by the eager look on Ayda's face that the actual conversation was about to begin. She wiped remnants of the spicy sauce from her lips and took a few sips of the room-temperature water to lubricate her vocal cords. She wasn't a singer, but she'd need a bit of moisture to fight off the dryness of her nerves.

"Well, Layla, now that we've broken bread together, I'd like to discuss why we're here today. And I have a surprise for you before we end our meal with some of that nice dessert on the menu.

Ayda smiled warmly and searched Layla's eyes for confirmation that the young girl was still hanging in there with her. She was more than aware her potential new artist was full of nerves, but she was glad Layla seemed a bit more relaxed, considering the tapping noise had ceased. After hearing her pitch, Ayda prayed to G_d that the young woman wouldn't go into convulsions.

"Yes, thank you, Ayda. I appreciate this chance to meet with you."

"Oh no, Layla, the pleasure is all mine. As I said, I've been watching your social media feed. You are very charismatic with a great stage presence. And I believe you're ready to broaden your scope. Would you agree?"

Layla tried not to search the crowded restaurant for hidden cameras. But her eyes darted around the room a few times as she tried to soak in Ayda's words.

Was she being punked?

Her hesitation must have warned Ayda that Layla Joy wasn't buying what the talent agent was selling, not just yet. Her mother had taught her never to believe the *mouth of a gift horse* unless the bags were present when it spoke. Layla knew the actual proverb held a different sentiment. But she had learned the hard way not to trust the empty promises of many people who had crossed her path.

"Layla, dear, is everything alright?"

"*Ms. Kohn*, I don't mean to be rude, but are you sure you've got the right person for this conversation? It sounds like you're offering me a chance to pursue an acting career with your help. But I don't understand why you would do that."

Ayda sighed and then granted Layla another one of her warm, motherly smiles.

"Hakarat HaTov."

"Excuse me?"

"Sorry, Layla. I was merely thankful that you weren't prepared to turn down my offer before you'd even heard it. Hakarat HaTov is Hebrew. It means, *thank goodness*. But first, please, you don't have to be so formal with me, Layla. I have a feeling you and I will be good friends soon, even though I hear reservations in your voice. But I ask you, why wouldn't I approach you, Layla Joy?"

Layla couldn't contain her bitter laughter. She wasn't angry with Ayda but was more frustrated with the Queenmaker. Certainly, Ayda should be able to see what most people saw when they looked at Layla Joy. Instead, she pretended that a woman with her looks could glow up in a society that preferred a much lighter complexion.

"Because you have an A-list clientele, and nowhere do I see someone like me on that roster. I'm a Black girl, no name, with a less-than-impressive following, and I don't look like the Black Barbies. So, yes, I'm confused about why you'd be interested in someone who wouldn't even get picked for a Cologuard commercial."

Ayda almost sprayed Layla and the linen cloth on the table with wine as she tried to contain her laughter over the spunky young woman's response. She grabbed her napkin and dabbed the wine from her lips, chin, and fingers.

"Oh, Layla! You must warn this old lady if you're going to introduce this ballsy side of you!"

Layla's insides were in turmoil. Had she just insulted the Queenmaker with her unfiltered thoughts?

"I'm sorry, Ms. Kohn. I didn't mean to be rude. I don't think I'm the right person for whatever you're offering.

"And Layla, I want to assure you that I didn't get to where I am or represent the types of clients I have without faith and a sixth sense. Plus, a whole lot of ballsy behavior too. So, you and I are quite the pair. And if you're really sorry, please give me a chance to explain further and remain open to the possibility that this could be your chance. Okay, Layla Joy?"

Layla tried not to let the nerves resurface, but she

couldn't hide her embarrassment despite Ayda Kohn's sincerity.

"Yes, Ayda. I will hear you out."

"Good. First, I don't want you to think I'm not sensitive or aware of the struggles brown-skinned women have in a world that has a commercialized view of what beauty is. I also understand the struggles of the African American community and other races marginalized by the wealth and faces that don't resemble them. I'm not as naive as I may seem or have sounded since the beginning of this meeting."

Layla's face flushed as Ayda's earnest words and observation revealed the guilt of her earlier behavior and thoughts.

"I'm sorry, Ms. Kohn."

Ayda placed her hand on Layla's and ran weathered skin across smoother skin.

"No need to apologize, Layla. Everyone won't be as direct with you as I will, whether the truth is scary or potentially hurtful. I'm not here to sugarcoat the real world. I am here to give you the push to take on this world like the silent warrior I feel you are. So, answer me this. Do you believe in you, Layla? Do you find yourself attractive, talented, and worthy of success?"

Layla sat silently momentarily as she contemplated the answers to those weighty questions. She'd been feeling like a puppet for so long, powerless to influence how the world saw her or what it would deny her from achieving, even though she'd given it her all.

Earlier today, Layla was sharply reminded of how insignificant she felt. But Ayda's wise eyes ignited a fire in her belly and sparked the belief that one day she'd capture every damn thing she desired!

"I don't always feel that way, but I haven't given up yet, and I don't want to."

"Good, Layla! That's a start. Now, most successful people, especially in the entertainment industry, have gotten their start after many years of struggling or being discovered. In this era of overnight success stories from social media and influencers who make more money than some of your household brand names based on sharing their *real* lives, there is more than enough opportunity for you to succeed. We just need the right angle to help you get there."

Layla's eyes expanded with suspicion. Here it comes, that gift horse turning into a Trojan horse. Now, she could hear her mother's voice screaming in her ear. Unlike Grandma Bee's optimistic and maternalistic nature, Melba was shrewd and often a cold-hearted realist.

"I represent Nzinga Films, and they're in the development stage of a new movie. Have you heard of them?"

Layla's eyes sparkled with enthusiasm. She was a mega fan of the Morgans. Layla had celebrated her 21st birthday by watching her first Nzinga flick and had been hooked ever since. Their cinematic artistry and their dope way of putting people of color in authentic, mature roles made them unforgettable. Not to mention that she also had a massive girl crush on Carissa and Shantal Morgan, the boss baes behind the production company.

"I take it by your expression you are more than familiar with their work. Am I right?"

"Sorry, Ayda. Yes, I love their films! I've been a fan since *Nope, Not Today!* And the sequel, *Welp!,* was just as amazing! I admire their use of satire to bring home the injustice of Black women and their right to their feelings and ability to express them without being dismissed."

"Well, I'm glad to hear you're a fan. They've made a lot of headway since they started their independent production company 15 years ago. Now, they've joined a partnership with That Queen Films. This alliance with Nathan Queen and his mega cinematic productions has brought them major cash flow to broaden their direction. And their latest venture would be a great opportunity to introduce your talent to their audience. Don't you agree?"

Layla was speechless. She didn't know what to say or think. Did she really want this chance? Hell yes! But could she pull it off? She had no idea. Layla had so many questions. As she mustered the courage to rattle off each one, Ayda's cell phone interrupted their conversation.

"Sorry, Layla. That's my surprise for you. I want to explain my idea before we're joined by one of my other clients. Nzinga Films is scouting for new talent in the two main roles. I believe I have the two actors they need, you being one of them. Now, how do we get you noticed by them? Great question, right? Simple. We have to increase your social media presence and make you an influencer their audience will fall in love with and encourage them to see no one other than you as one of the main actors."

Layla was dumbfounded. She had no idea how Ayda could just sit there with that confident smile and rattle off an idea that seemed damn near impossible! But she was hooked and couldn't prevent herself from asking Ayda to break down this crazy scheme.

"How do we do that?"

"Easy, my dear. We make you and my other client the next best thing or even more influential than Da Brat and Jesseca Dupart!

afterword

THANK YOU

Thank you so much for reading *Cheryl - I'm Coming Back.*

To keep up with the latest releases and get free reads,
follow me on social media at:
Instagram - @onyxleepublishing
Instagram and TikTok - @auntgeorgialee_author
Instagram - @qwocbooks

If you enjoyed the book, and would be so kind to share your
feedback, please don't forget to leave a review.

Get up-to-date news by signing up for the Onyx Lee
Publishing newsletter at https://onyxlee.pub

To explore more queer women of color books, check out
https://qwocbooks.com.

about the author

AUNT GEORGIA LEE is an old soul but still young at heart. She is one of the South's best storytellers. The love of reading and writing romance stories have always been her passions. It pleases her even more, to share her original stories with the LGBTIQA+ community.

In her own words, "Can we pretend? Characters are my family and friends. Stories are what could have been or what should have been."

You can connect with Aunt Georgia Lee:
https://onyxlee.pub
Instagram - @onyxleepublishing
Instagram - @auntgeorgialee_author
Instagram - @qwocbooks

also by aunt georgia lee

Caught Up and Strapped Up

Hot for Teacher

The Bad Girls

Stalk Her Much

Old School Lovin'

Midnight Snack

They Call Me Dr. Feelgoode

Kiss and Tell

The Heart Doesn't Lie

A Missed Erection

The Social Circle